Her
Lisbon
Colors

Also by Cynthia Morris

FICTION

Chasing Sylvia Beach

NON-FICTION

*The Busy Woman's Guide to Writing
a World-Changing Book*

Create Your Writer's Life

Cross the Finish Line

The Graceful Return

Visit Paris Like an Artist

Write Your Travel Stories

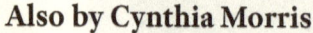

Her Lisbon Colors

A Novel

Cynthia Morris

ORIGINAL
IMPULSE
EST. • 1999

Published in the United States of America by Original Impulse, Inc.
www.originalimpulse.com

Library of Congress Control Number: 2025902880

Morris, Cynthia
Her Lisbon Colors: a novel/Cynthia Morris first edition

PRINT ISBN: 979-8-9929573-0-3
EBOOK ISBN: 978-0-9759224-1-5
AUDIO ISBN: 978-0-9759224-4-6

Published by Original Impulse, Inc.

Book cover and interior design is by *the*BookDesigners
The cover font is Cera Pro
The main interior font is Adobe Text Pro

FIRST EDITION

10 9 8 7 6 5 4 3 2 1

Dedication

———

To Lisbon, a city of beauty and grit, complexity, and tenacity. You and Lisboetas continue to inspire me.

Chapter One

Darla didn't enjoy crowds, especially those so bright and well-intentioned. The priest was the only other person in black, apart from her. Darla wore her work outfit: white shirt, black pants, a blazer, a pair of shoes that weren't quite heels but looked professional enough. She felt out of place among the dramatic patterns and drapey cuts. But it was a funeral. Feeling off was normal. She shook off her discomfort and took a seat at the back of the yurt.

The room filled slowly. Murmurs accompanied the gentle sitar music. Boulder's irrepressible cheer had taken a day off. It was uncharacteristically gray outside, contributing to the somber mood. At the front of the yurt, a small podium was framed by two giant bouquets and a poster-sized picture of Lauren.

Darla inhaled the Nag Champa smoke and pushed down her anxiety with righteousness. Lauren would have hated all of this, she thought. She would have done away with the seating, put on a bumping tune, and demanded they all rise up and dance with her.

Darla wanted to think of Lauren that way. But when she last visited, she'd found Lauren frail and surrounded by pillows. Her friend had been far from dancing.

"I'm almost outta here, Darla darlin'," she said when Darla came into her room.

Would anyone else ever call her Darla darlin'? She smiled

and took Lauren's hand. What to say? Something meaningful, something fitting a final goodbye. Nothing came out.

"Tell me something good," Lauren had said. Her brown eyes were as kind as ever, if a bit tired looking.

Darla had struggled to think of anything good. On the way over, she'd been ruminating about Gregory, wondering about the restless energy she'd detected from him lately.

"I think Gregory might propose," Darla said.

Lauren grimaced. "I don't think he's the one."

Her words pinched off a bud of hope that had been striving to bloom inside Darla. "How do you know? I mean, how do you know who's the one?"

Lauren reached for her cup. Darla moved it toward her. Lauren sucked from the straw before pressing on.

"When I was dating, I didn't get hung up on whether he was the *one* or not. I just collected PMEs."

Darla tilted her head.

"Positive Male Experiences."

They laughed.

"Enough about this," Darla said. "You need to conserve your energy."

"For what?" Lauren said. "This is it, darlin'." She waved her hand and continued.

"Let me say it straight. You are living at half ass. I know you like to play it safe. I can tell you want more but don't dare let yourself have it. That time you came to Avalon and danced with me—you were lit up."

Darla smiled. She'd had a blast, despite the crowd. Getting lost in the trance music made it easy to be around people. Any setting where she had to make small talk was just awkward.

"I see you," Lauren whispered. She struggled for breath.

"You deserve to be seen and loved for who you are."

Darla teared up. Damn it. She grabbed a tissue.

"But who am I? After forty years, I still don't know. You lived your life so *you*, Lauren. How do I do that?"

"You will figure that out. But I don't think Gregory is helping you be *you*."

Darla suspected that more than one friend thought he was a hard pass. They had been together for almost three years now. Sure, he wasn't perfect. But he was great. Tall, handsome, successful, kind. They had their routine.

"I don't know what would happen if I weren't with Gregory," she confessed. "I don't have much faith in finding someone better. What should I do?"

She could hardly get that last sentence out.

"It's less about what you do. It's about what you love," Lauren said. "Find what you really love and want. No matter what anyone else thinks. That's what I did. That's how this Ivy League professor became a hairdresser."

Darla was really crying now. What did she love? She loved Lauren, and the pain of losing her was starting to get real. She wasn't even old, in her fifties, with so much left to do. Darla took in the wisdom and surrender in Lauren's eyes. She seemed at peace. For a moment, there in Lauren's house nestled among the aspen trees, Darla had felt a release of worry, of all concern siphoned off.

But here in the yurt, without Lauren's presence anywhere she could detect, all of it was back. Cat, her best friend, slipped in. His long blond hair and gypsy pants. Darla wished he dressed better, but there was no controlling Cat or even suggesting anything different. He put his arm around her and squeezed. She closed her eyes and let herself briefly feel the warmth of his support. She'd told both Cat and Gregory about the service, but of course, it was Cat who was here. Darla hadn't even asked him to come.

"You okay?" Cat whispered as the priest took the podium. She nodded, trying to focus.

"Lauren was special," the priest said, his voice too soft. She caught snippets—Avalon, clients, hair. The mention of Lauren's phrase made her throat tighten. Around her, people were already crying, but she held it in. One speaker followed another, all sharing stories of Lauren's wild energy. Darla's head buzzed. Her chest tightened. She needed to get out of there. Finally, Lauren's brother took the podium. She searched his face for a resemblance to her friend. There, the same crinkly lines when he smiled, the same dusky brown hair, the same gentleness. He spoke about Lauren and how she'd always had her own rhythm in life.

"No one was surprised when she quit her job and moved to Colorado, because Lauren will be Lauren. But I tried to talk her out of it. I thought she should stay the course of her career. Was I wrong. Lauren belonged here. She flourished here."

His voice hitched a little, and he had to pause. The room seemed to hang suspended, basking in the shared feeling Stephen showed. Darla glanced around. The yurt was packed, people standing all along the curved back wall.

"Lauren thrived here because of all of you."

A chorus of sniffles rippled through the crowd. Darla's face grew hot. She wouldn't let it out. She wouldn't. She had to go back to work. She snuck a peek at Cat. Tears streamed down his face and caught in his hair.

Afterward, everyone clustered on the patio. Kombucha and gluten-free cookies were served alongside a stack of

Lauren's Live Full Ass stickers. Most people had one in hand like flags of a new world being waved. Tears and hugs were liberally shared along with the 'buch. Was everyone living more full ass than she was? Darla and Cat made their way through. She had to get out of there and into her car before she broke down. She saw Stephen, Lauren's brother, put down his drink and rush toward her.

"Darla! Can we talk later? It's about Lauren's will."

"Uh, sure."

They arranged to meet at the Trident, which had bitter coffee but a bookish feel Darla appreciated. After a quick hug with Cat, Darla managed to slip away from the service without crying.

Back at her office, Darla tried to focus. Her boss, Terry, had blithely tossed a new project on her desk while she was at the funeral. She usually liked the start of a new project. Working with a client and gathering information for their annual report was like starting off on a new adventure. What was this company about? What was their year like, and what drove sales and success for them? Interviewing different people from the organizations and turning data into stories had been engaging for Darla for years. But now the thought of a new client just felt like a slog. She didn't like this new perspective on work. She hadn't given it much thought, but now she wondered how she could stay in this job until retirement.

A shiver passed through her. The sun had slipped behind the Flatirons, leaving Boulder huddled in the cold shadow of evening. Darla sighed and crunched her shoulders up. She prepared for the meeting to introduce her new client to their process. It saved a lot of hassle down the road when she showed them the ecosystem they'd be working in: the software, the expectations, the deliverables. She customized their intake process based on what they'd discussed to be their big challenge. Darla was all prepared, makeup on, ready to join the online meeting, when a message came in. The new client had to reschedule. *Argh!* She hated last-minute changes, especially when she'd planned her day around it. She would have preferred to go home, or for a walk, after Lauren's service. Not come back to the office.

Darla shut it down for the day, now able to pay attention to what was really on her mind. Was she in Lauren's will? It was likely. Lauren's generosity wasn't new. After a haircut once, she'd slipped Darla a gift card with a note: *Ditch those Target undies.* Lauren had insisted that life was better with better underwear. So, Darla had bought herself a teal lace bra with matching panties. Wearing better underwear did give her a lift, she had to admit.

She keyed into her apartment. The dismantling: keys in the vide poche, jacket and hat off and pegged, shoes off. The rest of it came off in the bedroom, all items stowed immediately so she didn't have to see the office wear that now felt like a prison uniform. Reclothed, she splashed water on her face. In the kitchen, Darla reached for a bottle of wine and a corkscrew. What did she love? Was it evident in her home? She'd decorated it sparsely when she'd moved in a few years before. It felt temporary, and it was. Darla wished she could be like Lauren. But she wasn't. Why couldn't she just be happy with what she had? She sat back with her glass, sipping the wine, letting the day settle in. An idea flared. She remembered what she'd loved as a girl. Could she try that again?

On the couch, she searched. There! She clicked. A beginning drawing class tomorrow at a paper shop downtown. Her heart thumped. The screen blurred behind her tears. "Live full ass," Lauren's voice echoed in her mind. She clicked "register." Time to forget her high school art teacher, Sister Quinn. No one would tell her she couldn't be an artist. She could almost feel Lauren's high five on her palm as she got out her credit card to pay for the class.

Chapter Two

The next afternoon, she found Stephen in the café's bookshop. He crouched at a tiny table at the back in the children's section. A black leather folder and a cup of black coffee were out of place in the colorful kids' zone. That's gonna hurt later, Darla thought. She took one of the children's chairs, her legs folding like a mantis.

"There weren't any spots in the café, so here we are," Stephen started.

"That's fine." She shifted in the seat that barely held her. "How are you?"

He fiddled with the edge of the folder.

"As good as can be expected. We weren't close."

"Everyone adored Lauren," Darla said. "I don't understand why life is so cruel sometimes."

He shook his head. "I don't understand much these days. Especially what we're here to talk about. Do you want a coffee or something?" He seemed to be stalling.

"Nope," Darla said.

"Well, let me get to it. Lauren left you something."

She hoped it wasn't a piece of furniture. She didn't have much room in her apartment. Maybe the dream catcher?

"Brace yourself," he said. Sitting in the miniature chair, there wasn't much for bracing. She leaned in, eager to get this over with.

Stephen opened the folder and pulled out a paper. He tucked glasses onto his nose, cleared his throat, and began reading.

"I leave Darla Clarke $25,000."

"Whoa!" She reared back, almost falling off the tiny chair. Her eyebrows shot up and stayed up. She righted herself, feeling a bit dizzy. Twenty-five thousand dollars!

"What the—?"

Stephen paused, smiling. "Do you know about Thrill Money?"

"Sure," Darla said. "Thrill Money was something we talked about. Lauren believed that some of the money we make should be used for frivolous, fun things."

"Lauren bequeathed a bit of Thrill Money to a few friends. Exciting, no?"

Darla liked the idea in theory. But she also relished the feeling of seeing her 401K add up. She was behind on savings, having spent too many years knocking off debt.

"Well, that's a lot. I don't even know . . . I mean, that kind of cash."

"Well, you don't need to know. Because the money comes with a directive." Darla thought she saw a little smile at the corners of his mouth. She felt dazed. The words *twenty-five thousand* kept repeating in her mind.

"Lauren liked to be in charge. When we were kids, she was always the boss in whatever game we played. I didn't mind. She was usually right about most things, so it was easy to go along."

Get to it, Darla thought. But she could see that Stephen was savoring this memory of Lauren as his playmate. He finished his coffee.

"So . . . here's the deal." He continued reading. "I believe Darla would benefit from a break from her life. And I know just the place. Darla gets the money if she takes some of it to go to Lisbon."

Darla shook her head. "Lisbon?! Why Lisbon?"

He held up a finger and kept reading. "When I was in Lisbon, I felt the magic of the city. It was beautiful and gritty, hilly and low to the river. Lisbon held all the contradictions of life itself in that one small city. I loved it, and I know Darla will too."

Had Lauren ever talked about Lisbon? Darla couldn't remember. She sat immobilized, stunned by this news. She pushed back from the table.

"I can't go to Lisbon. I know nothing about Lisbon. That's Portugal, right?"

Stephen's lips tightened.

"That's right," he said. "You don't have to accept this money. Or the directive. Though I don't know what I'd do with it if you didn't."

"There are plenty of charities I am sure Lauren would want this to go to. Why not one of those? Like Planned Parenthood?"

He shook his head.

"Already taken care of. She gave money to them too. This is for you, Darla dear."

Crap, Darla thought. She respected Lauren and missed her. But she resented someone telling her what to do. She had enough of that at work. She gripped the seat of her little chair.

"Can I think about it?"

"Sure you can. Of course. But this needs to be taken care of this month. I am wrapping up her estate. After I sell her cabin, it's going to be mostly handled. I need to get back to New York."

They chatted for a few minutes, reminiscing about Lauren. Stephen texted her his details, and she promised to get in touch. Walking in the brisk evening, Darla felt numb. Leaves were just starting to form on the trees lining Pearl Street Mall. She had never been to Europe.

No one had ever given her an inheritance. Her mom was still very much alive, and she hadn't seen her dad since she was a toddler. The idea of someone looking out for her like this was sudden. She didn't like it.

"I've done just fine on my own," she huffed to no one. "What did Lauren mean, 'Darla would benefit from a break'? I can't take a break."

Taking breaks hadn't gotten her where she was now. Darla had done all the right things. She'd gone to a good university, gotten good grades and an English degree. She'd spent time in the editorial trenches in New York before burning out on the city. A job in Boulder had come up serendipitously. It wasn't the job she wanted, but she could deal with it. She chose the lifestyle of Boulder—mellower days, nearby hikes—over the perfect job. She'd planned to find something better once she'd settled. But she hadn't. She'd been an annual reports project manager for years now.

Darla entered Two Hands Paperie accompanied by the jingle of a bell above the door. One step in, and she was unable to go farther. Her breath caught; how had she never been here? The space was a kaleidoscope of color and texture and paper. Calendars and cards. Pens and ink bottles and shelves of blank notebooks. Where to start? She'd given herself extra time before the class to check it out.

"Welcome in! Can I help you?" a friendly voice spoke from behind the counter.

Through all the paper goodies, Darla saw a petite woman with cropped black hair smiling at her.

"I'm here for the beginning drawing class?"

"Great! Classes are in the back. Feel free to settle in and look around."

Darla moved through the store, past the display case lined with fountain pens and the open cupboards stacked with fresh, pristine notebooks. Her whole being wanted to stop and look at every single thing. The back room was packed with even more fun things, the walls covered with racks of paper of all colors and patterns. A table was set up with handouts and a few objects. She approached, and a woman with long dark hair greeted her.

"Are you here for the class?"

"Yes, I'm Darla Clarke."

"Welcome, Darla! I'm Cara, the instructor."

Cara smiled, and Darla immediately wanted to be her friend. She set her stuff down and wandered over to a table full of watercolor paints, brushes, and paper. She wanted everything, even the things she didn't know how to use.

Before long, Cara launched the class. Darla took her seat along with several women. Suddenly, Darla felt intimidated. What if she were terrible at drawing? What if she didn't do it right? She had been good enough at drawing but couldn't get perspective right. She just couldn't see it the way she was supposed to. She failed every art exam, forcing Sister Quinn to give her a D. She'd given up art and focused on practical things she could succeed at. Cara introduced herself and told them about how she had gotten into drawing.

"I found a book about drawing and meditating," she said. "So, I got a sketchbook and found that drawing helped me feel calmer and more centered. I've been keeping a sketchbook for twenty years now and also making paintings and other things."

Darla's skin tingled, and she could barely sit still. Cara was cool! Her calm demeanor and friendly eyes told Darla that she was living full ass. Cara moved on to give instructions on basic drawing. Darla's shoulders dropped an inch when she realized accurate perspective drawing was not going to be part of the class. Soon, guided by Cara's prompts, Darla and her fellow students were engrossed in making marks on the page. The hours flew by. At the end, Darla popped her head up. Something was different. The room was still a flurry of color, texture, and possibility. But something had changed. The colors seemed brighter. The air felt crisp. Everything was more in focus. She felt lighter. As they went around the circle to debrief, Darla was shocked to hear what she said.

"For the first time—ever—I didn't think about work for two hours. I don't know that I thought about anything!" She blushed and glanced at the others. They were nodding, and Cara wore a big smile. She continued.

"After the first scribble exercise, I even forgot about making it good. I can't believe this, but now I love what I drew."

Darla held up her sketch of a leaf. It was gorgeous. Intricate lines and shading gave it depth. When Darla looked at it, she felt a fondness, a joyfulness that reminded her of drawing as a girl. If this was meditation, she'd take more of it.

"How do we keep going?" she asked.

"I was just about to talk about that, Darla," Cara said. "I'll share how I keep drawing as a practice. Let me know what questions you have."

She got out her sketchbook and paged through it, holding it up to show the students. Darla sat up straighter on the hard stool. Cara's pages revealed an explosion of color, line, and story. Cara shared a fat, worn sketchbook from her daily life in Boulder. Sketches of everyday objects and little bits of writing, it showed a life observed, a life savored.

"One thing to consider is contrast," Cara said. "The thing that makes art interesting is variation. Differences in size, texture, line weight, colors—contrast is the thing that holds our attention."

Darla took notes when Cara discussed ways to make drawing part of everyday life. She really perked up when Cara mentioned travel sketchbooks.

"I'd like to go over a few methods I like to use when I am traveling. This is from my most recent trip to Italy." She began riffling through, the pages alive with color and shape and words. Darla's whole body wanted that. She wanted to be in that sketchbook, absorbing those colors. She wanted to be in Italy with her sketchbook leading the way.

She tuned back in. Cara was showing a page that recounted the story of how she'd befriended a flower vendor at a market.

"Everyone thought I was Italian," she said. "This hair and my dark eyes make me fit in almost everywhere I go."

She showed pages of her drawings of people at the market, accompanied by scraps of words, poems, and stories.

"Filling a sketchbook on a trip helps me to process all the things I am taking in. I'm sensitive, and all the input of a new place can be overwhelming. But when I have this"—Cara waved the fat black Moleskine—"I somehow am able to manage all the stimuli better."

"And then you have something cool to show afterward," the woman next to Darla piped up.

Cara laughed. "I enjoy people's reactions," she said. "But the act of doing it is the real prize. It's really not about how other people see it. It's about me and my relationship with the world. It's a big part of making me feel like *me*."

Tears crowded Darla's eyes. That was it exactly—the

change she'd felt from the class. She wouldn't have said it that way, but it felt like something had been returned to her after a long absence. Drawing made her herself. She would keep going. She had to keep going. At her job, she was herself—kinda. But not all of her got to show up. She lingered with the others as they packed up, not wanting to leave. Before heading out, she bought a notebook just like Cara's.

On the way home, Darla thought about how Cara fit in wherever she went. She had never felt that way. She hadn't fit in at Catholic school. The daughter of a single mom, living in an apartment, was not the same as the other kids who lived in subdivisions. She hadn't fit in in New York, a bitter disappointment after the long-held idea of New York being the answer to her childhood boredom. Would she fit in anywhere? Almost home, the concept of contrast sparked a new idea. Maybe that was why she should go to Lisbon. It stood out apart from the places she wanted to visit. It was different. She had no story about it. Maybe the contrast would make her life more interesting.

She took a picture of the leaf she'd drawn and texted it to Cat.

Look!

Groovy! Looks like the class was good?

LOVED it.

A wave of hearts floated onto her screen. She smiled, glad she could share this with Cat. She was intimidated to show Gregory. He was the definition of a perfectionist. He would never reveal a first draft of anything. She'd wait until she had something better to show him.

Chapter Three

That week, Darla took every free moment to fill her sketch-book. During online meetings, she'd doodle people's faces. In the evening, after work, she'd add watercolor. This became much more fun than reading *Don Quixote*. Much as she tried, she couldn't finish the book.

Driving to Denver for book group on Saturday, she let herself imagine going to Lisbon with a sketchbook. She hadn't said anything to Gregory about Lauren's bequest. Merging onto I-25, she realized she didn't want to tell him. This surprised her; usually, he was her confidante. But she'd never forget a walk they'd taken together one Sunday morning. She'd been going on about how she dreaded work the next day. Then, Gregory slowed and waited for her to finish.

"I want to tell you something," he said.

Darla smiled up at him.

"My aunt died and left me some money. So, I bought this." He gestured toward a brick bungalow they were standing in front of.

Darla gaped at the small house. Maybe this was his big proposal—he'd bought the house for them.

"Wow, well, what, I mean . . ." she stammered.

"It's going to be a rental property. There are tenants in it already."

She gazed at the neatly trimmed lawn, the established

peony bushes up against the house.

"When did this happen?"

"Last year. It took a bit to settle her estate and find the right place. But here it is." He smiled as if to fend off further questions. Darla felt sick.

"Wow, why didn't you tell me when it was happening?"

He shrugged and moved along, pulling her with him.

"It didn't seem important."

"You get a big inheritance, and that's not important?"

They walked for a bit more, talking about it. But they never came to a seamless understanding. One of the things Gregory had told her once when they were talking about money was that people should keep their finances private. They'd been playing, "What would you do if you won the lottery?" The only thing he was sure of was that he wouldn't tell anyone. Darla couldn't imagine holding that kind of information in.

Now, almost at Gregory's, she knew why he'd said that. Darla decided she wouldn't tell him about Lauren's bequest. Or that she was considering going to Lisbon. None of his business, she thought, maneuvering the car into a spot in front of his house.

Gregory greeted her at his door with a big smile. No matter what she thought of him when she was away, either missing him or wishing he was more chill, Darla still had a full-body reaction when she saw him. Everything in her wanted to lean into his strong, tall body. His eyes were always bright behind his glasses when he saw her. She felt he genuinely loved her. He just didn't show it easily.

She kissed him and shed her overnight bag. She hung out and sketched while he got ready. They chatted about their days, and she shivered in his cold house.

"Chilly?"

She shook her head. He liked to keep the temperature low. It didn't do any good to complain about it. She tried to wear warmer clothes when she visited him. Later, they knocked at Marco's door, a classic Arts and Crafts house in Wash Park. She cradled her hefty copy of *Don Quixote* and her sketchbook. Gregory held a bottle of wine. Inside, Marco and Paula hung out in the kitchen. In a flurry of greetings, Darla inhaled the yummy smells.

"Lasagna?"

"Of course!"

Marco smiled. He was famous among them for his lasagna. It was a small book group. They didn't enlist new people often. Not many wanted to read the classics they chose. If she were honest, Darla was losing interest in old stories from the past.

They gathered in the dining room. Paula brought in the salad, and Marco hefted the lasagna onto the table. Gregory opened the bottle he'd brought and poured it around. She felt like they were a family of sorts. Paula, a friend from university who had moved to Colorado well before Darla, had introduced her to Gregory. They chatted about the book while they ate. She had only made it halfway through the novel.

"I wish I had read farther," Darla explained, "but work was particularly intense."

"Further," Gregory said. Darla blushed, glancing at Paula. But no one seemed to notice. She forked more salad in, mortified as always when Gregory corrected her grammar. They discussed the plot, and Darla started relating more to the character. She wanted to do something more interesting in her life. She wanted to have some kind of grand, foolish adventure. They relocated to the living room with key lime pie and tea.

Darla snuggled up on the couch. She sketched to keep herself occupied during the discussion. She could listen and chime in here and there and also sketch the teapot, cups, and pie plates with crumbs and forks. She made notes in fun lettering about what they'd talked about.

On the way to Gregory's place afterward, Darla thought about the art class at Two Hands Paperie. She tried to tell Gregory what had happened to her, but as an uber-practical architect, he didn't seem to get it when she said it made her *her*. Still, he tried to be supportive.

"That's great, Darla. I'm glad you found something fun for yourself."

"Me too."

Sometimes Darla felt like he was reciting from a book of *What to Say to Be Polite*. Like he was performing politeness and masking what he really thought.

"What do you think you'll do with that? The sketching?"

"Do? Like what?"

"Like a side hustle? Maybe sell paintings?"

Cara's sketchbook was just a piece of her art. She also made abstract paintings and sold cards with her drawings on them. She'd figured out how to make a living as an artist. Darla really wanted to see Cara's studio, but Darla hadn't even considered making money from art. She shrugged.

"I don't know. I'm just doing it because it feels good. For me. Not for anyone else."

"Uh-huh," Gregory said. Clearly, he didn't get it. She didn't want him to say anything else, so she changed the subject.

"Good discussion tonight."

"Yes, I enjoyed it. *Don Quixote* was even better than the first time I read it."

"I can't believe you've read it more than once. I could barely get through it! I don't have as much time to read as I used to."

"That's a shame. I think you'd get more from the discussion if you read the whole book."

"Well, sometimes I just can't. Deadlines at work, you know."

Gregory had his own architecture firm and made his own schedule. He had enough time to read *The New York Times* every Sunday, plus books for book group. He pulled into his pristine garage, glancing at Darla. He had that tightening around his mouth when he was going to say something she wouldn't like.

"You seemed more interested in drawing than the discussion."

She unbuckled and got out. She *had* been absorbed in her sketchbook. But she'd been with them, had participated. Sketching while hanging out made the time more pleasant. She got impatient sometimes, especially when she wasn't on top of the conversation. Drawing offered solace in this and other situations, like when on a conference call at work. She didn't want to think about Lauren's bequest. She couldn't leave work, but the thought of letting Lauren down was unbearable. She kept her grief tucked deep inside, and sketching helped her pretend it was all just the natural flow of life.

Moving through their evening routines, they tucked into bed together. After uninspiring sex, Darla couldn't stop thinking about Lauren.

The next morning, they had breakfast in his unadorned kitchen. His whole house was bare of decor. He hadn't hung up his art. He claimed to have a collection of paintings, but she had never seen it. Darla had always thought that when they got married and moved in together, they would decorate and make a real home. Now she pushed down how much she wanted to share a home. It had been fine living solo in her twenties and thirties, but now, just past forty, she wanted more.

Gregory filled the teapot and set out the muesli and yogurt. He had three things he made at home: muesli and yogurt, burritos, and spaghetti. He didn't drink coffee, which Darla tried to forgive him for. She took tea when she stayed with him but always stopped at a café on the way back to Boulder to get her much-needed cappuccino. They ate quietly, Darla pausing between bites to sketch the muesli and berries. It was too detailed, though, and her lines looked shaggy, trying to capture the chaos of muesli.

After breakfast, they headed out for a walk in Washington Park. From one week to the next, winter was reluctantly giving way to spring. When they got to the lake, Gregory pulled her hand to sit with him on a bench. Her ass was instantly cold. They watched a giant gaggle of geese approach and splash down on the lake. Even in March, there were tons of them populating the park.

"Darla, I want to talk with you about something."

She braced herself. Was he kicking her out of the book group for being a slacker? But no, he was fishing around in his pocket. A small green velvet box was tucked in his hand. Her heart thumped. Was this . . . ?

"Darla, I love you very much. I think we're good together. I'm ready to do what you've wanted all along." He opened the box. She gasped. Her whole body retracted. She couldn't hide her shock.

"Oh, um, wow," she stammered.

He pulled it out and held up the key.

"Wanna move in with me?"

"Wow, that's not what I thought you were going to say. I thought that was going to be a ring." She was shocked to discover that she felt not disappointment but relief. How could she have said no to a proposal? She'd been waiting for this kind of commitment for years. But now she couldn't feel anything but a desire to flee. If only she were one of those geese, she'd be able to disappear in formation and fly far, far away. Or at least across town.

"Oh." Gregory paused, the key pressed between two fingers. Recognition sparked in his eyes, and he tucked the key back into the box.

"I thought it was a cute way to ask you to move in."

"But not get married?"

She clapped her hand on her mouth. She had just proposed to him in a backhanded, half-ass way.

He pushed his glasses up his finely sculpted nose. He couldn't meet Darla's eye. He was so damn handsome, Darla thought. All the things—tall, dark, gorgeous hair. Why couldn't he be the one? She realized, in that green velvet moment, that this would never work out the way she had hoped. There was no way forward with Gregory. She'd wanted this clarity for a long time, but now, it almost blinded her.

"Let me sleep on it?"

She could barely nod. She just wanted to leave. They made their way back to his house in silence. She put her few things in a backpack and rushed a goodbye. Suddenly, she was wiped out. Her eyes were heavy, and she just wanted to take a nap. He hugged her. She could tell he didn't know what was happening.

"Call you later?" he said.

"Sure." She waved and jumped into her car. Darla made her way to the coffee shop, where this time, she took a seat inside and got out her sketchbook. The cappuccino bolstered her mood. She sketched and journaled, losing some of her anxiety in the lines that appeared on the page. When she drew her coffee cup and the biscotti she couldn't get down, a calm settled over her. Ah, there it is, she thought. This was the body feeling she wanted. This was how she wanted to feel. Not tense and as if she weren't smart enough for Gregory and the book group members. She popped onto her phone and quickly found what she was looking for. She gathered her things, buoyant with her new bold move.

On the drive back to Boulder, Darla called her mom. It rang forever. She was about to bail when her mom's voice came over the line.

"Hellooooo! I was just thinking of you! Weird, isn't it?"

"Hi, Mom! What's up?"

"Not much. Henry just left, and I was about to start a bridge game. How are you?"

"You're not going to believe what Gregory did. I hardly believe it!"

"He finally proposed! Congratulations!"

Darla tensed up. She couldn't get words out. It was a mistake to call her mom so soon after the disappointment. She changed lanes, slowing behind a delivery van.

"Uh-oh. He didn't propose."

"Well, he kinda did in a sorta not really committed way." She told her mom about the velvet ring box, the key, and her unquestionable no.

"Oh, honey, that stinks. I'm sorry he's not the one for you."

"That's what Lauren said. Does everyone think Gregory is a bad match for me?"

"I don't know who Lauren is, but I can't say I ever warmed to him. I always saw you with someone more fun. But don't worry, we'll find someone for you."

Darla gripped the steering wheel.

"I haven't broken up with him yet, Mom. Maybe there's hope. Maybe moving in with him is a great first step. And then we get married. And live happily ever after."

"You know, your father and I were never married."

Darla startled, her car swerving toward the shoulder.

"What?"

"Nope. If I'm honest, we were together just because of you. But he couldn't take it. Didn't want to have a family that young. He left."

Darla couldn't believe her mom was saying these words. As if telling a stranger.

"Okay, well, thanks, I guess?"

"Don't you worry about Gregory. He's not the only fish in the sea."

Darla rolled her eyes at the cliché.

"Love you!" She signed off. Approaching her exit, she shook her head. Mom. She'd never change.

That afternoon, Darla took a long walk, savoring the creek path's shaded quiet. She got home just as night settled. She sent a text, the whoosh sound exhilarating her. A text came back from Cat:

Whatcha doin'?

Leaping off the edge of my life.

Coolio! Can I watch?

Come over! I have big news.

K. Be there soon! Dinner?

Sure. Bring Thai!

Thumb up emoji.

Later, Cat arrived in a flurry of cold air, with his usual grin and a bag that smelled of pad thai.

"What's the news?" he asked.

Darla took the food into the kitchen. "Not so fast! More suspense won't kill you. Wine?"

"Sure." Cat shed his jacket of many colors and slipped his shoes off. He accepted the glass Darla gave him, a small French tumbler she preferred over wineglasses. They caught up on life incidentals while she assembled the food on a tray.

"I'm starving. Thanks for bringing dinner."

They tucked into the spring rolls. The sauce was her favorite. The comforting flavor of peanut butter knocked into action with the spiciness. They ate for a minute before Cat insisted she tell him the news.

"You won't believe this. Remember Lauren?" She took a bite of pad thai.

"Of course!"

"Well, her brother contacted me after the service. It turns out Lauren included me in her will."

"I'm not surprised. She was kinda your fairy godmother, wasn't she?"

"I hadn't thought of her that way, but yes, I suppose she was. Guess what! She bequeathed me money. A lot of money."

"Like, how much money?"

"Twenty-five thousand."

"Holy crap," Cat said through a mouthful of noodles. "That's awesome!"

She nodded, sipping her wine. She didn't plan on telling anyone except Cat.

"It's awesome, but it comes with a stipulation."

"Oh, things are about to get good." Cat smiled. "Whatchu gotta do for the cash?"

"Lisbon! I've got to do Lisbon."

"What? Tell me."

"I don't know any details. Lauren said I needed a change." Darla paused, poking at her food. "I can't disagree."

"I can't either. You've been in a rut for a while."

"I have not! I like my job. And I've got this now, which I love." She waved her sketchbook.

"It could be a fun trip for you and Gregory. I've heard Lisbon is awesome."

"Well, that's the other thing. Gregory and I—"

"He finally proposed!"

"Not exactly."

She told him about the key and how clever Gregory had thought he was. She tried to describe her full-body no. Cat shook his head, but he didn't seem surprised.

"Oh man, that sucks. Did you break up?"

"No, not yet. But I don't think I can stay with him. And now this Lisbon idea. I suppose I could take my vacation time for this."

"Two weeks isn't very long. And $25K? There's no way you could spend that in two weeks."

Darla's pragmatism had already worked through the math. She couldn't imagine spending that much money in one place.

She could probably save at least $20K and still splash out in Lisbon. Maybe Cat would go with her. But these ideas deflated as soon as she floated them. It was as if Lauren were there, saying, "Nope, nope."

"I think you've got to go a little bolder there. From what you told me about Lauren, she would want more than a fun vacation for you."

He was right, as usual. As funky as Cat was, he was also astute about what was usually going on underneath things. She began to clear away the dishes and leftovers.

"I've barely ever heard of Lisbon. I'd prefer to go to Paris."

"Do both! You could move there. With that money, you could live for at least six months."

She sipped her wine and tried to imagine leaving Boulder, maybe for good. Could she really move away? She would miss Boulder's quaint side streets lined with funky old houses and rickety porches. She'd had a decent time in Colorado.

It was better for her than New York. The noise had worn her down. She was certain there had never been one single moment of silence in the city, ever. The infinite number of things to do—museums, parties, bookstore events—was both thrilling and daunting.

But she wasn't advancing at her job. And she couldn't afford a home in Boulder. She'd been looking in Denver, near where Gregory lived. If she admitted it, part of the *hell no* to Gregory's proposal was Denver. Visiting and hanging out with Gregory was fine, but she didn't want to live there. She surprised herself with this knowledge. Weeks ago, she would have been sure that Gregory and Denver were the next best thing for her. And now the news that her parents were never married. She opened her mouth to drop that bomb for Cat but stopped. She didn't know how to think about it, or feel about it, let alone talk about it.

"Six months! I think not. A few weeks is better. Maybe I can go to Paris after Lisbon."

"Well, whatever you do, don't do it half ass." Cat grinned.

They talked about other things before Cat's girlfriend pinged him for a ride home from work.

"Gotta go!"

At the door, they hugged.

"Lisbon! Lisbon!"

She swatted him. "Oh, stop! I probably won't be able to get away from work."

Getting ready for bed, her mind wandered across the sea to Lisbon. Her phone pinged. Stephen. She also saw a text from Gregory, which she ignored.

"Thoughts on your inheritance?" Money emoji, heart emoji. She hadn't pictured Stephen as an emoji guy.

Her palm grew sweaty. Who would pass up that kind of gift? If only it were not contingent on going to Lisbon. But why not, really? Why not take a trip to Portugal? Truth was, she hadn't been out of Colorado in a long time. She knew she didn't fit in. Sure, she had adapted, but most people she knew here were crazy for it. Had relocated here because they wanted the lifestyle of the mountains. She had defaulted there because of her job, and the ease of living in Boulder had allowed her to stay, coasting.

She texted Stephen back. "I'll get back to you right away."

Could she do a short "sabbatical"? Maybe a month? She struggled with getting up in the morning. She wanted to blame the sadness of losing Lauren that permeated her days. But if she were honest, this had been going on for a while. She didn't spring out of bed every day, not even close. It was more like a slither out of bed and into the world suit she wore but resented.

A conversation from a few years back with her coworker Tami came to mind. Tami had turned forty and was feeling it—not physically but existentially. Her mom had died, and she'd just returned from dismantling her estate.

"I just realized that there are some things I won't do in this life. I have to let them go."

She'd looked so sad, and Darla had felt sorry for her. Darla had also been suspicious. Was life really over at forty? Probably pushing it to have kids. But she didn't want kids anyway. No clock was ticking for her to hurry up and do what she wanted. Until now.

Brushing her teeth, she caught sight of herself in the mirror. Her curly hair was getting long. Time for a cut soon. It overcame her that Lauren would never cut her hair again. She already missed the salon, which Lauren had decorated wildly and filled with upbeat music. Going there had been a sort of therapy for Darla. Being in that vibrant space gave her a sense of her own fun spirit, which she had kept under wraps for the sake of making a decent living and getting by. Darla couldn't imagine going there without Lauren. How would she find a new hairdresser? She was crying, the toothpaste drooling down her chin, any hope of brushing her teeth gone. Sobbing, she rinsed the brush.

She crawled into bed, desperately wanting to talk to Lauren about the inheritance and directive. Why had she done that? Where was the note going along with it? Why Lisbon?

Chapter Four

At work after hours, Darla tried to care about the new client she'd been assigned, a nonprofit helping eradicate food deserts. This was the kind of cause she wanted to be part of. But today? Nope. She bumped her knee against her desk and shouted.

"Crap!"

"You okay?" her boss called from his office.

"Yep, thanks." She limped into the hall. "You're here late."

"Trying to stay ahead of it all," Terry said.

"Do you have a minute?"

"Come on in." He waved her into his office, where he ran the ship from his standing desk.

It felt weird to be there at night, just the two of them and the cleaning guy in the main office space. But this might be the time to discuss her trip plans.

"I wanted to talk to you about my vacation time," she said. "I have several weeks saved up."

He didn't respond.

"I'm thinking of going to Portugal this spring."

He grimaced and shook his head. "Okay, but that's not going to work for us. Timing-wise, it's off. Wait till summer? We have the big MacDonald project due in June. We always count on you to make sure the client narrative interviews are all edited."

Darla twisted her pen.

"I was planning to leave in May. So, I'd be able to contribute to the project, no problem. And then have a nice vacation."

"Why don't we hold off on vacations until summer," he said. He went back to shuffling papers.

She slumped inside, a gnarly ball of resentment in her stomach.

Back in her office, she packed up her thermos and donned her sweater. Crap. She didn't want to wait. Now that she saw a cliff to leap off—at least for a vacation—she couldn't stop peering over the edge. Spring in Europe sounded better every day. Maybe she could speak to Mel in HR. But going behind Terry's back might not be a great idea. It certainly wouldn't help with the promotion she'd been hoping for.

On the walk home, the sky was clear and sparkled with stars. The trees on the Pearl Street Mall were twinkly with lights. Few people were out. She fumed. Terry! Gregory. How disappointing that moment had been. What was with these guys? Why didn't they seem able to understand what a woman wanted, what *she* wanted? For the first time, she was aware that she hated being controlled by her job, restricted by her boss's agenda. Lauren hadn't seemed controlled by anyone. Darla thought about her careful plans for saving and retirement. How far $25K would take her. How much time would it buy her? She had no delusions about a vacation fixing her life. She wasn't under the illusion that life would magically be better in Europe. But it sure sounded fun to get away.

Darla drove up to Chautauqua. She wasn't much of a hiker. She wasn't much of a Boulderite, if she were honest. She didn't meditate or drive an EV. She didn't do yoga. But the Enchanted

Mesa Trail was her happy place. The noble pines made her feel like she was in a magical forest. She parked and headed up the incline toward the dining hall. Her thoughts were on Europe. A month seemed so daring. Finally, doing something. The last big thing she had done was move to Boulder.

She passed the barn where concerts were held in the summer. A few hikers and dogs were on the trail ahead of her. Her heart was starting to really pump now. But was that the terror of making a big change? Alongside the possibilities, an orchestra of fears played on. Waves of doubt on repeat, riding a crest of thought and then fading. She was trying to not sing along to those thoughts but to let them wash over her.

As a child, Darla would lie around reading about exotic places, powerful people and adventurous women braving the rigors of New York City. She decided that when she grew up, she'd live in NYC. So, after graduation, she made the move and got a job as an assistant editor. The publishing house was okay. She liked the conversations about what to publish and why, but she hated to admit she did not enjoy living in New York.

Boulder wasn't *bad*. She was surrounded by the best things, near the creek path and the library. Wild Oats and the Dushanbe Tea House were right there with the farmer's market. She couldn't ask for a better box. But it was still a box.

She reached the curve of the climb where a view over the plains opened up. Pausing to catch her breath, she felt a burst of appreciation for Boulder. The fresh air, the views, and the pines gave her energy and clarity. Still, she didn't feel this was her place, despite living in Colorado for years. Her adventures were lived through books. She read for pleasure and escape. But she also wanted to travel as much as possible. Somehow, she hadn't managed to take the trips she wanted. Now, the damage to the environment, the political climate, the mud-slide of the dollar against the euro all planted fear seeds in her: go now or you may not be able to go. As she walked, edges started to form around her future map. By the time she finished the hike, a plan had formed. At the bottom of the trail near the picnic pavilion, she saw a familiar form. Cat stood in the shade, checking his phone.

"Hey!"

He looked up and smiled. "Yo!"

"Fancy running into you here. We should have planned to hike together."

"I'm meeting Sara soon."

Darla took off her hat and wiped sweat from her hairline. "I'm thinking of going to Lisbon for two weeks, then Paris for two weeks."

"Okay, that's big. Tell me more!"

His phone pinged. "Sara's going to be late."

They sat at one of the picnic tables under the pavilion. An older couple played cards nearby, their thermoses and sunhats on the table next to them. They had a little transistor radio that played the local jazz station.

"I can't believe I've never been to Europe."

"Now is the time! You have to go. Lisbon! Why not?"

"Why not? I haven't come up with anything other than because of . . . inertia. Ever since I got the inheritance—I love saying that!—my mind has been on a possibility party. I haven't felt this excited since I don't know when."

"Well, I'll always vote for adventure," Cat said. Darla smiled. Yet she didn't want to count on his enthusiasm. Lauren had died. Anyone could die.

"So, I've got big news."

"I'm sorry. I've been so wrapped up in this Lisbon thing I didn't even ask how you are. What's the news?"

"Well, my parents are selling the cottage."

"What?! I thought they were going to retire there."

"They did too. But it's kinda remote, and as they get older, they think they need to be near town more."

"Wow."

She felt stupid that she didn't have something better to say. Her memories from the cottage were some of the best of her life.

"How are you taking it?"

Cat shrugged. "I always wanted to have that cottage in my life. But now that I'm older, I realize I don't want to live there or take care of it either."

He checked his phone. Darla resisted reaching for hers.

"I guess certain things have their own lifespan, and this season of my family's life is over."

"Someone good will buy it. It's such a special place."

A complete picture of the cottage and the lake lit up in Darla's mind. This was where she had become a water baby, saturated to her core after a day in the water. She wished she could buy it, but same as Cat, she didn't want the responsibility. The idea of owning a house now seemed moons away from taking off for Europe.

They talked about his parents' plans. He'd have one more chance to spend time there and help them pack up. Darla might not ever go back. The only thing she missed about Michigan was the water, the abundant lakes, and the ability to go swimming in nature all summer long. Boulder's dryness was starting to eat away at her. She spent way too much money on lotions and serums, fending off dry skin and dry sinuses.

Lisbon had water—a river. And lots of coastlines. Portugal was starting to be more appealing to her.

"Would you go with me? To Lisbon?"

Cat tilted his head. "Mm, probably not. I'm saving for my Sprinter van."

"I'm on my own then."

"You'll meet people!"

Darla couldn't imagine it. She wasn't outgoing like Cat.

"Here's Sara."

He gave Darla a quick hug, and they said goodbye. Darla headed to her car. A wave of sadness surged up, thinking about losing Cat's family cottage. She hadn't been there for years, not since she'd moved to Colorado. But knowing it would no longer be a place she could go to made her feel really old. Doors were shutting. She needed to find a way to get water into her life. Maybe a water aerobics class?

In her car, she texted Stephen.

I'm sorry it's taken so long to get back to you. I accept Lauren's generous gift, even Lisbon.

She was driving downhill toward her apartment when a reply came in. She pulled over.

A thread of exuberant emojis, followed by, *I'll be in touch.*

Chapter Five

——

She took everything out of her carry-on. Again. Once she'd accepted Lauren's bequest, things had happened quickly. It had taken a couple of months to set everything up, places to stay in Lisbon and Paris, a few friend dates, a bit of research about coffee shops. Now it was taking forever to pack. Once she'd gotten into her closet, she couldn't help but sort out the things she never wore. She made a giant pile of clothes she never wanted to see again. Donate them, she thought. When the trip clothes were laid out on the bed, they seemed necessary. But her carry-on didn't agree, refusing to shut with everything inside.

Her phone rang. Mom.

"Halloo," Darla sang.

Her mom dove right in, peppering her with questions about work and Gregory.

"It's over with Gregory," Darla confessed.

"You didn't get past that key thing? Come on! How could you pass that up?"

Darla couldn't believe her mom had changed her tune about Gregory. Had she forgotten her earlier comments about never really liking him? Darla shook off a creeping concern about her mom. She didn't want to recount the breakup scene with her mom. It had been awkward and awful, if she admitted it. She'd never broken it off with anyone. At Racine's, she'd been unable to hold back. Out poured all her resentments. Gregory had been silent, a look of astonishment on his face giving way to tears. Darla had never once seen him cry. She almost backpedaled. But Lauren's voice in her head said, "You go, girl."

She took a deep breath. "Mom, saying no to that and breaking up with Gregory felt like the first real thing I've done in a long time. I want you to be happy for me."

"Oh, poo. You've done all kinds of things that are real for you. New York! Your great job."

Darla knew her mom would prefer that she focus on the practical. She changed the subject. She didn't want her mom to see how much she was still bummed it hadn't worked out with Gregory. Just because she'd initiated the breakup didn't mean it didn't hurt. She'd never be able to go to Racine's again. No loss there, but she was surprised at how much she missed Gregory.

Before her mom could launch into plans for finding a new boyfriend for Darla, she spoke up.

"Mom, I'm taking a long vacation."

"Oh? You can take time off work? How long?"

"I'm using my vacation time. They'll be fine without me." Darla had negotiated with Mel in HR, who'd spoken to Terry on her behalf. It hadn't been easy, but everything was arranged. She'd be back in four weeks, refreshed.

"Well, where are you going?"

"Lisbon. Then Paris."

"That sounds like a big trip. You must have a lot of vacation time saved up." Her mom harrumphed. "Who are you going with?"

"Me. I'm going with me."

"Is that safe?"

Darla groaned. "Safe compared to what? To never doing anything that I want to do?"

She wouldn't tell her mom about the inheritance or Lauren's directive. No matter what. She steeled herself against her mom's onslaught of questions.

"Why isn't Gregory going with you?"

"Mom, we broke up, remember?"

"Pffft. I could see you getting back together."

Darla firmed up her lips. She wouldn't have this conversation. She wouldn't.

"I don't know about you in Lisbon. All by yourself?"

"I'm an adult, Mom. I can travel alone." She brought Lauren to mind to bolster her courage.

"What if you have another panic attack?"

"It wasn't a panic attack. Geez, Mom!"

Before she'd left New York, there'd been an incident on the subway. Work had been particularly stressful. She'd almost arrived at her stop when she had a weird sensation in her body—she felt immobilized. Her stop came and went, and with it, her heart beat faster and faster. She had no idea what was happening. No one in the subway car took notice. It took five more stops before she could move. She reversed direction and made it home safely, if quivery. Nothing like that had ever happened again, but she added it to the list of reasons to move out of New York. Now, she wished she had never confided the incident to her mom.

"Well, whatever it was, you decided cities weren't right for you."

"That's why I chose Lisbon, Mom. It's not too big."

She told her mom what she'd read about Lisbon and how she'd rented a room there. As she talked, her excitement grew.

There were still a lot of details to sort out, but she liked organizing things.

They hung up, and Darla folded the last item into her suitcase: a cute purple jacket. Wrapping up Lauren's estate, Stephen had hosted an open house at Lauren's and invited her friends over to take anything they'd wanted. Most of the stuff was too flowery for Darla's taste, but this purple jacket would do. It fit perfectly. When she put it on, she knew it would be her shield against her own doubts and fears. She'd also gotten a sexy lace dress. Someone had urged her to take it, intimating she might have a fling in Europe. Darla couldn't imagine it, but she was happy to have a bit of Lauren with her always.

In her journal, Darla kept lists of things to do and places to check out. When she mentioned her trip, friends and coworkers had chimed in with recommendations. Someone had suggested Globalkin as a way to meet locals. Globalkin was a nonprofit that believed in the human family and offered ways for travelers to connect with locals for events and even homestays. Darla loved the idea of being part of the big human family and wanted to participate in cultural exchanges with others. She collected a few names of people—Globalkins—to connect with.

Hopefully she would get to the coast. The sea's vastness had great appeal for her. But along with her excitement, a mounting terror kept pace with her plans. She got out her journal and expunged her fears onto the page. This became a running list. At some point, there were so many that they became ridiculous. Darla had to laugh at herself for being such a scaredy cat.

She took every fear and reversed it, turning it into a blessing. "You eat with caloric impunity." "Security and customs officials love you and let you pass." This list of blessings boosted her up. What if good wishes really did make a difference in life? What if these blessings could really work some magic? She liked that sparkly feeling she had when something fun or surprising was happening.

Darla turned this into an art project. She made a set of the wishes and trimmed them into little pieces of paper, like from fortune cookies. She printed sets of them and put them into little coin envelopes, naming them Journey Blessings. She made a bunch of them to give away if she met people.

She carefully selected her art supplies. She'd only carry a small day purse, a stylish sporty thing that wasn't too big but would take her sketchbook in a side pocket. She reminded herself that she could buy things in Europe. That it would be fun to visit an art supply store in Europe and buy pens and paper. Her book group had gone in on a gift for her: a special Retro 1951 pen with postage stamps depicted on the barrel.

Finally, her departure day arrived. Cat came to take her to the airport. She picked at her cuticles, waiting outside for him. What would happen in Europe? What if she hated it? She tried to shake it off. Whatever it was, she would be back in a month. She had been predictable for years, in a rut with Gregory. She wanted something totally off her radar. To make an actual change. She couldn't imagine what would change in a month, but time away would give her a boost to be able to cope with work.

In Cat's ancient Mercedes on the highway, Darla was antsy. She felt like she could leap out of the window. She turned the conversation to Cat.

"When are you buying your van?"

He shrugged. She could never get a specific answer from him. She hoped he did someday quit his job and go Sprinting around the country.

When they pulled up at the airport, Cat reached into the back seat and produced a rumpled paper bag.

"I know you're not taking much, but I thought you'd need this on your trip."

Darla sagged inside. She had no room for anything else. The bag looked big. Inside was a small pillow with an embroidered message. Tears came up and her heart clenched.

"Cat!"

"I know you love your comfort stuff, and I thought this would help you stay cozy wherever you go. And Lauren's message to you, so you don't forget."

She ran her fingers over the lettering. *Live Full Ass.* Like she could forget that. She was really crying now. Cat handed her a tissue. She grabbed him for a hug, the pillow smooshed between them.

"You're going to have a great time," he said.

"What if I don't?" she wailed.

"Then no big deal."

She sniffed and clutched the pillow. She felt bad for wanting to reject it before she'd seen it. The embroidery was badass, the slogan something she would try to live up to.

Chapter Six

Darla's first view of Lisbon didn't sync with the bright photos she'd seen online. In a taxi from the airport, she zoomed past Soviet-style apartment buildings from the days of the dictator. Her body was electrified, pulsing with fear and excitement. She felt like a house with all the rooms lit up unnecessarily. All of the switches had come on when she walked up to the passport control. It was her first passport stamp. Would he question her about her purpose in Portugal? But he'd barely glanced, stamped, and waved her on.

"Your street, up there." The driver had pulled to a stop and pointed up the hill.

"Are we there?" she asked.

He pointed again up the street. "Thirty euros." He got out.

She'd been told it would be much less than this. She protested. He responded by yelling loudly in Portuguese. Darla shrank back. He opened the trunk and turned to demand the money. She wasn't interested in an argument with him. She gave him the cash, and he exchanged it for her suitcase. She tried to get better directions from him, but he just slammed the trunk and waved up the hill. Sheesh, she thought, hopefully all Portuguese people aren't this cranky.

Darla clunk-clunked her carry-on through her new neighborhood, Bairro Alto. The streets were cobbled with irregular white and black stones. Her suitcase loudly rumbled and bumped, catching in the cracks. Graffiti scarred the walls of the narrow streets, not all words or tags but artful images of people stenciled in black paint. Balconies dripped with succulents, burro tails draped over railings. She arrived on her street, Rua da Atalaia, and sensed the gaze of several old ladies roosting on their balconies. She felt vulnerable and obvious, carting her luggage, not nimble, not quick, clearly an outsider. Darla wanted to believe that without the suitcase she could blend in anywhere, like Cara. She knew she looked like the tourist she was.

She pressed the buzzer at the address. A voice came over the intercom.

"Darla?"

"Angel?"

"Third floor on the right!"

The buzzer sounded, clicking open the door. She pushed into a dark hallway. Darla huffed up three flights, arriving with her clothes sticking to a layer of sweat. She raised her hand to knock when the door opened. A buxom woman wearing a dressing gown and a lot of makeup began talking.

"Welcome! Come on in! You must be exhausted. You came from the US, right? Liza! Judy! Stop that! You know Mommy doesn't like that."

Two thin, scared-looking dogs huddled nearby, yipping. The women bottlenecked in the foyer, Darla's carry-on at her feet.

"We're in a bit of a disarray here. I'm headed to Berlin. I've got some shows lined up there but have a few things to do before I leave here. Yes. I'm a performer," Angel said, and now the makeup and dressing gown made sense to Darla, understanding she'd rented a room from a prima donna. Her nerves continued the twanging they'd started when she landed in Lisbon.

"You're leaving?" Darla suspected something wasn't quite right about this. Angel plunged on, eyeing Darla.

"Not for a week still. What's your birthday? I'm an astrologer. I can do your chart for you."

Darla didn't know what a chart was, but she didn't want to give Angel more info than necessary. In the living room, a mess of clothes, makeup, and stuff cluttered every surface. It smelled of incense and something unpleasant she couldn't identify. The dogs followed them, looking back and forth at the women with wet, anxious eyes. Darla felt sorry for them.

"This is Judy and Liza." Angel pointed to the dogs. Darla reached toward the small one, but the dog shrank away. Angel plowed on. "The couch is here, and you can put your stuff here. The kitchen is in here . . ."

The kitchen was also a wreck, with food boxes on the counters and dishes in the sink. A few tiny flies traced a circle in the air above the mess. A moist, mildewy scent crowded the dark room. Darla's heart sank. She had planned to economize by cooking at home at least a couple of times a week. She couldn't imagine spending any time here, let alone cooking and eating in this mess. The small bathroom, with a shower and tub and a high window, would do. Through the open window, she heard children shouting; there must be a schoolyard next door.

Angel showed Darla to her room, a cramped box. There was a mattress on the floor, barely covered with a rumpled blanket, and a dressing table coated in dust. She thought of her Journey Blessing—*Your beds are like pillows of the gods*—and couldn't help giving a small snort. The window looked onto an abandoned building. An open closet full of clothes drew Darla's attention. Angel saw her looking.

"Those are Mary's. She's still here but will be moving out in a few days. You'll be staying in the living room until then."

"That's not what I signed up for," Darla said.

Angel put her hands on her hips. "That's what we've got. Sorry."

Darla snorted. Angel wasn't sorry. Darla didn't want to go out into Lisbon with her suitcase, trying to find somewhere safe to stay. Her instinct was confirmed. She experienced a fleeting triumph, washed over by a greater sense of dread about the apartment. She glanced at the couch. A wave of panic washed over her. Where would she go if she left? She was stuck here, at least for the next two weeks. She could sleep there for a few nights. Then she'd get her own room.

Back in the living room, Angel got down to business. "It's 250 euros for the two weeks. Can you pay me now, in cash?"

She didn't want to pay ahead of time. Steeling herself, she forced out a reply.

"Sure. I need to hit an ATM." She silently pushed her luggage to the corner of the room, eager to escape from the oppressive atmosphere of the apartment.

"Okay, no problem. You can leave your stuff. Here are the keys."

Angel showed Darla the downstairs door key and the apartment key. "Can you go get the cash now?"

"Sure."

Angel told her where to find the nearest ATM, and she headed out. It felt good to be free of the luggage. Now she could look around a bit. The neighborhood was quiet, uncluttered with cars or bikes. Hardly anyone was around. Her street had several closed bars, plus a few shops selling artisan goods. A bit unbalanced and woozy from jet lag, she picked her way carefully along the black cobbled streets, bits of glass crunching underfoot. She smelled something burning and heard sounds from open windows up high. Silverware clattered; a radio broadcast in rapid Portuguese. Nothing looked like the images the internet had fed her. What had lured Lauren to this place?

She found the ATM and hustled back, nervous about carrying a lot of cash. She passed a group of guys clustered on a stoop, eyeing her, then discarding their interest like the flakes of tobacco that fell from the cigarettes they were rolling. Angel pounced the minute she came back. She was what Darla called "can't *not* talk." Angel kept up a monologue mostly about herself, with a few tidbits of advice about Lisbon. The men were short and hairy. Beer was cheap, and bars stayed open late. She bragged about her gigs and told Darla where they were and insisted she come. Darla had little interest in Angel's shows nor in her perspective on Lisbon, but she tried to be polite. Finally, she escaped to explore the neighborhood, hoping her stuff would be okay in the apartment.

She wandered the narrow streets, quiet in the late afternoon. The small cobblestones were everywhere, not just in her neighborhood. The black and gray stones were often arrayed in intricate patterns. Pity the fool wearing heels. At a *pasteleria*, she ordered a glass of white wine and a *tosta*, a grilled cheese sandwich. The wine, from a spigot behind the bar, fizzed in her glass. The sandwich was hot and cheesy, unremarkable but adequate comfort food for the moment. She regretted not getting a hotel room or her own apartment. How could she get out of it now? She'd paid Angel the €250. Maybe it wouldn't be too bad. She sat there in a daze, wondering why she hadn't used some of Lauren's Thrill Money. A lifetime of economizing and saving wasn't broken in a day. The flight over and her Paris lodging had cost her more than she'd expected. She'd try Angel's and see how it went.

After lunch, Darla walked and walked. Up and down, leaning into the hills, everything at a slant. Her body, used to Boulder's thin air and her hikes at Chautauqua, seemed to recognize and appreciate Lisbon's hills. She came upon a mirador and paused. Here were the stunning vistas. Palm trees and tile and tourists, oh my. The views of the river from up high were stunning. Now she had a glimpse of what drew Lauren here. She wrote in her journal, wanting to capture impressions for later sketches.

It was growing dark when she made her way back to her apartment. She found Bairro Alto changed. Bars were now open, with people clustered outside. Too tired to join the party, she headed upstairs. The effects of jet lag were fierce. Luckily, Angel wasn't home. Mary, the woman occupying her room, wasn't there either. Darla took a shower and set herself up on the couch in the living room. It's not too bad, she tried to convince herself. It took a long time to dim all the lights that were still turned up bright inside her, but she finally fell asleep.

A loud cheer woke Darla. She looked around the living room, unsure where she was. Her back kinked up against the rough sofa cushions, and her mouth was dry. The smell of incense and dog brought her back: Lisbon, Angel's apartment. Party sounds from the street filtered through the large windows. It sounded like a rager—shouts, bottles clanking on the cobblestones, pumping bass. At the window, she peered out. A sea of people flooded the street as far as she could see. Everyone had a drink, and people danced and hugged and sang. She had no idea when she'd booked the room that she would be in party central. She padded into the bathroom and then back to her couch. Fuck, she thought. Why didn't I bring earplugs? She made a mental note to get some.

Sleep seemed as far away as her life in Boulder. She squirmed around on the couch, trying to get comfortable. Her worries clustered around her pillow, driving away any sanity or confidence in her decision. She rolled over. She fluffed her travel pillow under her head, hoping sleep would invite her back in. But it didn't. The noise outside raged on. Instead, her mind began a parade of fears. Why had she listened to Lauren? Why did she leave home? Now, in this smelly room on a couch in a stranger's home in Lisbon, she wondered what had been so bad about her life. The fears surged through her, making her gut clench and her jaw tighten. She took a deep breath, held it, released it slowly. What would Lauren say? A new set of blessings floated through her mind.

Everything works out better than you imagine.
You're in the right place at the right time with the right people.
It's gonna be okay.

She didn't know if these affirmations actually did any good, but imagining them inked on cards somehow soothed her. Soon, she was asleep.

Chapter Seven

The next morning, Darla had a few things to do online. She wanted to be out of the apartment before anyone got up. The thought of Angel pushed her into action. She fired up the internet, her fingers trembling, searching for something—anything—to do that night. At the Globalkin website, a fado dinner was scheduled for that evening. She didn't know what to expect other than live music and Portuguese cuisine. If it was terrible, she could leave. She scribbled in her sketchbook the meeting spot at Praça Luís de Camões. A quick search for another place to stay yielded nothing. She didn't want to stay with any of the Globalkin hosts for two weeks. No matter how friendly they looked, that was too long. She uploaded photos onto her laptop. She dashed off an email to her mom and Cat, letting them know she'd arrived and was already meeting people.

Darla finally nudged herself away from the safety of life online and headed out. She lunched at a *pasteleria*. There weren't many vegetarian options, so she ordered cheese *tosta* again. The tables were full of people, and waves of Portuguese flowed through the room. She nibbled her sandwich and tried to enjoy the idea of a day ahead of her with no one to answer to or work to be done.

After lunch, Darla walked everywhere. She made her way to the São Jorge Castle near the harbor. Not her thing. The view over the city, however, pulled her into a moment of wonder. This was a far cry from where she was staying. She wanted to sketch the view. She wouldn't know where to start. Other tourists lingered around the mirador. Most people were coupled up. Everyone seemed armed with a guidebook, many of them in French.

She trudged up and down, taking breaks at the miradors that offered a flat expanse to rest. She walked up Bica, a narrow street with a cable car poised at the top as if ready to release and plummet down the hill. Lisbon was unlike any city she'd ever been in. Some neighborhoods were navigated on narrow streets like Paris's oldest quarters. The hills gave the city a curvy shape. Small parks with benches and sometimes cafés made the miradors wonderful spots to take in the view of the Tejo River. People lounged on benches and took photos of the view. Big puffy clouds over the river, networks of electrical lines crossing the sky above the streets, giant cranes on the docks along the river. Some miradors were seedier than others. The one near her apartment, Santa Catarina, attracted a lot of shady characters, so she didn't linger.

People she encountered were friendlier than the taxi driver. After a few exchanges, Darla felt comfortable with *bom dia* and *obrigada*—hello and thank you. She bought a public transportation pass. She nabbed a window seat on the #28, a yellow tram that crossed the city. Tourists packed the few wooden seats. Two girls rode on the back, clinging to the doors. A little gray-haired Portuguese lady wanted on, but the driver signaled there wasn't room. The tram squealed along its tracks, winding through the city, giving Darla a great tour of Lisbon. The wooden seats and open windows lent it an old-fashioned feel. Signs in Portuguese and English warned about pickpockets. She careened through the city, taking it all in. The gentle movement and sunny day lulled her into a trance. She might have slipped into a jet-lag nap; everything became blurry and warm like a fairy tale.

The tram passed through narrow streets and curved around gentle hills. Here were the colors she'd expected. Every corner hosted blooming trees and painted apartment buildings. If the walls weren't tiled, the plaster peeled away in big chunks. Or they were latticed with graffiti. Some buildings boasted youthful colors: pink, yellow, and turquoise. Others were dilapidated, surprising Darla. She couldn't imagine derelict real estate like this in the center of an American city. She couldn't help but wonder what the buildings could be. Gregory would have ideas. On their walks, they'd talk about architecture. Darla had grown more confident voicing her opinions about some of the hideous new houses that were replacing small homes in Denver. Maybe these decrepit buildings were better than shiny new high-rises.

At one point, they stopped for a long time, logjammed behind an ambulance. She gawked along with the others, trying to figure out what had happened. It seemed that a lady had been hit by something falling off the building. Darla wasn't surprised, given the state of some of the buildings. The medics used gauze to partition off part of the sidewalk. Other riders had jumped off the tram, but Darla stayed on. She relished the feeling of not being in a hurry, not being irritated, not worrying about anything. She lost herself in sketching the inside of the tram. Finally, the ambulance took the victim away, and they creaked onward. She rode to the last stop. Everyone had to get off the tram, so she wandered into the cemetery. She felt sleepy walking among the graves. She found a bench and sketched a few tombstones and crypts. Darla dug cemeteries, ideal for sketching and getting a rest from the noise of the city.

After a tram ride back, in Bairro Alto she was lured into a colorful shop. The saleswoman told her that everything was made by Portuguese artists. The jewelry, clothing, and other art from Portuguese artists gave her a lot to look at. She seized upon a fun necklace made of big balls. It was colorful and intriguing. She asked what it was made of, and the shopkeeper told her colored string spun into balls. She bought a skirt and the necklace, forsaking her self-contract to travel lightly. She tried to pretend that the exchange rate wasn't so bad. She didn't care; she wanted some of the creativity of Portugal on her.

In a good mood, feeling free, she made her way to the fado evening meeting point. She was nervous about meeting new people. She clutched her sketchbook. At the fountain, she saw a suave young guy smoking a cigarette. She approached with a wave.

"Globalkin?"

"*Olá*," he said. He leaned in to air kiss her.

Darla replied, "*Bom dia*."

He smiled. "It's technically *boa tarde* now, but no matter."

She felt corrected. She tried to be grateful, but she was reminded of Gregory's grammar hammer, always nailing any incorrect usage. They chatted, exchanging basic info. Rafa introduced himself as an architect and writer for the local paper.

"Lisbon could really use your enthusiasm for urban development," she said. He nodded, distracted by more people joining their group. Soon, they were a crowd of about fifteen, mostly locals and a couple of German Globalkins. They headed to the restaurant a few blocks away, Rafa leading the way.

Vai Tu had no fancy pretensions. Just the opposite. In one room, the restaurant was a nonprofit social club. Posters of fado singers hung on the walls. They settled in at a long table along a wall. They introduced themselves. Everyone seemed younger than Darla and spoke English. Darla got out her sketching pen and sketchbook. Wine arrived in little ceramic pitchers. Next to her, Anita, a young Portuguese woman who lived in Lisbon, took charge and poured wine into little terra cotta cups. Darla passed them around. They toasted, settled in. Anita pointed at Darla's sketchbook.

"What's that?"

Darla opened the pages. She flipped through a few and then on to the next blank page.

"Wow," Anita said. A few others had noticed and remarked on her sketches.

Darla shrugged it off.

"It's a fun way to remember my travels," she said. All the attention made her uncomfortable. She asked Anita if she hosted people at her place from Globalkin. The conversation broke into small groups. Darla relaxed, surprised to find herself enjoying the small talk. The Globalkins were interesting. Everyone was open and seemed genuinely interested in others. Her dinner mates were especially surprised that she was a solo traveler. Darla hadn't realized going it alone was such a big deal. Maybe meeting people in Europe would be easier than in Boulder. Food arrived, plate after plate passed family style. Her introduction to Portuguese food was a bona fide cod fest.

Cod with potatoes and onions swimming in oil. Cod with potatoes and cream. *Bacalao*, salted cod in a shallow dish with what seemed like a lot of cheese—like the artichoke mayonnaise dip back home but saltier. Darla practiced pronouncing the names like the locals did, spitting words out with the kind of emphasis you'd use to spit out fish bones. Cod was

Portugal's national food, eaten everywhere on any occasion. She tried some of everything but couldn't finish the cod she'd taken. Where were the green vegetables?

She spent more time in her sketchbook than with her plate. Anita and Rafa gave her the Portuguese names for things, and she added those to the pages. Other dinner mates commented on her sketchbook and asked her about it. She didn't mention that she felt terribly self-conscious about it but also needed it to make friends. Instead, she got out her Journey Blessings and handed the envelope around. Her new friends read their Blessings aloud.

"You eat with caloric impunity!"

Darla laughed. "That's my favorite!"

More food came. Bread in little plastic baskets. Wine in tiny pitchers with little terra cotta cups. They feasted and chatted. Then, it was time for the fado. Darla hadn't noticed the stage because it didn't exist. Instead, a woman in a red sweater and black pants stood near two guys armed with guitars. They strummed a few notes, tuning their instruments. A collective shushing and conversation tapered off reluctantly.

Two guitarists and one singer. A wail, a moan, a supplication to be released from this dolorous suffering! She didn't need to understand the words to recognize the pain of a broken heart. It could have been the wine, it could have been the relief of the easy camaraderie, it could have been the music, but sitting there in the crowded, dim restaurant, tears rose up. She let them fall, not knowing what made her cry. She was fully immersed in the music, in the swell of feeling it evoked in her. For a moment she lost track of where she was and just floated in feeling. It felt good to not hold it back for once. Her face was wet with tears.

A glance around revealed that other people were moved, dabbing their eyes and clearly overcome by the music. Everyone seemed lost in the rise and fall of the notes and perhaps in their own painful memories. Many of the group were also teary. She caught the eye of a young guy with cropped hair at the end of the table. His hand came up to his face, and Darla thought he was going to wave or wipe a tear away. Instead, he curled his hand into a fist and turned it at his cheek. Darla drew back. Was he implying she was a baby because she was crying? She wiped her face and looked away, a hot flush rising up her neck. What a jerk, she thought, trying to refocus on the performers.

The show went on, a series of singers taking the "stage," not emerging from a green room backstage but rising from seats around the restaurant. Ordinary people stepping up to sing the Portuguese songs. An ancient-looking man in a green V-neck sweater belted out a song about his bed. Somehow, Darla was completely present and filled pages with the singers' words and sentiments. Later, she'd color it in from her studio. The music infused her lines with melancholy and meaning.

The best singer came last. A woman surely over eighty sang with such fervor that she brought the crowd to its feet. They all stood, swaying slightly from the wine, from the trance state, from the spell of the fado. A roaring round of applause and much wiping of eyes closed out the fado show.

Rafa and a couple of other locals went to settle the bill. After a long discussion with the lady in charge, they came back and announced the price they each owed. Seven euros. Darla could barely contain her shock—ten bucks for all that food and the singing. The cheap price of the meal shocked her. No one said anything about it. She didn't want to be the gauche American, so she didn't comment on it.

She packed up her sketchbook and pens, full and content from a surprisingly good evening. The guy who'd made the baby fist was making his way toward her. But fuck him. She said quick goodbyes to Rafa and a few others and hurried out into the night.

Chapter Eight

The week passed. She wrote a bit in the mornings and wandered around with her sketchbook in the afternoons. She was finding her new rhythm outside of obligations like work and friends. She missed her friends but only slightly longed for Boulder.

Her apartment was central, near Chiado and Baixa. During the day, the streets seemed almost her own. She greeted her neighbors who lurked around the stoops, *Boa tarde*. Lisbon's funky brokenness intrigued her. For all the beauty of the city and its harbor, the pale pastel-painted buildings, the city was also cracked out, empty derelict buildings in the center of town like gaping, rotting teeth. The graffiti was cool and creative but added to the feeling that the city was in a semi-rogue state. It wasn't so much that the brokenness disturbed her. Still, it was unfathomable that buildings in the center of the city hadn't been reclaimed by creative enterprises, by entrepreneurs who were ready to take the opportunity to build new ventures in places with perhaps lower rent.

Darla could only bear Angel's apartment for brief stints. She'd hoped to spend more time at home, cooking and writing. She'd have to get over her inclination to make herself cozy no matter where she was. What would Lauren say? She'd be out there meeting people and seeing things and probably getting a tattoo or something radical. Darla wanted to see as much of Portugal as she could in two weeks. This shitty apartment would force her to get out and socialize. The Globalkin site was a great place to find in-person meetups. An upcoming expedition to Sintra intrigued Darla, so she signed up. She could stay a few nights. She had no idea what Sintra was, where it was, or how to get there. This new way of jumping into things gave her the feeling of truly being on an adventure. She was slowly getting used to the freedom away from her Boulder routines.

She asked in the conversation thread if anyone wanted to commute to Sintra with her. A guy named André messaged her to say they could go on the train together. Could she trust him? She read his reviews on Globalkin. He was a charming and generous host. Plenty of kind remarks boasted how meaningful the experience with André had been. She decided to go for it. Meeting someone through Globalkin seemed safe. Everyone at the fado event had been super friendly. She arranged to meet André at Rossio train station.

Darla wore her light blue cargo pants and a flowery linen blouse from the clothing swap. Her new purple jacket gave her the feel of a bright flower. She slung her red string market bag over her shoulder. But her enthusiasm drained away when she got lost and ended up in a warren of narrow streets in Alfama. Her phone was useless; the data speed was so slow that she was wasting precious time waiting for the map to load. She finally emerged from the maze. She darted around Rossio Plaza, searching for the entrance to the station. Waves of black cobblestones seemed to rise and fall as she walked across the plaza. At first it threw her off-balance. Then she delighted in the trompe l'oeil. But she couldn't dawdle. She was never late. She didn't want to miss André because, without him, she wouldn't know how to get to Sintra.

She finally saw the train station, its entrance framed by two large carved ovals. At the top of the stairs stood a young man wearing a dark striped hoodie and carrying a large backpack; was that him? He turned to go inside. She ran toward him, shouting, "André?"

He turned and smiled. Oh no, she thought. It's *that* guy. The jerk who made the baby face with his fist at the fado night. Fuck. She got hot under her jacket, her heart pounding. No. Not again, she thought. Not another panic attack. Could she duck and flee, hide and wait for her heart to return to normal? No. He'd seen her and was waving. She feebly lifted her arm. Taking a deep breath, she made her way to him. "It's going to be fine," she assured herself, forcing a smile.

"Darla?"

She nodded. He leaned in to kiss both cheeks. He had a stylishly geeky look, and she couldn't decide whether he was attractive or dorky. She pulled away, her mind darting around. Could she find an excuse to bail?

"Let's go," he said. "We don't want to miss our train."

His voice, deep and sure, went right inside her. He sounded like he was on the verge of laughing. Like he was in on something, and she wanted to be in there with him. She followed André into the station, where they bought tickets at a kiosk. On the train, they sat opposite each other. She sized him up. He wore a dark beret, dark eyeglasses, and a giant watch that poked out of his sweatshirt cuff. He asked what she was doing in Lisbon. She didn't want to reveal much, so she kept her answers short. He nodded as he listened, seeming interested in her travel plans.

"How long are you staying in Lisbon?"

"Two weeks."

"You are from where?"

"Boulder," Darla said. "In Colorado, against the Flatiron Mountains." She didn't expect Europeans to know American geography. But he nodded as if he knew Colorado.

"There are lots of rock climbers in Colorado," he said. He spoke very good English.

"Definitely lots of rocks," Darla replied. She didn't know any climbers in Boulder. She was nervous talking about herself. She turned the conversation to him.

"So, what is this Sintra thing?"

He leaned forward, arms on his knees. "It is a magical place. You will see."

Darla tilted her head. She wanted to drill down, ask for details, have it all mapped out. Preferably in writing. Magical? Show me that on the map, she wanted to say.

The train swayed along the scintillating coast. Glimpses of the bright, sparkling water excited Darla. She started to relax a little. At one point, André leaned down and picked up a tiny piece of paper from the train floor. She hadn't even seen it until he drew attention to it. He held it between two fingers. She kept sneaking glances at him. He was cute and young. One time he caught her looking and smiled. She blushed and tried to smile back, mortified that he'd seen her sizing him up. She didn't want to like him. She didn't need another person in her life who thought she was too emotional. But he didn't seem to remember his slight, so she tried to put it aside. She got out her sketchbook.

André perked up. "You're an artist?"

She wanted to say, "Yes, I am a successful artist." But instead, she blurted out, "I just started. I love my sketchbook!"

André raised his eyebrows and smiled. "I want to know more."

The train began to slow. He gestured at the door.

"Our stop."

On the platform, André threw the scrap of paper into a garbage bin.

"Let's go for a coffee?" he asked.

Darla nodded. She took in the town, the crowd from the train dispersing. Sintra was quieter than Lisbon, less dense. They walked along thick stone walls that were covered in vines and moss. The smell of cool stone was a welcome relief after the heat in Lisbon. Every few paces, there'd be a gate through which she could see trees and lush gardens of *quintas*. The streets were quiet, tourists flowing toward the palace. André stopped to chat with an older man in a brown cap sweeping the sidewalk. Darla understood nothing. Not even a hint of a word or a sense of what they were talking about. They spoke for several minutes. When he came back to Darla, she raised an eyebrow.

"Directions," he said.

Seemed like more than that. Surely, in all that talk, André had gotten the man's life story. But André just shrugged. They made their way through the town. She wouldn't admit it aloud, but she liked being escorted by a handsome young man. At a bustling café, they stood in line to order.

"Try a *travesseiro*. It's the specialty here."

She nodded, turning her tastes over to him. She hadn't for-given his mockery. They found seats. Casa Piriquita was more a cafeteria than a café, with tile floors and small tables where all kinds, ages, and shapes of people gathered over coffee and pastries. It had nothing in common with the hip cafés in Boul-der, where people huddled over laptops, gazing at screens instead of talking with their friends. Waves of Portuguese flowed around her. She tuned into the river of language that sounded sometimes French, sometimes Russian, its shhsss sounds completely hiding meaning from Darla.

She got out her sketchbook and pen. She'd only been away from home for a few days, but getting the sketchbook out was now always her first move. André scooted closer.

"Can I see?"

"Sure." She flipped through the pages. Line, color, story passed before their eyes. They gazed together, entranced in the pages.

"You *are* an artist!" André said. "Who is this?" He smiled.

Her book was open to a page where she'd sketched Judy and Liza. She'd depicted their large, doleful eyes, their skinny ribs. In the background, the wall of French windows, a thriving plant on a low stand nearby. She worried about the dogs and had tried to make them look more well off than they were. The date was stamped at the bottom with her library date stamp. In large letters, she'd written the word for dogs in Portuguese.

"Those are the dogs where I am staying, Liza and Judy. After the singers, I assume. My host is a performer."

"You're good. I like your drawings."

Darla murmured a thanks and flipped to a blank page.

"Do you mind if I sketch while I'm with you? I'm still here with you."

"And I'm with you," he said like a Catholic prayer response.

She began making the shape of the moment in lines on her pages. She made one continuous line, tracing the backs of the café goers bent over pastries, tipping back cups of espresso, following the scene across her page in black ink.

"You spell *travesseiro* how?"

He laid out the letters for her. "It means 'pillow.'"

"*Obrigada*," she said. She wanted to tell him about her travel pillow, but that would probably make him think she was even more of a baby. Darla asked him about his job while sketching. André told her he worked as a software engineer and was a rock climber. The pastry, shaped like an éclair, had a dusting of powdered sugar on top. André gently tapped his pastry against the plate, shaking off excess sugar. She drew his gestures. The long, pillow-like pastry, his strong fingers, the sugar falling in a cloud. He paused, holding the pillow in the air. Darla focused on his hand, the soft dough. She watched as his lips destroyed the perfection, his bite sending shards of crust and avalanches of powdered sugar everywhere. She wanted to watch, and she wanted to try it herself. She set down her pen and picked up her treat. She bit in, almond paste melting sweetness on her tongue. Crunchy met mooshy, creating a texture party in her mouth. She wanted to draw this moment, this flavor of discovery, trying something with no idea what it would taste like. She wiped her mouth with a thin napkin pulled from dispensers on each table. The napkin was more paper than cloth.

They also tried the *queijadas*, but Darla didn't love them. She had more fun drawing the cupcake-shaped treats. Certain she had powdered sugar all over her face, Darla asked André, "Do I have . . ." She gestured to her face.

He smiled. "Just a little there." He pointed to her mouth. She wiped her lips. To her dismay, a hot blush spread across her cheeks. They laughed. She was glad to be away from Angel and the smelly apartment. Could she last for two weeks? Maybe one of the Globalkins could help her find a new place. And despite herself, she was enjoying André's company.

She worked up her courage. "Listen," she said, "I didn't like it when you made fun of me at the fado night."

André frowned.

"You basically called me a baby."

He shook his head, still frowning, as if trying to remember. She made the fist at her eye movement.

"Oh!" he exclaimed. "What do you mean, 'baby'?"

"That's the gesture for crybaby in the US."

"Crybaby? No, no. I meant 'I am crying too.'"

Darla *psshhed*. Some things were universal. Surely everyone thought that meant crybaby. But he seemed sincere. He reached out to touch her arm.

"I wouldn't do that. It was sad. Everyone was feeling it."

She nodded. She appreciated that he had noticed the feeling in the room and that they were all riding the fado wave of melancholic bittersweetness. She smiled and ducked her head back to her sketchbook. His phone pinged.

"The others are here." He looked at her intently. "Are we good?"

She smiled. "We're good."

Chapter Nine

A car idled in the main street near the café. André waved at the driver, a smiling young man. They piled in the backseat.

"Olá!" the driver said. "I'm Luis. I'm leading this expedition."

André and Darla said hi. André knew Luis but not the woman in the front seat, Amalia. Luis guided the car into traffic while they introduced themselves and chatted. Soon they'd left the village. Giant trees flanked the road. The cooling green enveloped them. Relief from the urban jungle of Lisbon overcame her.

"So, what is this expedition exactly?" André asked. Darla was glad he did; she didn't want to appear ignorant.

Luis smiled and glanced at them in the rearview mirror. His dark eyes were friendly, and Darla warmed to him immediately.

"I'm testing a group training with you all today," he said. "Don't worry!" He'd caught Darla's eye. She couldn't believe he'd read her so quickly. She didn't love group activities and was wishing she and André were alone.

"This will be fun," Luis assured them.

Amalia concurred. "I haven't done this with Luis, but he's led some great things at my work."

"Where are we going?" Darla asked.

André told her about Monserrate, a park that had been the estate of a wealthy British industrialist. He had built the palace to be a refuge from the heat and bustle of Lisbon.

"There's a big palace and many gardens. It's known as a place of many microclimates. It's a special place," he said.

They pulled into a crater-filled parking lot. Special. Magical. Huh. She'd believe it when she felt it. A group of people gathered under the shade of a tree. After introductions, they chatted among themselves in Portuguese. She recognized a few people from the fado night. Darla lingered at the outskirts, feeling skittish. She shifted awkwardly. Finally, Luis got everyone's attention.

"*Olá, tudo bem?*" Everyone nodded and murmured something. Darla nodded too, a half beat off the rest of them.

"Welcome to my happy place, Monserrate," Luis told them in English. "Thank you for coming to play this game with me in this most beautiful place!"

They murmured thanks and other words Darla didn't catch. Luis explained the game. She had a hard time focusing. Jet lag? Proximity to André, who was standing close by? Something about pairing up and exploring the garden, looking for clues. They should keep track of their clues and at the end, Luis explained, they would compare scores to determine the winner. She glanced at André, who seemed to be paying close attention. He caught her eye and winked. Darla blushed.

Luis broke them into groups of two. Darla was happy to be paired with André. They entered Monserrate, a world away from the tourist crowds in Sintra. A few other people strolled the gardens. Plants and trees made a kaleidoscope of shapes and colors. Darla itched to draw everything. A gentle fog hovered over the top of the trees. Darla was certain they'd stepped through a magical portal. They inhaled the delicate scent of jasmine and wisteria in the fragrance garden. Darla closed her eyes, intoxicated by beauty turned into scent. André led her through the park, clutching the notepad and pen that Luis had handed out. She tried to follow along but was happy to let him find the clues. They came upon what seemed to be an ancient Indian arch crowning the path. A real portal! André touched it. Darla thought he would scale it. She took a photo of him.

It seemed to Darla that there were a million versions of green. She inhaled them all into her lungs, through her skin, soothed and calmed after the intensity of Lisbon. Ferns waved in a gentle breeze. Maybe green spaces were her place. Boulder had been both—a city with cafés and bookshops, with access to outdoor walking paths and hikes.

In the Mexican gardens, the fog fell away. They strolled past the giant agave plants, mesmerized by the peace that imbued the space. It wasn't crowded, and they sometimes had the place to themselves. Like they'd entered into a fairytale landscape. André read the plaques here and there and told her the story of the gardens. He filled in the bingo card on the pad, engrossed in the game. He didn't seem to mind that Darla was just tagging along. Usually, her competitive self would kick in, but today she was happy to wander around the park, which stunned her at every turn.

A giant Australian banyan near the chapel beckoned, and André climbed it. Darla wasn't sure this was cool in a public garden, but she didn't feel it was her place to say something. André seemed to want to climb everything. His giant watch didn't get in the way of reaching up to test anything possible for a climb. He got more handsome to Darla by the minute. Being outside in the gardens seemed to be where he belonged. The calm and beauty of the garden gentled him too. He was younger than her; she didn't know by how much. That didn't stop her from appreciating him. She sketched the tree, his legs dangling from a giant horizontal branch. Another team came along and shouted up at André, laughing. The Globalkins were so friendly, and Darla was glad she had come.

They walked through Moorish archways into the palace of Monserrate. The intricate tile patterns mesmerized Darla. A simple thing like walking indoors shifted her from the mundane to the magical. Now, no one but them was inside. They stopped speaking, absorbing the sacred beauty of the palace. In a large, round room, the light poured in through the windows. Darla lay on the floor, gazing up at the round ceiling. She'd finally landed, in her body, in the moment, in Monserrate of all places. André got down next to her. They lay still for a long time, gazing at the ceiling of the rotunda, with a hole open to the sky. Clouds floated past, and Darla may have dozed off. The next thing she knew, André was crouched next to her, his hand on her shoulder. He smiled. She clambered upright, laughing.

She followed André through a narrow, pointed arch. Inside, they gathered at a pool of water. In the calm space, every sound was amplified. A drip of water. Her breath. André right next to her. There was no way she could sketch this. No way to capture its beauty and shape. He was leaning right next to her, and together they pulled back from the well. They looked at each other and smiled. As if they both knew no words would add to this moment. She gazed into the well and dropped into it a fervent wish that some of this magic would stay with her forever.

It came time to meet the other Globalkins. In the parking lot, they began to compare their scores. Luis told them they'd debrief over a picnic nearby. Darla reluctantly left the gardens. She would love to come back and sketch here. Back in Luis's car, they curved along country roads, and the open sky and movement of the car lulled Darla into a light sleep. Images of the well and the Monserrate Palace flitted through her mind.

It wasn't long before they pulled into another park. Everyone got out carrying picnic supplies. Luis led them into the park. They set up on a green field near a lake. It was a bright, idyllic day. She loved nothing more than eating outside. Still under the spell of Monserrate, she started to feel at ease with the group. People had brought cakes and soda and plastic containers filled with fruits and vegetables. Breads and cheeses. She hadn't known to bring anything. *"Não faz mal,"* they told her. André translated—"No worries." She got out her sketchbook and drew all the shapes on the blanket.

André had collected flowers from the ground in Monserrate. Peach-colored petals formed the shape of delicate cups. Everyone cheered when he brought them out and placed them around the food. Darla put one in the center of an apple cake. The flower entranced her, and she photographed one, cupped in her hand. Like she could hold all the beauty of the day in her hand. She couldn't wait to capture the colors in her sketchbook too.

They settled in to eat and chat. André sat next to her. For a brief moment, Darla felt like she was in a couple. She liked the ease of it. Luckily for Darla, most of them spoke English, except for Elise, a Brazilian. Elise's boyfriend, Jerónimo, also from Brazil, translated. Jerónimo studied psychology, focusing on consumer behavior. They all seemed so interesting. Their work sparked Darla's curiosity. At one point, André leaned in close and recounted his love for flowers. Once, he told her, he had placed rose petals all around the bath for his lover. A full body heat rose up in her, and she had to take her jacket off to cool down. Had he just given her a look? The look that says, "I'm into you." She remembered that look from her last young boyfriend. Thomas also had gorgeous eyes with long lashes. They'd met at a record shop in Boulder. One day they had lunch together. Stopping to chat on the mall, he'd given her that look. Before long, they were having sex and going out.

André opened his water bottle a little bit and gently dribbled the water over the tomatoes he'd brought. He carefully dried them with a small cloth from his bag. Darla recalled the tiny fleck of paper he'd picked up on the train. Was he always this anal?

Conversation flowed easily while they got to know each other. Globalkins united around the love of travel. Soon, they didn't feel like strangers. Mostly university graduates and professionals, they were young, in their twenties and early thirties. Darla enjoyed their company, even as she felt self-conscious about being the oldest person in the group. They were all doing big things: studying, traveling, exploring, and learning. She relished being the only American. It gave her a small, false sense of almost being European herself. She already felt different being away from Boulder. Even though it was a small, mellow city, the American drive of push, push, push for the dollar permeated everything.

Margarida, who in her spare time made soap and danced with a traditional Portuguese dance group, asked about Darla. She told them she was on a long vacation from her job and life in Boulder. She didn't tell them that she hoped to find a reason to never go back. Darla could barely admit that to herself. It sounded so foolish to her. Boulder seemed so far away. The person she was at work hadn't seemed to come on this trip at all.

"And you're an artist," Luis said, nodding at her sketchbook.

"Having fun with it," she said. She shrugged off the artist label. She didn't want the pressure of having to make "good" art. Right now, it was all about playing in the sketchbook to capture her experiences.

"How long are you in Portugal?" Luis asked.

"Just a couple of weeks," she said. She told them about her plan to visit Paris.

"Cool to do this on your own," Jerónimo said.

"We hope you love Portugal," Luis said. "Maybe you'll be convinced to stay here." They all laughed.

"I like it so far, but I don't plan to stay." While she had everyone's attention, she worked up the courage to ask what else she needed to see while in Portugal.

"I'd love to go to a beach."

"Alentejo!" Luis said, and others agreed. He told her about the region. Alentejo extended from the western coast of Portugal inland. The interior part of the region produced wine and cork. The coast, known for its cliffs and beaches, was ideal for surfers. Darla wrote down the names of villages to visit. She'd have to investigate where to go and how to get there. The well-beaten path of the Algarve seemed easier.

Margarida said, "I have a room for next weekend in Odeceixe, but I can't make it. Maybe you could take my reservation?"

"Yes! Thank you," Darla said, even though she didn't know what Odeceixe was. Margarida told her about her special connection with the place.

"When I was a child, my family would pack camping gear

for a month and camp by the river that feeds into the ocean. My sister and I would play all day at the beach." Darla imagined the Portuguese girls, wild and free and scrubbed bright by the ocean breezes and sand.

"I always felt like a gypsy there. It's one of the most beautiful beaches in Portugal."

Margarida explained that she had rented a room in Odeceixe with her sister, but now neither could go.

"It's twenty-two euros a night, including breakfast," Margarida said. "I think you will like it."

"Where is Odeceixe?" She tried to get the consonants right.

"It marks the border between the Alentejo and the Algarve," Margarida explained. "Almost all the way to the bottom of Portugal."

"I'll do it," Darla said. Another chance to get away from Angel and close to the water, which she craved. Things were falling into place easily, and she was happy riding the wave. Maybe letting go of control was the way to go. A little sparkle, the feeling she called mojo, passed through her.

At the end of the meal, Darla got out her Journey Blessings. She passed the small coin envelope around for everyone to choose a blessing. They seemed delighted, reading their blessings aloud. "You have tons of fun." "Your shoes are like Mercury's wings." André read his. He nodded. "The music makes you dance." Margarida clicked her fingers and made a little dance move.

"Do you like to dance?" André asked her.

"I love it," she said.

"Me too." Some part of her was ticking a list inside: Gregory versus André. She caught herself doing it and shook her head. She dipped into her bread and cheese to cover it up. She was not going to get involved with a younger man. And certainly not someone in Portugal.

When the picnic ended, everyone stood, gathering their stuff and shaking out blankets. André cleared away the small amount of trash.

"Thank you, spot," Darla said. André looked at her with a question in his eyes.

"I always have to thank the spot that hosts us," Darla said. She'd never told anyone this, never did it aloud in front of others. Until now.

She had enjoyed it, but it was late. Wondering where she would stay that night lingered at the back of her mind. Nothing seemed to happen quickly here. Darla wished she could bail and head home. But she was in it. They struck off into the park, following Luis. Darla and André tackled a small hill with brio. The two of them taking on something together. They laughed and chatted. The forest was cool and green, its trees mossy. Giant boulders also enrobed in moss gave André something to climb over.

She kept saying to herself, "I'm in Portugal!" Dislocated from her home and everyone she knew, she reminded herself where she was, away from Boulder and on a grand adventure. At the top of a hill, they convened near a church that had fallen into ruin. They gathered at a small lookout surrounded by a short stone wall. The ocean billowed out below them, turning the sunlight into an undulating bed of jewels. Her first glimpse of the sea in Portugal made her heart skip. She soaked in the endless view. The wind whipped her hair and stung her face. Darla's muscles relaxed as if being recognized. And yet she was also energized. Was this the feeling of finding home? The ocean always stoked this in her, its soothing blue expanse and mesmerizing repetition taking her in. She stood entranced, taking in the view, when suddenly she heard André's voice in her ear, very close.

"Look out over there. Do you see that?" He extended his arm, and her eyes followed his direction. She nodded, even though she had no idea what he pointed at. Unable to focus on anything, she gazed out at the sea. He was so close. She could get used to his voice in her ear. It intoxicated her but confused her too. Was he making a move? She couldn't tell. Perhaps in Portugal, they had a different concept of personal space. She stood still, not wanting this to end, the moment she saw the sea and the moment a tiny door opened in her heart to him.

The group broke away from the view and gathered for a photograph. They lined up along the wall to pose. André leaned away and down from the wall as if falling. The group grabbed for him, laughing. She liked his kooky playfulness. She liked her playfulness. When had she last laughed with others like this? She couldn't recall.

Back at the parking lot, Margarida asked Darla where she was staying. Darla shrugged. "I planned to find something in Sintra for tonight."

"You can stay with me," Margarida said. "I have a room for Globalkins."

Darla accepted gratefully. When the group made to leave, André approached her. He air kissed, the stubble on his face brushing her cheek. He took her hands in his.

"I enjoyed being with you today, Darla," he said.

"Me too," she replied. Her heart beat faster when he said he'd like to get together again. She played it cool or hoped she did, nodding and wanting to hug him American-style.

She'd only brought a toothbrush and a change of underwear, so getting ready for bed didn't take long. Tucked in her bed at Margarida's, she replayed the day in her mind. It had been fun to be with a group, to discover new things, to play and explore. And André. The tingly feeling she'd had when he had stood behind her, pointing toward the ocean, wouldn't leave her. She savored it, surrendering to its possibility even as she pushed away the idea of a romance. She wasn't going for younger men anymore.

Thomas had been fun. Lots of dancing and drinking and sex. Most of her friends had children, and their party days were over. But she'd always known she and Thomas wouldn't last forever. He had never said it, but she sensed he wanted children. The partying was less appealing the older she got, and along with that, the younger men were not so much of a match.

Gregory, a bit older than her, had seemed like a better fit. Maybe age didn't play into it as much as she thought. She rolled over in her bed. No matter. While she planned to have fun in Portugal, she wasn't interested in falling in love.

Chapter Ten

The next day, she made her way around the tourist sites of Sintra. At the Quinta da Regaleira, she came upon a deep hole. Peering in, she saw a spiral stair descending to a well at the bottom. The moss-covered walls and pillars gave it an ancient appearance. A sign described an initiation well. Darla shivered. She wanted to initiate herself in something. To initiate herself into a new life, a new way of being in her skin and in the world. She wanted to be part of not just the world but the world with herself in it. What was her true life? How could she have lived to forty as someone not really herself? Lauren had reminded her it wasn't too late. Tears sprang to her eyes, and she leaned over the wall into the well. It was too late for Lauren, but not for Darla. She took a deep breath and let herself feel what she wanted. She wanted to stay in Europe. She wanted to be an artist. She wanted, if she dared admit it, to find someone fun and loving to be with. Someone like André. As soon as she had the thought, she stuffed it deep inside.

After, she walked up a tree-lined hill where she found a bus stop that would take her to the Castelo dos Mouros. She didn't mind waiting in the sanctuary of the tree-lined road. She absorbed the peace and beauty while sketching the road. She wanted to remember everything. She thought about the Globalkins. How nice they'd all been. How welcoming to a stranger.

Was André friendlier than the others? Maybe more than just politeness and being a good host? She replayed the last thing he'd said to her. About getting together again. She shook her head. Be here now, she said to herself. That's all future tripping. She took a deep breath, enjoying the fresh air and the happy feeling she always got when outside in a beautiful place.

Finally, the bus came, and she got on board. Crowded with tourists, they chugged up many switchbacks. The tiny but mighty bus groaned its way around the tight curves. She doubted they would make it, but the driver just kept spinning the steering wheel to maneuver the tight curves. They arrived at the top of the hill, and the passengers tumbled off the bus. Darla breached the castle walls, wandering along its exterior corridor. She tried to lure the cats in for a head rub, but they kept to the walls, regarding her with suspicion. The bright May day exhilarated her. At this height, the brisk wind shook her hair in all directions along with her thoughts. At the top of the castle, she surveyed the town. She wrote a haiku in her notebook.

Flags rippling in the wind
on Moorish castle tower
I reign with my pen.

Back in town, she chose an Indian restaurant for lunch. She got out her sketchbook and her special Retro 1951 pen her sketching group had given her as a goodbye present. It had postage stamps depicted on the barrel. She ordered a curry and a beer.

"Large or small?" the indifferent waiter asked.

In a good mood, she ordered a large. She always wanted more. More of everything. She couldn't help but love food. The textures, colors, flavors and nuances of eating endlessly fascinated her. When the beer arrived in a giant, German stein, she regretted her choice. She sipped it, ate her curry, and made notes in her journal. One other person in the restaurant ignored her, a man who wiped his mouth fastidiously after each bite. She headed to the restroom. Back at her table, she finished her meal, paid, and went back out into the town. She debated going back to Lisbon. But for once she wasn't in a hurry.

She strolled in the late afternoon, taking more pictures. An inexpensive room was easy to rent at a pension in the center of town. After more exploring, she returned to her room to rest. She watched Portuguese TV, not understanding a thing. She relished the solitude of the small room, its neatly made single bed and its tidy bedside table. She wasn't hungry for dinner, but she wanted to see Sintra at night. She strolled the streets, enjoying the views. Back at her room, she conked out early.

The next day, back at Casa Piriquita, she pulled out her sketchbook and searched for her pen. Nowhere. Not in any pocket of her bag. Not in her small green bag, nor in her pocket, and certainly not in her mesh shopping bag. Just a backup Pilot pen. Panicked, she finished her coffee and dashed back to the room where she'd stayed. The woman was in her room cleaning. Darla told her in English and gestures that she'd lost her pen. The woman nodded and helped search. She overturned the small table and crouched down to look under the bed. Nothing.

Another ray of hope emanated from Darla. It must be at the Indian restaurant. It wasn't far. She ran back there, but it was closed. In the café across the street, she asked the man behind the counter when it would open.

"Eleven," he said.

She ordered a coffee and took a table, overcome with despair. She couldn't have lost the pen; she couldn't have. It had to be found. She couldn't accept that it was gone. She used her other pen to ink her despair into her notebook.

When the restaurant opened, she hurried in and tried to communicate with the man that she'd lost a pen. It was a different waiter than the day before. He telephoned the other waiter, and she waited hopefully. But he came back shaking his head. She slumped, begging him to ask the staff if they had seen it. No one had turned it in.

Despairing, she pushed past flocks of tourists. She couldn't believe it had disappeared. Someone must have taken it. Who would do that? She stopped to check all the pockets in her bag once more. Nothing. Her mind refused to believe an incontrovertible fact. Overcome by the loss, she fought back tears. Boarding the train to Lisbon, she wished she had someone to tell about it. Someone who could help her let it go. Tears spotted her jacket. She brushed tears off her cheeks, embarrassed to cry in public. But no one seemed to notice. The other passengers looked out at the sea view or chatted. The farther away from Sintra she got, the more upset she felt. A true cry burst forth, and she was helpless to stop it.

Chapter Eleven

Darla let herself into the apartment on Rua da Atalaia. Mary had moved out, and Darla took possession of her room. Dust bunnies huddled along the baseboard, and a stained white shirt hung limply in the closet. She doubted anyone had cleaned after Mary left. It wasn't ideal, but she had abandoned the idea of finding a new place. Paris would be better, and she could suck it up for a bit longer in Lisbon. She unpacked and hung up her clothes. Arranging her notebooks and books on the small desk made it seem like home. She wandered into the hallway. No one appeared home, but the smell she'd detected before was stronger now. Entering the living room, she saw the source—two neat piles of dog shit. The dogs looked at her guiltily, and her disgust and anger quickly turned to pity for them. It wasn't their fault they were trapped in the apartment.

She cleaned up the mess. They stood at attention, tails wagging, pitifully skinny rib cages shaking. She caught sight of their leashes hanging near the door. She could take them for a walk, give them a chance to be outside. Who knew where Angel was? They weren't on "leave a note telling me where you're at" roommate status quite yet. Would she be mad if Darla took them for a walk? They seemed to sense what she was considering, their tails beating harder, their eyes wet with hope.

"Okay," she said. "Let's do it. Let's be crazy." She took the leashes down. The dogs leapt in the air, coming to life like she hadn't seen so far. She snapped the leashes on and grabbed her keys. She trip-ran after the dogs tugging her down the stairs, laughing and entreating them to slow down. Outside, they scurried ahead, pulling her down Rua da Atalaia. She was buoyed by their exuberance. They led her through the neighborhood, sniffing everything and leaving a squirt here and there. Their joy passed on to Darla. She was lighter, her steps more confident on the uneven streets of Bairro Alto. People smiled at her, and some stopped to pet the dogs, who quivered with excitement. She'd never had a dog. Now she realized they were great friendship ambassadors, making it easy to connect with passersby. Walking back, she thought of a business idea. You could rent a dog for a walk or two while traveling. You'd feel like a local and experience the place through the dog's needs. In Paris, it would be called Rent a Chien.

She was giggling about her idea and nudging the dogs back into her building when she heard her name. She turned, her foot on the step, the door open, the dogs sniffing the air. Angel came up. The dogs leapt on her.

"Down, you naughties! Mommy's gonna punish you."

"Oh, no, they were great," Darla gushed. "We had a great walk." She went into the entryway, followed by Angel, who snatched the leashes from Darla's hand.

"Who said it was okay to take my dogs? What if something had happened to them? I couldn't bear it."

Darla was sure she would find a way to "bear it." To milk Darla for money or worse. Her buoyancy deflated.

"They needed to go. I cleaned up a big mess they left. No harm was done. They're happy."

Inside the apartment, Angel huffed and put the leashes away. The dogs slunk to their beds by the window, ignoring

Darla now that Angel was back. Darla wanted to slink off to her bed too. Anything to get away from Angel.

The buzzer rang, and Angel answered. Someone below spoke in Portuguese. The only thing she understood was Angel's name. But Angel shook her head, saying that person wasn't here. Darla slipped away, pretending she hadn't been eavesdropping.

In her room, she shed her bag and kicked off her shoes. What a creep! Was that the police? Still stinging from the loss of her pen, annoyed by Angel, she flopped onto the bed. She mulled it all over before surrendering to a nap. When she woke, she was in a better mood. She wasn't going to let anything overshadow the fun she'd had, especially with André.

At her makeshift desk, she fired up her laptop. A few minutes to check email, and then she logged into the Globalkin site and saw a message from André.

He'd enjoyed the time they spent together, he wrote, and wondered if she wanted to go out sometime the next week. She blushed reading the note and logged off to give herself time to compose a reply. In the shower, she shivered with delight. He was attracted to her as she was to him. She hadn't made that up.

In the few months since she'd broken up with Gregory, she hadn't had any interest in dating. In Europe, however, maybe she was open to meeting people. She didn't need to get into a long-term relationship. She could have some fun.

As she dried off, she tried to rein herself in. She was done with younger men, right? Don't even mess with that, she scolded herself. But catching sight of herself in the mirror, she saw a spark that she hadn't seen in a long while. She was even barely sorta smiling. After just a few days in Lisbon, the difference in her skin was noticeable. The breeze from the Tejo and the moisture in the air made her face soft and smooth. She somehow looked ten years younger.

She logged back in and sent a reply. In several messages, he suggested dinner. They chose a date and a meeting place. Buoyed up by how easy it was to connect here, she emailed Julie, an American living in Lisbon.

Chapter Twelve

A few days later, the women met at a bright café in Cais do Sodre. Darla had gotten used to being the only American at the Globalkin events. Now she was happy to meet a fellow American. Julie greeted her with the cheek-kissing ritual.

"Coffee?"

"Sure," Darla said. "But not a café au lait with a lot of milk."

"How about a *pingado*? It's an espresso with a few drops of milk. I drink it all the time."

"Great."

Julie ordered for both of them.

"Your Portuguese sounds perfect," Darla marveled.

Julie laughed. "Well, it's not perfect, but I have gotten a lot better since I moved here." They chatted, the usual. How did you end up here? How long have you been here? What do you like? And of course, what do you do?

"I work for an organization called Paint the World," Julie told her. Darla perked up and asked for more. Julie downed her pingado and took a sip of water.

"I help artists organize murals in places that need an uplift. It's amazing how much a neighborhood can change when there's art on the walls. We also sponsor residencies for artists. Another pingado?" She signaled the barista for two more.

"That sounds cool. Are you an artist?" Darla added a bit of sugar to her tiny coffee. Julie laughed and shook her head. Her blonde hair shimmered in the sun coming through the window.

"I studied arts administration at university. I always believed that art can change the world. Now I get to see changes happening every day. I've been working for Paint the World for almost a decade now."

Darla had never met anyone like Julie. She knew making art was changing her, but she couldn't put into words exactly how. She just knew that filling pages in her sketchbook filled her up. The idea of making a difference in the world with art seemed way better than spending time writing annual reports. She finished her pingado. Their second pingados arrived.

"How did you end up here?"

Julie laughed again. Darla hadn't been around anyone this lighthearted since Lauren.

"I fell in love with a Portuguese artist doing a residency in LA. When he left, he invited me to come visit him here. Then I fell in love with Lisbon."

"Still together?"

Julie nodded. "Yep. I somehow manage to love him more every day. How about you?"

Darla recounted the story that she'd been telling the Globalkins. She asked for recommendations of things to see outside the usual tourist haunts. Julie gave her a bunch of suggestions. Darla wrote them in her journal.

"Have you met some people here?" Julie asked.

"I have. I used Globalkin to meet people and go on excursions." She told her about the fado evening and the Sintra outing. She mentioned her date with André.

"I have no idea how old he is," she confessed.

"Be careful with these Portuguese men," Julie cautioned. "You'll fall in love and end up staying like I did."

Darla laughed. "I doubt it. I'm going to Paris and then back to Boulder."

"Maybe just a fling then." Julie smiled.

"I'll do anything to keep me out of the place I rented."

"What's up?"

Darla paused. She didn't want to unburden herself on a stranger. She liked Julie. But she also needed to get it out.

"I rented a room from a crazy person."

"Crazy how?"

"It's a borderline scam. The first two nights I slept on the couch because she'd double-booked the room. Then she has two dogs whom she neglects. I don't think she minds that they crap in the apartment, and I don't think she takes them out for regular walks. I feel so sorry for them."

"That sounds awful! How long are you going to be in Lisbon?"

"Not much longer. I paid for the whole time." She sighed. "I'll get through it."

Julie's phone buzzed. She glanced at it, picked it up, and quickly tapped on the screen. She set it down and looked at Darla.

"I may sound crazy now, but I might be able to help you."

Darla perked up.

"I have a spare room in my apartment. You could stay with me. I wouldn't charge you anything."

"What? That's so generous. Of course I would want to pay you."

Julie shook her head. "I keep it for guests and the occasional artist who needs somewhere to stay for a few days. Do you want to come by and see it? I have a few minutes now, and it's just around the corner."

Darla couldn't believe her luck. This could be better than Angel's. She didn't want to spend her inheritance on a hotel. It would be too expensive. Even Lauren's Thrill Money, she couldn't let go of that frivolously. She agreed to come with Julie. They chatted while Darla imagined this as her neighborhood. The wide sidewalks and streets with trees were a far cry from Bairro Alto. She didn't see as much graffiti here.

Once inside the third-floor walk-up, Darla fell in love with Julie's place. She felt immediately warm. Giant windows turned a wall into a framed portrait of sunlight. A collection of plants basked near the windows, giving the room a cozy, vibrant feel. Art hung on every wall. Darla wanted to spend time with each painting.

"Wow," she exclaimed.

"I love it here too," Julie said. "It's my first apartment all to myself. In LA I couldn't afford anything close to this."

Darla tried to take everything in. The art books on the coffee table, the cushy sectional couch. The vibe was open and creative, a complete 180 from the feeling she had at Angel's.

"Let me show you the room."

Down a long hallway, Julie pointed out the bathroom and a separate tiny room for the toilet. At the end of the hall, they entered the guest room. Darla gasped. One wall was painted with a jungle mural, alive with different greens and leaf patterns.

"Wow!"

"One of my visiting artists painted it. You like?" Julie smiled.

"I love!"

The room was spacious and uncluttered. A bed, a bedside table, and a dresser. It was ironic how her room at Angel's also didn't have a lot of furniture but felt neglected. This space seemed fresh and clear, the windows open, the breeze rustling a set of sheer white curtains.

"You really can stay here," Julie said. "I'm going to be pretty busy these next two weeks, so I won't be around much."

Tears threatened Darla's cool. She wasn't used to this much generosity. Maybe Lauren's bequest had started a trend for her. She took a deep breath.

"I'd love to stay here. Thank you, Julie."

"You can move in right away if you want."

"I'm going to the beach this weekend. Maybe after that?"

"Sure. Let me show you the rest of the place."

They toured the kitchen and peeked into Julie's bedroom. A third bedroom had been converted into a study, lined with books, outfitted with a desk and what Julie called her reading lounge. Darla wanted to move in and stay forever.

Chapter Thirteen

The whole Sintra adventure could easily be chalked up to a group outing with a nice guy, a guy as friendly as all the other people on the caper. She tried to downplay her nerves, but she never felt comfortable on first dates. Familiar racing thoughts and feelings threatened to bring on a panic attack. Darla brought Julie to mind. Her carefree way of being, her easy laugh. She seemed so relaxed.

Darla shook her nerves off as she emerged from her apartment on Rua da Atalaia. Her skin opened to the fresh air, or as fresh as it could be in Bairro Alto. The smell of dog was replaced by the odor of stale beer. She waved at the ladies on their balconies and was no longer surprised by the guys on the corner smoking spliffs. She wanted to both hurry and dawdle. Her stomach morphed into a troupe of little acrobats, throwing flips and twists. She hoped she'd be able to eat. Right now she couldn't imagine relaxing enough.

Darla arrived at the Praça de Luís de Camões a few minutes early. She wondered what he saw in her. Sure, they had fun on the Sintra excursion, but when he spoke so closely to her ear, she knew something more was going on. When she saw André, a jolt of attraction coursed from her crotch up her torso. He strolled toward her, jacket open, no tie, and a smile. This was his professional look, and she noted his Italian shoes with appreciation. How old was he, anyway?

She'd have to figure out a way to ask without being rude.

They cheek kissed, and Darla blathered on nervously for a few minutes about how she was glad to be out of her dark room at Angel's apartment. André smiled as if he empathized. He didn't seem nervous at all. He suggested a restaurant.

"Whatever you want," she said.

"What do you want?" She couldn't meet his sure gaze. She shrugged and told him to lead the way. They strolled through the neighborhood. She was still nervous but happy to be with him. He was funny and easy to talk to. They walked along narrow sidewalks to the restaurant he'd chosen. At a corner, a car drove by, close to them.

"I always think a car that close is going to roll over my foot," Darla said, pressing back against the building.

"I have had that thought too," he said.

At Jardim de Sentidos, a grandma-like woman ushered them to a seat in the garden with a pat on André's arm. Candles lit the tables. They were surrounded by potted plants and twinkly lights. Appetizers arrayed on the table tempted them: octopus salad, bread, butter, olives, some thinly sliced meat, and several slices of cheese. Darla exclaimed over the array. But André pushed aside several items, and when the waitress came, she took those away. Darla was surprised; that would never fly in the US, she thought. Once it left the kitchen, it was unretrievable. He'd kept the octopus, but she was unsure. Mostly vegetarian, she would eat fish now and then if she had to. André ordered a bottle of red wine from the Douro. She didn't know anything about Portuguese wine. André was happy to explain.

"The Douro is one of Portugal's biggest wine-producing regions. It's a river with a valley with lots *of quintas*. It's beautiful there. This is where they make port."

"I've never had port," Darla confessed. "What's a quinta?"

André smiled. He seemed happy to tell her everything. He explained that the hilly valley was full of wine estates, or quintas.

"It's the oldest dedicated wine region. They even made it a UNESCO World Heritage site."

She let André put some octopus salad on her plate. She inspected the colorful salad. Sliced octopus, green peppers, tomatoes, onions. She forked a bite, savoring André's gaze as much as the taste of the food. The garlic, oil, and vinegar were delicious, but it took some chewing to get used to the texture of the octopus. André noticed and laughed.

"You are just like a Portuguese explorer," he said.

She laughed. "How so?"

"Trying new things, having new experiences."

"What will I pillage and take back to my land?"

He shrugged mysteriously and gave a winky smile. The wine came, and while the waitress opened the bottle and offered him a taste, she took him in. He seemed older now, dressed in his work clothes. His super short hair and dark glasses still appealed to her. She sipped her wine, trying to taste the essence of the place in her glass. It was rich and bold, as good as any Italian or French wine she had had.

"Have you been there, Douro?"

He nodded. "My family has a home there."

"A quinta?"

He laughed. "Not quite. More like a farm that no one goes to anymore. I haven't been there in a while."

They nibbled on marinated olives and octopus salad. It wasn't too terrible. She probably wouldn't order it on her own, but for now, Darla was happy to try new things. She asked him about his work. He told her what he did as a systems engineer, but after the first sentence, she was lost. She didn't understand the role he played, and she was distracted by his gorgeous hazel eyes. He was funny, and soon she was laughing naturally and not nervously. A sense of humor topped the list of traits Darla appreciated in a man. Good-looking, young, well-dressed, and funny. Gregory had a wry sense of humor that he rarely exposed to anyone. But André seemed comfortable sharing himself. She still couldn't believe he was attracted to her. Not that she didn't have a lot to offer herself, but she was tired of doubting everything. She wanted to enjoy his company. Her critical mind reluctantly curled up behind a potted plant.

A stuffed eggplant dish arrived, along with scalloped zucchini in a creamy sauce and some kind of grain with nuts and seeds. André poured more wine. They talked about the ingredients, singling out flavors and sharing appreciation for the creativity of the chef. He asked if she did any sports.

She shook her head. "I like to bike."

"I'm taking a massage class."

"Why?"

"Because it's important to relax," he said. "I like the idea to exchange massages with my lover."

He had a lover! She didn't want to ask specifically. She couldn't help but think of his hands all over her. She forked the last bite of eggplant to cover up her thoughts.

"Do you like massage?"

"I love massage," she said. "Who doesn't?" She'd love to have a massage from him, but she didn't tell him that.

"How often do you get to go climbing?" she asked.

"As much as I can. Not every weekend but almost."

They chatted about climbing, and she was glad to have the

attention off her. He told her there were lots of places in Portugal, and he also went to Spain. He went on his own, with friends, and also went to climbing festivals. He asked about her life in Boulder.

"It's okay. But I don't want to stay there forever. I want more than okay." She surprised herself, telling him this. She had barely admitted it to herself, let alone said it aloud to anyone else. She didn't really care to go back to Boulder.

"I don't want to stay here either."

"Lisbon?"

"Portugal. I can get better jobs other places in Europe."

She nodded, but inside she ticked off another thing they had in common, wanting to explore more of Europe.

They finished all the food and wine. Darla thought it was time to go, but André didn't seem in a hurry.

"Let's try some port, yes?"

Full and flush with wine, Darla couldn't say no.

"And dessert?" He gave her a naughty smile.

"Why not?" She and Gregory never splashed out like this, certainly not on a weeknight. She had no plans for the morning. She was having fun. He signaled to the woman who had seated them. Darla sat back and relished hearing him speak Portuguese. She was surprised to not need to know what he ordered.

But she did want to know more about Portugal. Before she'd come to Lisbon, she'd known nothing. He was from a city in the north she'd never heard of. She could talk to him all night. They stayed at the restaurant until ten, when the staff gently told them it was time to go home. She insisted they split the bill. He didn't want to but gave in. Slightly drunk and completely buoyant, they wandered toward Bairro Alto. They paused to take in the view at a mirador. Darla hadn't been out at night. The gold glow from the streetlamps and all the lights spread out over the city, the colors making a collage of shapes on the hills opposite. It all took her breath away. André seemed to relish her delight.

"I love Lisbon!" she said.

Back in Bairro Alto, the streets were again clogged with young, drunk Europeans, dancing to the music pumping out of tiny clubs. "Lebanese Blonde" pulsed. The drunken, spring break-like crowd made Darla feel old. She'd never been a festival, party-type person. She preferred small gatherings where she could talk and share ideas and laugh. Darla and André threaded their way through the throng. A crowd gathered in the middle of the street. A woman lay in the middle of the street, her shirt pulled up around her midriff. A young man was crouched over her, drinking a shot from a glass perched on her belly. Darla and André exchanged a glance and moved on. The sexy feeling that she'd felt early on seemed to grow. They were almost at her apartment when André paused.

"Do you want to get a drink?"

She didn't want the good feeling of the evening to end, so she agreed. At a jazz club, André got beers while Darla headed to the bathroom. When she came out and saw him, she could hardly believe it. She had not expected to be on a date, let alone with a hot younger man. She sat down, and they toasted. They talked and laughed for hours, getting drunker and goofier. He was fun. Sweet and responsive. He seemed to want to know all about Darla.

With a few drinks bolstering her, she plunged in.

"How old are you?" She sipped her beer, trying to appear nonchalant.

"I'm twenty-six." He smiled.

Darla hid her surprise behind her beer glass.

"And you?"

"Forty-one." She was sure this would end the date. But no. He smiled wider.

A fierce heat spread over her face.

"What? I thought thirty-one."

"Stop!"

"What? You look great, Darla. I love your blue eyes."

Darla demurred.

"No! They're penetrating." He looked mischievous as he said this.

She got all hot all over. He hadn't said anything like this yet. Used "love" and "you" in the same sentence. It felt good and also made her squirm.

"I'll be back," she said.

In the restroom, she checked herself. Was this really the flirty thing she thought it was? Was she losing touch with reality? He seemed interested in her, no matter how old she was. At the mirror, she fluffed her hair. Maybe it was the Lisbon humidity, but she thought she looked pretty good. She didn't look forty-one. Maybe the age difference between them wasn't such a big deal. She winked at herself in the mirror, cracking herself up.

She took her time washing her hands. Where was this going? The biggest age gap she'd had with her younger lovers was ten years. But sixteen years? André wasn't even thirty. A baby! He didn't seem to mind. Maybe older women turned him on. But Darla didn't really think of herself as an "older woman." She loathed the cougar moniker. She was just past forty, for goodness' sake.

Back at the table, they picked up the conversation, easily talking about other things, mostly nonsense and silliness. They shut the jazz bar down too.

They found themselves back in the street, still crowded with partiers at 4:00 a.m. Flashing lights from a police van made a different mood. Police were herding people. She grabbed onto André's arm. He escorted her away from the scene.

"What's happening?" she asked.

"I think someone got shot," he said. "That's what I just heard, anyway."

André didn't seem concerned. Darla made a face. Did this happen all the time in Lisbon? Around a corner, they arrived at her doorstep, the crowds and flashing lights gone. She stood on the step above him. Her initial nervousness was back. Her stomach clenched on all the beer. She had to use the bathroom again and wanted to end this quickly so she could get upstairs. Now that she knew his age, she definitely wasn't going to consider another date with him.

He took both of her hands. Darla smiled tightly. Much as she'd enjoyed this, it was time to end it. But he wouldn't let go.

"Darla," he said, "you're a very special person. You're amazing."

She shrugged, unsure what was so amazing.

"You're amazing too, André."

She tried to pull her hands away, but he tugged her toward him. It had been a long time since she'd had a stranger's face so close to her own. When was the last time she'd been kissed like this, years? Pressing against him so close, so intimate. Right now, kissing André was the only thing she could think about.

After what seemed like an extended-play kiss, she keyed into Angel's building. They stumbled up the stairs and into her apartment. Removing their shoes at the door, they slipped into her room.

"Just a minute," she said.

In the bathroom, she tried to chase her drunken thoughts. Words of caution careened with thoughts of how hot André was and how fun the evening had been. Would she? No, she wouldn't have sex with him on the first date. But maybe there wouldn't be other dates? She finished peeing.

Back in her room, she found André looking at her sketchbook. Safe territory, she thought. But he turned to her and resumed where they had left off, holding each other close and kissing like they would never stop. They fell to the mattress on the floor and continued making out in the dark. André's hands were up Darla's dress.

"I've been wanting to explore here all night," André said.

"So you haven't been listening to me? Just wanting to get to my panties?"

"Your panties? Your *xoxota*!"

She was ready for him. "Show showta," she repeated, not understanding the word. Soon their clothes were all off.

"Oh, wow," André said, taking in her body.

Darla discovered his giant cock. It took a second to get a hold of it fully. It was the biggest she'd ever experienced. And he was uncircumcised. That was less shocking than his size, but she said nothing. Being naked with him was easier than being at the bar or restaurant. Naked, the age difference melted away.

"Darla," he said, his lips against hers.

"Mmmm . . ."

"I have condoms. Should I get them?"

"Get them! Yes."

He reached over her for his pants. His body pressed against hers, and for a moment, she was pinned to the mattress. The anticipation heightened her sensation. His hardness against her leg made her impatient. He sat up, kneeling next to her. The light from the window backlit him. His broad chest, slim waist, and muscly arms turned her on. She sprawled, wanting him in her. He got the condom on and guided himself into her.

"Okay?" he asked.

She nodded. But when he put himself fully into her, she lost her breath for a second. He pressed, slowly making room for himself. Before long, they were in a rhythm that she didn't want to stop. She surrendered, opening and pulsing on him. Now she'd arrived, fully landed with her first orgasm in Europe. André came too, and she held his hips until he collapsed on her.

"Well," he said, his lips against her neck. "*Bem-vindo a Lisboa.*"

"*Obrigada.*" She hated the moment of pulling out. He took care of the condom. She waited in the near dark, wondering if he would stay the night, wondering if she wanted him to. It was already 6:00 a.m. He came back and climbed into the bed with ease. He grabbed her and held on, turning her so he spooned her from behind. It took a while, even drunk, for Darla to relax into his embrace.

Chapter Fourteen

They woke a few hours later. Rain spotted the window.

"*Bom dia,*" he said, smiling and reaching to hug her.

She snuggled up to him. "What time is it? Don't you have to go to work today?"

"Catholic holiday. Don't know what it's about, actually." He smiled. "Let's celebrate our bodies," he suggested.

They used more condoms. They couldn't stop kissing and touching. Darla never wanted to stop. For the first time, she wanted to stay in the apartment. With André, the room had become sexy. Not just a mattress on the floor and a place to escape from. They made love slower, exploring each other, finding each other's pleasure. It was slower this time, and with more light, she saw his gorgeous body. She ran her hands over his back and touched his head. His hair was shortly cropped. She wondered if it would be curly if left to grow. That would do her in—she was a sucker for curly hair on a man. Finally, they moved to get dressed. She slipped into the lacy bra and panties she'd bought with Lauren's gift. She peeked to see if André noticed, but he was looking at his phone. Time to move on, she thought. She had no plans for the day other than to go to Odeceixe that evening.

André helped make the bed, the sheet flying in the air between them. It threw Darla off-balance. She fell to the bed, and he was on her immediately, kissing her and touching her face. She laughed. She felt so hot and sexy, her chin rubbed raw from his facial hair. His kisses were so loving and fun. He seemed open, unafraid, willing to try things. Darla appreciated that. When she mentioned it, he called it exploring.

"I want to go everywhere, see everything, taste it all," he said. His words were a beacon, lighting up something inside her that recognized him. She wasn't afraid to let him in. They already knew each other so well, it seemed.

They made the bed again. He stood in his underwear, tight, short black briefs. He was fit and compact. He was about the same height as her. She liked how their bodies fit. Gregory was tall and thin. She never felt this kind of physical match with anyone else. Darla stared. André gazed back, smiling, confident.

"No tattoos?" she asked.

He shook his head. "Maybe someday. I don't know what I would want permanently on me."

"Me neither. No tattoos. I don't want the pain or the permanence."

He laughed. She busied herself putting the pillows back, tucking her travel pillow on top. He read the slogan.

"Live full ass?"

She blushed. She respected Lauren and the slogan, but now it felt like one of those cheesy sayings on an inspirational poster.

"Don't hold back. Live life with gusto," she translated.

"Ah," he said. "In Portuguese, we say '*Quem não arrisca não petisca.*'"

"And that means . . ."

He thought about it. "I think in English it is, 'No risk, no gift.'"

"No risk, no reward?"

He snapped his fingers. "*É isso!* That's it."

He pulled her close for a kiss.

"Coffee?" André asked.

"Of course! And maybe one of those Portuguese pastries."

In the hallway, she bumped into Angel. Had she been listening at the door? Her blonde hair was disheveled, and she wore a drapey silk robe. Gripping a cup of coffee, she raised her eyebrow and cocked her head toward Darla's room. Darla blushed and made to get past her.

"Enjoying all the Portuguese flavors?"

Darla cringed inside. What was it to her? She was sure Angel was a master of the one-night stand. She pretended to go along, forcing a chuckle. Please, god, let André not come out now. She was about to close the bathroom door when Angel leaned in.

"The room is for one person. It costs extra for guests."

Now Darla couldn't fake friendliness. She closed the door in Angel's face. On the toilet, she fumed. She wasn't moving to Julie's until after she got back from Odeceixe, so she didn't want to tell Angel yet. Paying more for guests was bullshit. Back in her room, she dressed quickly.

"Let's go."

André was ready but in no hurry. He pulled her close for another kiss. But she just wanted to get out before another encounter with Angel. By the time they left the apartment, it was noon. The rain had stopped, and Bairro Alto was again quiet. At the top of the street, the three crones were on the lookout, watching the street coming up as if it were a TV upon which any kind of drama could be played out. Darla wondered what they thought of her, emerging with a young man in a suit and Armani glasses. As they passed, a wave of chatter rose from the ladies. Darla blushed, both embarrassed and proud. Surely they were used to seeing morning moments like this, the smell of sex oozing off mismatched couples. Was this a common thing—young Portuguese men and older women? She didn't think of herself as older. What had Angel said about Portuguese men? Darla shook her head and gripped André's hand more tightly. She didn't care what they thought. She was so full of them—young lovers, talking, laughing, staring at each other. Surely everyone around them noticed. Surely their love lit up the world.

Darla's deep body satisfaction of being sexed up informed her every move. She walked differently, her center of gravity lower in her hips. They held hands. He had big hands, and she couldn't help but think of that cliché about big hands, big . . . . They stopped to kiss several times. They seemed unable to pull away from each other. She wondered when he had last had sex. She wasn't used to random sex with people she'd just met. Was he?

They went into a *pasteleria*. It reminded Darla of a classic American diner—sparse décor, Formica countertop, simple setting, simple food. There wasn't any ambiance or charm, just simple coffee, food, pastries. People of all ages sat at tables and at the counter.

Darla and André ordered coffee and pastries and sat at a table. This was a different coffee date than the one they'd had in Sintra. She felt both excited and calm, full and hungry for more of him. She followed André's lead and pulled a paper-thin napkin to wipe the powdered sugar off the pastries.

She was distracted by the tension between them, a drive to connect, wanting to touch him everywhere, wanting to touch him all the time. An agreement that bound them together had been made without words but with kisses and caresses.

She went to the bathroom, enjoying a break from the intensity between them. She didn't know what she'd do that day. Maybe check email or look for other events for the following week. When she came back to the table, André was looking at his phone. He had two. When she asked, he told her one for work and one for home. Darla stifled the impulse to check hers. She'd forgotten it all evening and this morning hadn't cared to share any of her attention with a screen or even her sketchbook. She wanted all of it for André. They talked about her trip to Odeceixe.

"I can't wait to be at the beach," Darla said.

"I love the beach!"

"It's my happy place." She liked that she had something going on, that she was doing something on her own. It seemed good to be unavailable to him for the weekend. This wasn't a game; it just seemed like a good idea not to get totally absorbed.

"Have you been to Odeceixe?"

André shook his head.

"You should come with me." It burst out without thought. She wanted to snatch it back. Even as she was fine going away, there was a magnetic pull between them. She hadn't known she was this sex starved. André hadn't said anything, and now she wished she could pull back the invitation.

"I have to work tomorrow."

"Oh, of course." She moved back into the lane of being independent. She was fine on her own. She'd come all this way alone, after all.

"But maybe I can come Saturday morning?"

She thought about it as she wiped powdered sugar off the

table. The diner had cleared out, and they were almost the only ones there. Coming Saturday and going back Sunday? It was a three-hour bus ride. Would he really do that?

"Sure," he said when she questioned him. "I could do that." He leaned over and kissed her, and she swore he licked a little powdered sugar off her cheek.

She couldn't deny that her heart beat a tad faster. She wouldn't be in Lisbon much longer. This way, she could spend a few of those days with André.

Chapter Fifteen

She had been excited to be near water in Portugal. Living in Colorado made for a pretty dry life—dry skin, landscape, arid climate. Darla had always gravitated toward water and was happiest when she was floating or swimming. Margarida's reservation in Odeceixe had given her a chance to go to the beach without having to plan much.

From her laptop, she called the number that Margarida had given her. She spoke with Claudio, whose English was good enough to confirm she was taking Margarida's reservation. Searching online, Darla found where to catch the bus to Odeceixe.

She tried to text Cat to fill him in on her date but didn't hear back. The seven-hour time difference made it hard to connect. She missed telling him everything.

Her mind was full of thoughts of André, her body feeling his presence like a palimpsest—her chin rubbed red by his stubble, her inner thighs stretched and tightened. Full of the feeling of having been sexed up, she savored the wonderful buzz of a new romance. Maybe it was time to explore a little, not be so hung up on relationships but experiences instead.

Somehow, with André, it hadn't been a big deal. She'd been flattered by his attraction to her. She couldn't deny there'd been a chemistry between them that she rarely experienced with anyone in the US. Whatever happened with André, she'd had a PME. But she couldn't help but want more.

She made her way to the bus station and boarded the bus going south. They pulled away from central Lisbon just past dinnertime. The bus passed through urban corridors and then floated along a green, green world. As they broke away from the city, she felt free and open. She gazed out the window, soaking in the Portuguese landscape. She wanted to breathe in every molecule. Everything seemed greener. Even riding the bus, surrounded by others, was a glorious adventure. Whizzing by pine forests and cresting hilly curves, Darla replayed all the moments of her date in her mind.

She heard André's voice, deep and accented, his English so good and so sexy. The heat of his face on hers lingered. Her skin prickled with goosebumps at the idea of him. Of kissing him. Of sex with him, and laughter. She wished she had taken a picture of them. The farewell in the plaza near her place framed itself like a picture in her mental gallery of good moments. A long kiss, drinking from a fountain without knowing when the next sip of water will come.

"I will tell you if I can come to meet you," he had said.

She gave him her phone number. It seemed like a long shot that he would meet her. She didn't want to get her hopes up. She was perfectly fine on her own.

She had no idea what Odeceixe was like or what awaited her. She only knew Claudio would be her host at the hostel. She hadn't brought much except a few essentials and a sketchbook. This new way of throwing a few things into a bag and hitting the road lightly felt good. Back home, she would never be this open and unplanned. She always needed to know where she was going, where she was staying, and what she'd be doing there. So far, things had worked out well enough, despite the setbacks of losing her pen and having to sleep on the couch for the first few nights. And having a room at Julie's when she got back–what a relief.

The bus moved along with the sunset through the lush countryside, full of pines and sand along the side of the road. The day unspooled its brightness, loosening its grip and surrendering to evening. She didn't see the water much, so her anticipation was building. She napped, catching up on the sleep she'd missed.

She woke as they pulled to a stop. Odeceixe was pitch dark. Just steps off the bus, she heard her name. She turned. A large, bald man waved.

"Claudio?"

"Yes, of course." He laughed. "Do you have luggage?" He looked behind her.

She swung her string bag. "Just this."

He looked impressed. "*Tudo bem.* Let's go."

He led her up a winding road. At the distant edge of her hearing, she made out the rhythm of the ocean. She sniffed deeply and caught a scent of sea. No urban smells or light cluttering up her senses, the night sky holding up the star sheet above. The utter quiet. Her shoulders released a notch. The hostel, a simple building painted white, glowed on a hill. They entered a veranda with tables set for a meal. Claudio took Darla into the office where he checked her in.

At her room, he flicked on a bright overhead light, revealing her home for the weekend. The white space sprawled large and sparse, with a giant bed in the center. He instructed her to put all the toilet paper in the garbage can. She'd never heard of this. The best feature of her room was the balcony with a cheerful yellow hammock inviting cloud gazing. She imagined floating there, relaxed and free. This weekend, she just wanted to relax, sketch, and touch the sea.

Back at the front desk, Claudio gave her dinner suggestions. She wasn't used to eating this late, but she was starving and hadn't brought any snacks. She wandered the narrow, windy streets of the village, trying to follow Claudio's directions. Despite the quiet, her pulse skittered. It was so dark. Her earlier sense of adventure now wound itself into a coil in her gut. Hungry and nervous, she finally found the town square. One little restaurant seemed open. She took a seat on the outside terrace under the stars, the only guest except for a group of older men at a table nearby. They ignored her, which was fine with Darla. A man wearing an apron came out and took her order. She couldn't decipher much on the menu. She settled for shrimp and a glass of wine. She started to relax, sipping her white wine. She checked her phone but had zero bars.

She got out her journal and wrote about her day, including her feelings for André. They really enjoyed each other's company. It seemed they had so much to talk about. She couldn't believe it had been just one date. Sure, a long one. She couldn't help but crave more of what she had this week in Lisbon. To have a life where she explored and discovered and met interesting people. She wanted more. More laughs, more sex, more kissing, more conversation. To be happy and loved. She had so many questions for André. She wanted to know about his life in Lisbon.

When her meal came, her buoyant feelings about André deflated. Shrimp, a handful of them, heads and legs intact, swam in oil and bits of garlic. She wanted something delicious, and this was not it. She called the waiter back and asked if there was something else she could order.

"Vegetables?"

"Fries?" he countered.

"*Sim, por favor,*" she complied, really wanting vegetables. So far, the food in Portugal hadn't been that great. She'd kill for some steamed broccoli.

Back in her room, she flopped on the vast bed. Her old friend, loneliness, joined in. She'd felt this as a girl. An existential void she couldn't explain. No one to talk to. No one who understood her. She'd learned to stay busy to keep this unwanted companion away. What was she doing here all alone? She had exhausted her thoughts in her journal and didn't feel like doing anything. Except kissing André. He dominated her thoughts. His hands and lips and tongue all over her was hard not to obsess about. It had been so sudden and unexpected. It was just a fling, surely. A fun fling. She wondered if he was in the habit of seducing Globalkins. PME, one-night stand, whatever. She tried to shake off the obsessive track her mind was taking with him. She fell asleep hugging a pillow, wishing it were him.

The next day, a gray sky waited dully outside. Rain spotted the windows. Her idea of a beach day deflated. Down in the dining room, loud Brazilian music played. Claudio cheerfully called out *Bom dia!* She responded, practicing her Portuguese accent.

On the veranda, a few couples ate and talked quietly. No one paid any attention to her, and if it was odd that she was there alone, no one mentioned anything. She poured weak coffee and arranged a plate with pastries, bread, cheese, and yogurt. She took an apple for later.

Without the sun and promise of the beach, an empty feeling replaced her sense of adventure. What was she doing here? She munched her breakfast and suddenly had the oddest sense of detachment. Detached from her life, from her job, from everything she knew. The rain pelted the window. What was she doing here? Lauren's inheritance had made for a fun leaping off point, but now that she was free floating, without the distractions of Lisbon, she was unmoored.

For a minute, she couldn't catch her breath. Back in her room, she huddled in bed, unable to load anything on her phone, listlessly sketching. She wished she could text Cat, but it was the middle of the night back in Boulder, and the connection wasn't great at the hostel.

Finally, the rain broke. At the front desk, she got directions to the beach. Claudio warned her that it was a long walk, but she was restless and had a day to fill. She packed her string bag with her bathing suit and sunscreen. Once she cleared the village, she walked along the roadside. Few cars passed by. Wild fennel and unidentified grasses shivered in the wind. The sky grew darker. Soon a river accompanied her, and its rushing hurried her steps.

She turned a curve in the road and came upon a small crescent of a beach. Tucked in a cove, the lagoon was framed by the river at the back and the sea in front. It was almost empty except for a couple of surfers and a few families. An older guy with bleached-blond hair strolled the edge of the water. She laid out her towel and settled in. But the sky had other plans. A gentle rain let loose, darkening the sand. If she were in Colorado, she'd just wait it out, but the rain showed no signs of letting up. Muttering, she packed up her stuff. Spotting a cluster of buildings at the top of the cliff, she headed toward it.

Darla went to a small joint called Restaurant Dolores. She shivered, loving these random synchronicities. Dolores, not a common name in English, was her grandmother's name. Her mom had once told her that her dad had wanted to name her Dolores, but they chose Darla instead. The small restaurant was full. A wave of anxiety flared up. There wasn't room for her. She stood alone near the door, fidgeting. She considered leaving, but an employee made room for her at a table near the door. She ordered tuna steak and rice. Thunder rocked the air, but no one in the café seemed to mind. Her food arrived, and she settled in. Would she get used to so few vegetables?

The persistent rain now made a shield between her, the world, and any need to think, or plan, or do. Pausing to look out at the beach sky, she relaxed a bit. Contentment settled over her. She had nowhere to go and nothing to do. For the first time, all the stress and intensity of getting ready and traveling to Portugal melted away. Finally, after all the sadness over Gregory, after all the planning to make this trip, a sense of satisfaction had replaced all that gunky stuff she'd been hounded by. Sometimes, she imagined she had been dropped into a moment to observe. She wasn't completely part of the scene herself. Just an observer, notetaker, sketch maker.

She ordered coffee—no fancy cappuccino here. She noodled around in her sketchbook. No one in the restaurant paid any attention to her. She dashed off an ode to the rain. Trying to capture the scene, she practiced describing things in writing, not relying on photos. André continued to haunt her thoughts. Spurred by caffeine, fantasies of abandoning her plans for Paris spun out on the page. Would she do that? She had everything set up for Paris. But what was that? Just a city with a two-week rented apartment.

Here she had found what could be love. She shook her head. It was just a fling. She had spent one night, one glorious night, with André. What made her brain think it was time to plan a long-term relationship?

The rain let up. Darla paid her bill and set out to the hostel. Instantly, the rain resumed. She slogged along, adding more ways to describe rain to the piece she had written in the restaurant. She set her mind to conjuring words for the rain instead of mulling over André. She arrived at the hostel so soaked that she'd long ago stopped noticing the wetness. She was one with the rain. In her room, she stripped down and dried off. The rain stopped, leaving a sad silence. On the bed, she added to her rain ode.

It's the kind of rain that sets sailors to consider taking up farming. The kind of rain that erases a month of drought. That beats upon the body in a deep-tissue massage from Father Sky. This rain drenches in an instant; it provokes melancholy; it stimulates excess. This rain engorges rivers, raises oceans, churns the depths of placid lakes. It empties streets and quiets cities, insisting on its own rhythm. It brings out not only umbrellas but galoshes and Wellingtons and rain caps and full-body parkas on those who dare its onslaught. It's the definition of wet. It surpasses wet. It turns the skin blue and speckles it with gooseflesh. It keeps everything moist and cold for hours. Chuva, in Portuguese. It coaxes out the greenest of green in flora and fauna. It makes children squeal delight, old ladies tut with memories of floods, and fearful people take cover. It's for being inside, for sipping hot drinks, for warm fires. It's for writing and reading and snuggling. Was there ever a dry moment?

After a brief nap, she stretched and went onto the balcony. Looking onto the village, she felt like something powerful had passed through the town and through her. Her hammock hung heavy and wet. She wondered what this would have been like with André, this kind of wetness. Her dark mood rolled back in. The bleak weather dampened her enthusiasm and ruined her picture of a wonderful beach vacation. Lauren would love this rainy day in all its imperfections. She would love having space to just be. Darla wished she could feel that carefree. She considered her options. She could catch a bus back to Lisbon the next day. Or she could call André and see if he could meet her in Odeceixe. Down in the breakfast room, she had enough bars to text André.

Olá.

Her heart beat madly while she waited for André to respond.

Finally, a smiley emoji.

Olá, Darla. How are you?

I'm good. It's nice here.

Did you go to the beach?

I did, but right when I got there, it started to rain!

She didn't want to ask straight out if he was coming.

How's work?

It's fine. I am thinking of you all day.

Me too.

She paused. Dare she ask? Full ass, Lauren whispered in her ear.

Are you coming to Odeceixe?

She watched the text dots pulse.

Yes.

She did a little skip in the breakfast room.

I can be there tomorrow around noon.

Great! I will see you then. Wait . . . how will we connect?

I will find you.

This seemed romantic, and Darla wasn't sure why. The vagueness of it should have bothered her, but somehow it was just romantic. She went out for dinner and found an Italian restaurant run by a German guy. She sat on the terrace and watched a little white dog stand on the porch, guarding the spot. She chatted in English with the German while she ate her pasta marinara. On the walk to the hostel, she basked under the stars sprawling over the entire sky. It was too early to go to sleep, but she had nothing else to do. She'd exhausted the contours of her own mind.

Chapter Sixteen

The next morning, the sky promised more sun than the day before. Thank god André was coming. It would be so much more interesting with him here.

She got ready for her lover. She liked thinking of André that way. Even if she only had another week with him, she could call him her lover if she wanted.

After breakfast, she headed out to walk the village. Only a few shops were open, selling beach and fishing gear. May was not yet full beach season, so the village was largely deserted. Signs pointing the way to the *praia* marked every turn. She fast-forwarded to July and August and imagined the streets crowded with people in flip-flops and bathing suits, children running after balls, and surfers nursing well-earned beers.

If André hadn't been coming, she would have tried to go back to Lisbon. Odeceixe was way too quiet for all the action she was experiencing in her heart. The low-slung, whitewashed buildings seemed deserted. Rows of potted flowers and plants lined up against the homes. She took her time, snapping photos of the abundant plants and flowers. The town center was still. She didn't see many people, mostly older people. Would this village die out along with its elder population and become another near-empty rural zone in Europe filled with expats seeking strong Wi-Fi and relief from the grind of home? She passed an old woman shrouded in black, inching her way along the narrow street with the aid of a walker. Darla heard her singing? Chanting? Mumbling to herself—she couldn't tell.

She made her way up the streets toward the top of a hill. She hummed a tune, breaking into words. Her heart beat faster and faster. She had faith in this day, that the sun would come out. A current of nervousness threatened her calm. André would be here soon. What would they talk about? She was comfortable with him but now was nervous. Would he still like her?

The narrow streets wound up and around. She arrived breathless at the top of the village where a windmill stood guard. Darla looked out over the valley. The wind whipped her hair. The sky cloaked a uniform pale blue over the valley. All the roofs of the village were terra cotta. The village was nestled in a valley of farm fields intersected by a curving river. It was green and quiet, the sky a flat expanse of gray blue.

The church bells chimed. She counted as she gazed over the valley. The peals kept going and going . . . twelve times! She startled. Noon had snuck up on her. She rushed back to the center of town. Around and around, she wound down the narrow, empty streets. Walking along a narrow corridor, she saw the plaza. There was André at a café, sitting at a table looking at his phone. A few others lounged, sipping beers and coffee. She rushed over, her heart beating fierce. He smiled when he saw her. He stood up and brought her close for a kiss. She smiled.

"Coffee?" he asked.

"*Sim, por favor.*"

He ordered from a stooped older man who moved slowly but with grace. She tried to catch her breath. Sitting in the plastic chair, she took him in. He was wearing the same hoodie he'd worn at the Sintra outing, with a dark beret. His glasses and a bit of stubble gave him a rugged, intellectual look. He smiled at her, and the knot in her stomach loosened. He took her hand.

"How is Odeceixe treating you?"

"Great, it's been . . . quiet."

He laughed. "These small villages are the definition of quiet."

Their *pingados* came. Darla added sugar, stirring with the mini spoon. They were flush with possibility. She felt that everything was good, everything was glowing. They kissed, the taste of coffee on their lips.

"How was the ride here?"

"Fine," he said. "I'm used to taking buses."

"Are there any trains in Portugal?"

"Not so much. Buses go everywhere and are cheap. What about where you live?" He sipped his coffee.

"There are trains and buses, but Americans really love their cars. They prefer to be independent, going where they want, when they want."

"Like you?"

"I guess. I'm here of my own free will." Saying it, she realized how American that phrase was. How they cherished being able to do whatever they wanted, on a whim. She felt privileged to be in Portugal, on her own, no ties. She bounced in her seat, unable to sit still. Her energy flooded her veins, her heart pumping. And here she was, with a man she hardly knew, on a whim.

"I'm buzzing with caffeine," she said. She'd left her sketchbook in her room. She could use it now, to help calm her nerves.

"You're almost Portuguese," he replied. She laughed. It seemed like they were always laughing, something always funny. How could it be so light and easy to be with someone she was just getting to know?

Her earlier nerves were gone. Back at the hostel, she introduced him to Claudio, who seemed nonplussed. Darla was self-conscious about being with a younger man. André and Claudio didn't seem to care. Up in their room, he shrugged off his bag and pulled her onto the bed.

They kissed and kissed. Before long, he had his hand in her pants. She pressed herself against his jeans, the bulge in his crotch tempting her. She melted, his fingers on her and his tongue running along her lips. But she pushed him away.

"Come on, let's go to the beach while it's still nice out."

He put his fingers in his mouth.

"I'll save this for later," he said.

The walk was more fun with him, cracking jokes, holding hands, and scampering into the grass to pick flowers. A few old men walked the edge of the road. She hadn't seen anyone yesterday. André stopped to talk. She stood nearby, watching their expressions, trying to understand what was happening. They pointed at the ground and their buckets. One of them reached in and pulled something out to show them. A snail shell nestled in his hand. Of course—after yesterday's rain, there was an abundance of snails. André told her that they sold them to restaurants in town. She had never eaten snails and never wanted to, but it was cool to see this countryside gleaning.

The sun shone brightly. It was a completely different place with André and the sun. Her dark mood from the day before seemed like a mirage. They arrived at the beach, nearly deserted. A few people lounged and walked the water's edge, but it was clearly not beach season yet. She laid out her fouta. He pulled out a picnic: bread, cheese, and tomatoes. A film canister.

"What's that?"

"Smell," he said. She expected pot.

"Oregano?"

"Yes." He smiled. "Oregano is the secret ingredient to life. I take it everywhere."

She laughed. His high-level picnic skills were unlike anyone she knew. He opened his water bottle slightly and dribbled water on the tomatoes to wash them. She asked him if he always washed fruit and vegetables like this. Always, he said.

She didn't have any food to contribute. They munched on nuts and tomatoes sprinkled with oregano and salt. The waves caressing the sand mesmerized her. After lunch, they lay down and made out. They pressed close to each other, kissing and touching. André's cock signaled its need for attention in his black undies. They might have been able to get away with more, but a family was at the other end of the beach. She pulled away and adjusted her bathing suit top. She wanted to keep going. Instead, she stood and stretched.

She funneled her sexual energy into stretches. He joined her. She moved and he followed, a slow and steady beach dance. An athlete, he had the muscles to improvise. All of his time rock climbing had sculpted his body. I could climb all over him all day, Darla thought.

They strolled along the sea's edge, the cold water tickling her ankles. After a while, they packed up. Atop the hill at the hamlet, they went to Dolores's. It was more fun with André and without rain. They sat outside. An old lady served them beers and a plate of little bean-like things.

"*Tremoços*," André said. He showed her how to place one in her teeth and remove the papery skin, like the skin on a garbanzo bean. They didn't taste like much, but somehow with the beer and the view and the feeling of lots of kissing on her lips, she was happy to eat them. She drew a picture of the beer and the snacks with the sea in the background, André's hand at the edge of the page. The day felt mythical to her: the sea stretching out in its timeless, endless waves; the clouds soaking up all the sun; the energy she felt of his masculinity, her femininity. Surely they were being used by the gods as playthings. She had been given a young lover to consort with. Perched on the top of the cliff, anything felt possible.

They made their way back to the hostel, happy and buzzing. Darla soaked up the beauty of the flowers along the way. Some walls in the town were covered with gorgeous fuchsia bougainvillea. She stopped to take a photo. André got in the frame, falling back on the wall of bougainvillea flowers, arms outstretched. She giggled at his impulsiveness. Like the photo with the Globalkins, he was willing to do something silly. His playfulness inspired her. They snapped a photo of themselves in front of the bougainvillea. Back in their room, they peeled off their clothes and made love. They took their time, touching, exploring, and kissing. She kept opening up and opening up, and finally she felt completely melted into the soft bed. They'd only known each other a few days, but making love with André somehow felt like a homecoming.

❈

She didn't want to leave the room, but it was late, and they were hungry. They went to the same restaurant Darla had been to on her first night. André ordered for them. She was getting used to him making decisions. The waiter brought a bowl of black olives and two wineglasses. He opened a bottle of Vinho Verde. Darla had never had this before she came to Portugal, but now she craved it.

They munched on the olives and sipped the wine. She started a page in her sketchbook, positioning the wine bottle at the side, practicing her lettering.

"What did you order for us?"

"*Arroz con mariscos.*"

She tried to repeat the crashing waves of shushing syllables. "What's that?"

"Seafood rice. It's delicious."

"Why didn't I see that when I was here the other night?" she wondered aloud.

"It's only for two people."

"Well, that sucks."

"It takes a long time to make. It's a big deal. You'll see."

"I will see, and I will eat!" She was hungry, and a rice dish sounded perfect.

They were the only people in the restaurant. Darla asked about driving. Did he want a car? He confessed he wanted a motorcycle. He told her about trying to pass his driving exam, not being able to slow down on the driving track and having to take the exam over. They laughed.

She had failed her driving exam too. She couldn't parallel park. She had to translate this with gestures. She said it made her determined to be good at parking, and now she was a master at it. He said he'd like to see that in action. He was still determined to go fast, he confessed, which is why he wanted to buy a moto. She wanted to know more about the moto, but the waiter was there, clearing space for the main course. He left a trivet on the table.

He returned bearing a giant pot. He situated it on the table and lifted the lid. Fishy-smelling steam wafted out. She peered in. Crab legs, shrimp with their legs and heads on, mussels in shells, and clams clustered atop rice. She wanted to draw it. She wanted to eat it! The waiter ladled it into shallow bowls. Darla inhaled deeply. She was so hungry that she didn't mind the lack of vegetables. André picked up the pair of crab claw crackers and held them up with a mischievous look.

"What are you going to do with that?"

He waved them theatrically and picked up a crab leg. Darla didn't want to admit that she had never cracked a crab leg, so she watched carefully. They set into the rice and seafood. She thought she tasted bits of fennel. The meal with its slightly fizzy wine was like eating the day, the sea flavors, the creamy rice, the tangy olives a palette of the sea. Full, she sketched the mussel shells and crab legs. The claw crackers and tiny forks for excavating the clams; the big ladle danced on the page opposite the seafood debris. If only she could capture flavors in her sketches, she thought. They sopped up the stew's gravy with pieces of flatbread. When the waiter asked if they wanted dessert, she shook her head.

"I couldn't fit anything else in," she explained to André when the waiter left.

They talked about what to do the next day.

"Margarida told me to take a bus to the Algarve," she said. "But is it far?

He shook his head. "Not far. We can do that."

She would have just headed back to Lisbon, not gone in the opposite direction to somewhere new. But with André, she felt even more adventurous and willing to explore. He had been to the Algarve and knew where to go and how to get there. She liked not having to make all the plans. For once, she could just go with the flow and follow him.

They wandered to a small plaza. It was empty but for the circle of benches and trees. They took a seat and absorbed the view. In the center of the plaza was a small fountain. The paving stones were in a lovely pattern not dissimilar to Lisbon. Palm trees waved their fronds. André produced a spliff. Darla was surprised. She hadn't thought of him as a toker. She smoked occasionally with Cat. She liked how pot lifted her out of her body, taking her mind above the mundane. She sometimes got wild ideas when high. They smoked it down to the end, laughing and chatting.

She didn't know how it started, but they took to the piazza and began dancing. There was no music but their smiles. They swung each other around and around, growing ever more daring and free. The night was mild. No one was around. They flowed, laughing and touching and moving in sync. They danced for a long time. She loved being high, being connected, playing together with their bodies. It seemed they were the only people in Odeceixe that night.

Finally, they stumbled back to their room, telling jokes and giggling hysterically. He was so goofy and playful. Suddenly, a knock came at the door. André opened it. It was Claudio. He spoke to André in Portuguese. André closed the door and came back to the bed, smothering a laugh.

"What did he say?"

"We're too loud. We have to quiet ourselves."

This just made them laugh more. She put her hand on her mouth and tried to stifle her giggles. They stripped down and went onto the balcony. The bright moon, the stars, the chill air on her nakedness—Darla had never felt so alive. Her body shivered. She spread a towel on the hammock. She lay back, and André nestled in the hammock with her. Their naked skin, her breasts pale in the moonlight. The hammock tilted and swayed, and Darla grabbed his waist to keep him from tumbling out. They moved together silently, aware that neighbors at the hostel might be out on their balconies above, or below, or even next to them. His mouth opened in a cry. Darla put her fingers on his lips. The salty air, the cool May breeze on her skin, Darla felt wild and free, the sea creature she was meant to be.

Chapter Seventeen

The next morning, they boarded a bus to Lagos. She'd heard that the Algarve coast along the bottom of Portugal was highly developed and overrun with condos, bars, and tourists trickling down from the north of Europe. André told her he'd been there a few times but didn't add much. Instead of talking, they cuddled and kissed. An hour or so later, they arrived at the waterfront. They got off the bus at a boardwalk. A surge of joy overtook Darla when she saw the beach. It was bigger than the scrap of sand at Odeceixe. People scattered, lounging on towels and beach chaises. Children scooped sandcastles, and young people played volleyball. This was another world from Odeceixe. André saw her smile.

"You like?"

"Very much."

"I see you in your happy place," he said. He pulled her close. He'd remembered her words. She leaned into him, savoring the moment, the sun, the intimacy. Her crotch was sore and satisfied from all the activity. What had he called it? *Show-show* something. She'd have to ask how he spelled that and what it even meant. They strolled along the boardwalk, holding hands.

"Let's find a boat," he said.

"Let's!"

André approached a boatsman at the wharf. She stood back

while he negotiated. He waved her over, and they climbed into a small-engined boat. The driver settled in the back of the boat and started the engine. A plume of diesel smoke set them off. Darla gripped the sides of the boat, the rocking boat thumping against the waves. They rode along the coast. The dinghy glided past ancient rock formations. She could tell André wanted to climb them. They made up names for the rocks, laughing and enjoying their creative play.

The buoyancy of the boat, the brightness of the day, the ease with which they flowed together lifted her up. Total joy washed over her, riding the waves, feeling André next to her, gazing at the horizon. The boat scuttled past the rocks, and then there was nothing but sea and sea for miles. This was the edge of Europe—the very bottom crust of Portugal. A thrill rushed over her. Her being felt electrified but not lit up and anxious. She was full and juiced up. Something melted inside her. She fully absorbed this aliveness she'd never had before. She felt so far away from the computer, from any thoughts of work, from any thoughts of the future at all. She was here, with André, bobbing on the sea, and for once, she had no desire to be anywhere else.

This was who she truly was, not the person working away every day on a screen tan. Tears rose up, and she let them fall away into the salty water. She glanced over at André. He was looking at her, a smile on his face like he had read her. She felt him seeing her. She felt and appreciated his perceptiveness. She liked it, and then it made her feel too seen. She wasn't used to having her happiest moments alongside someone else. She'd gotten used to having her own thrills, her own fun. Gregory liked serious things like classic movies and books. André not only wasn't stuffy, he seemed to really get her.

"We're at the edge of Europe!" she shouted over the engine noise. "We are hanging off the edge of the continent!"

"We are! Where water meets rock!"

They came ashore on wobbly legs and paused to kiss on the boardwalk. Darla's skin tingled from the salt air and from the heat André lit in her.

They lounged on the beach for a while. It was warmer here than Odeceixe. They waded into the water, splashing and laughing. They people-watched families toting coolers, chairs, and umbrellas and leading children to the ice cream shops. The sun drenched the afternoon in warmth. Darla finally felt like she had unhooked from home. Being on a boat gave her that freedom she'd felt at Cat's family cottage. Boats just made her happy.

"I love this day," she said.

"This day loves you. You look so happy. I mean—"

"No, I'll take it. I think this whole weekend loves me." She got hot all over. She wouldn't say it, but she already loved André, even after only a few days. Being with him felt right. Traveling together was a breeze. They set out to find a late lunch. At a beachside restaurant, they chose an outdoor table with a white cloth. André ordered, and soon the waitress brought a bottle of Vinho Verde along with a little round of goat cheese and a saucer of black olives. These were nothing like the black olives she and her mom ate from a can. They were slick with olive oil and speckled with rosemary. They started a pile of pits and worked their way into the bottle. They mopped up the runny cheese with bread and chased it with the wine.

She felt full even before the meal arrived, soaked from the ocean, dusted by the sand, kissed by the sun, appreciated by André. The sun was going down and the beach emptied out. It was a postcard-perfect date. Then their meal arrived. A whole fish, giving them the stink eye. Lemons ringed its head like a citrus daisy chain.

Darla had become a vegetarian at university. But the night before, she'd forged her way into sea life, cracking crab legs and sipping broth from mussel shells.

"I don't know," she said, glad she had eaten so much bread and cheese. She eyed the side of boiled potatoes. What would make those taste decent?

"Come, you'll like this." He pulled the platter closer. "I will show you the way."

His big hands deftly separated the meat from the fish's skeleton. He showed her how to eat the flesh so the tongue searched for bones before the teeth could crunch them. His elegance and patience made it easier for her to try something new. She leaned into the experience, nudging slightly past her fear of bones. The Blessing of the Throats ritual from her childhood church came to mind. Would the candles crossed at her neck and the mumbled blessing still be in effect after all these years? So far, no bones. She wondered about all the things she would try if she had more time with André. But this could well be it, this weekend, outside of time, at the edge of the continent.

They cuddled on the long bus ride back to Lisbon. They made the bus seats a cozy nest for the two of them, entwined. She offered André half of her headset, and they listened to *In Rainbows*, her favorite album. They kissed and kissed. They kissed like they'd invented kissing. They kissed like they could get inside each other, deep inside, through their lips. They kissed as if they might never see each other again. They were surrounded by people but oblivious to them. They didn't talk at all, it seemed. Darla felt like a different person than the woman who'd taken the bus alone, in the dark, to Odeceixe.

Back in Lisbon, André invited her to his place. It was after midnight, and she didn't want to go back to Angel's. She would move into Julie's the next day. After the short weekend together, she wasn't ready to leave him. After wandering a deserted Avenida da Liberdade, they came upon a pharmacy. A couple huddled at a little window in the pharmacy door. Darla saw a pharmacist inside. A taxi waited at the curb.

Peeking in, she saw wooden cabinets, paving stone floors, and rows of bottles. It felt like a special pharmacy, and she expected magic. When the couple got their goods, André stepped to the window. Darla hung back. She was in high school again when she and her boyfriend were too shy to buy condoms, so they stole them. André had no problem, though. He spoke with the pharmacist, who asked him some questions. A few minutes later, a paper bag and some euros were exchanged through the window.

"What did he ask you?"

"What size, what color, what flavor I wanted."

They laughed.

"He knows exactly what's going to happen with us now," she told André, her face heating up.

"Not exactly," André said, kissing her.

Six more days. She was leaving for Paris on Sunday. She'd leave him behind, because that's the way life was. With all this happiness must come a little melancholy, right?

Chapter Eighteen

The next morning, it only took a few minutes to gather her things at Angel's. She sent a message to Julie and arranged to meet. It wasn't far in a taxi to her new place. Inside, Julie had coffee and a plate of mini cardamom buns.

"I get these from the bakery downstairs," she said. "They're my favorite."

The women sat at the round table in the kitchen, nibbling the treats and chatting. Darla got out her sketchbook to capture the twists of the pastries.

"What's that?" Julie said from the sink where she was washing a few dishes.

"Just my sketchbook," Darla said.

"Let's see." Julie wiped her hands on a towel with a funky illustrated map of Lisbon on it.

Darla passed it over. She looked over Julie's shoulder while Julie flipped the pages. Her whole body tensed as it did when someone looked at her art.

"Wow, I love your style," Julie said. "You really captured the essence of Lisbon."

"Really?" Darla exclaimed. "It seems so messy to me."

"I don't see it that way. To me, your watercolors have a freshness that I crave. So much art is digitally made now. It feels plasticky to me."

"Me too!" Darla said. "I never thought of it that way. But

you're right, it's like a plastic version of art. None of the texture of an oil painting or a mural."

"Or watercolor. Even your watercolors have a lot of depth and texture. You're really good." She handed the sketchbook back.

"I'm just a beginner." But Darla felt herself relaxing under Julie's compliments.

"Well, keep going!"

She opened the sketchbook and began drawing the items on the table. Julie went back to putting dishes away. Darla felt so at home here. She basked in Julie's encouragement, followed by a twinge of longing. She wouldn't be here long. Then Paris and back to her life in Boulder. Her apartment and office seemed so far away, on a distant planet in a different time.

"I'm off!" Julie gathered her backpack and pulled on a cute hat. She flashed a smile.

"I don't think I have ever seen anyone so happy to go to work."

Julie laughed.

"I love my job. The commute! In LA, it took forever to get anywhere in my car. Here, I get to walk everywhere. So much better."

"For sure!"

"Enjoy your day. Make yourself at home, Darla." She leaned over for a quick cheek kiss. Darla flushed. How could some people be so easily affectionate and generous?

She spent the morning unpacking. Even though she wouldn't be here for long, she liked playing that she lived here, in Julie's home, in Lisbon.

She and André spent every minute of his spare time together. They texted all day, making evening plans and flirting. She set a special ringtone for him. Every time it went off, an electric current zipped through her body. His writing was romantic and dreamy, and Darla wasn't sure if it was because his English was imperfect and lent itself to poetry. Sometimes he didn't have a direct way to say it, so he had to say it slant. André was a dreamer, a lover of beauty.

She went to the tile museum. In an old convent, the museum both calmed and excited her. She gained a new appreciation for the tiles she saw in the city. She copied a few tile patterns into her sketchbook. After an hour in the space, she noticed her tension was gone. The repetitive patterns on the tiles soothed her.

It was her mom's birthday, and she wanted to FaceTime. Darla called from a mirador, with a view over the Tejo and Alfama clustered below her. Flapping sheets hung from clotheslines across the narrow streets. The rooftops a chaos of order. She sang the birthday song, her gaze roving the urban pastiche.

After the song, her mom started grilling her.

"How's it going? Where are you?"

"It's going great," she said. "I'm in Lisbon for a few more days." She didn't expect her mom to keep track of her itinerary.

"We miss you!" Henry waved from the background, moving out of frame. "Having fun?"

"I am! Lisbon is really cool. I'm getting lots of exercise on these hills. Look." She rotated with her phone to show them the view. The river and roofs pixelated, forming a semi-impressionist painting.

"Nice," her mom said. "I hope your money is holding out."

Darla grimaced, pretending to smile.

"I'm good. It's super cheap here."

She changed the subject, asking about their summer plans. Now that her mom and Henry were retired, they were hardly home. They wanted to adventure after a lifetime of hard work. Darla couldn't imagine another twenty-five years in her job or even in that industry. She didn't want to postpone joy until she was older. She pushed the thought away and refocused on the screen.

Once her mom was convinced Darla was okay, they signed off. She was ashamed to feel relief. She couldn't help it; she was a different version of herself than her mom knew. It was hard to put into words. Explaining felt wrong. Part of her wanted to keep these new experiences to herself. She didn't need anyone at home to understand. She breathed in the sea air, the ever-present breeze off the Tejo ruffling her curls. For a moment she wished she were staying in Lisbon. She had fallen in love with the colorful buildings, the funky streets, and most of all, with André. But maybe he'd come visit her in Boulder.

André had teased her all day via text about what he was going to cook for dinner but never revealed the menu. After work, they met on the Avenida da Liberdade, a posh avenue with a wide pedestrian strip in the middle. Trees lined the wide walkway. Darla soaked in the shady calm, strolling to meet André. He was waiting for her at the red lottery kiosk. The impulse to sketch it arose, but André was reaching for her, and all thoughts of sketching flew away. He kissed her cheeks and then her mouth. They kissed for a long time. Darla got hot underneath her purple jacket.

"It's great to see you," he said.

"Likewise. How do you say likewise in Portuguese?"

"Likewise means . . . ?"

"The same."

"*Também*."

She repeated it. She had no reason to take up Portuguese. But it was fun to learn words in other languages.

"*Obrigada!*"

She was getting the hang of *thank you*. The rule seemed to be to cut off the beginning of *obrigada* and the end of most other words. She was feeling more comfortable in Lisbon just when it was almost time to go.

At his place, André had a vegetable curry going. He had opened a bottle of red wine, now aerating in the decanter. A cutting board of chopped carrots, potatoes, and greens waited near the stove. A small pot of rice simmered on the back burner. She couldn't believe he cooked so well.

"Be comfortable," he said. "I just do more cooking here." He bent over a pan, the steam fogging up his glasses. He looked cute. But if he had that kind of posture, Darla thought, he wouldn't be cooking for long.

She took a glass of red wine he offered and looked around. Music was playing from upstairs. "Who's this?" she gestured upward.

"Manu Chao. Know him?"

She shook her head. The music was catchy and upbeat. He sang in what sounded like Spanish, but then she recognized some French. She bopped along while taking in the apartment. She'd been upstairs in the mezzanine when they'd come back from Odeceixe, but it had been late, and she hadn't looked around much. From the entry, it opened onto the living room. Black leather couches gathered around a coffee table on a shaggy black rug. A rustic staircase with no railing led up to the mezzanine. A card table served as a dining table with a few mismatched chairs scattered around it.

She excused herself to use the bathroom, where a spacious tub overlooked a window. A patchwork of Lisbon's terra-cotta rooftops filled the window frame. They were on the fourth floor, at the very top of the building. The apartment blended a modern and traditional vibe, with half-timbered, unfinished walls and rough-hewn beams at the ceiling. A closed door near the entry. André told her that was his roommate Ricardo's room. Sipping her wine, she relished being in Europe with a handsome European. He came up behind her, nuzzling her neck. She shivered and leaned back into him.

"Ready for *le dîner*?" he asked. They had been flirting in French. She never had the chance to practice the French she'd studied at university. With André, it was fun. It seemed like a common ground, both making their way not in their native tongue.

"*Oui, oui!*"

He invited her to the stove, where they assembled bowls of rice and coconut curry. It smelled great. She was usually the one to make a meal for friends. While she liked eating out, savoring someone's cooking was much more personal. Home-cooked food just tasted better.

They brought their bowls to the couch. André poured more wine. To Darla's delight, the curry tasted as good as it smelled. She didn't want to reveal her surprise; instead, she complimented him. He smiled but modestly deflected. How great it would be to not have to cook all the meals. How delightful to have a lover who shared her adventurousness in the kitchen. Over the spicy curry, they divulged all their favorite foods. They tossed around things they could cook together. Sushi!

Pizza! He told her about the Portuguese dishes he could cook: sardine rice and octopus rice. She told him her favorites: pesto, roasted vegetables, and smoothies. He didn't know smoothies, so she explained the glory of a quick and healthy breakfast.

"This is a great place," she said. "You scored."

"Scored?" He tilted his head.

"Got a nice place."

He nodded.

"Are you excited for Paris?

"I am. I've dreamt about Paris for what seems like my whole life."

He smiled, spooning in the last of his curry.

"Have you ever been there?" she asked.

His face clouded over, but he quickly recovered.

"You don't like Paris?"

He got busy with his food, chewing slowly before answering.

"I love France. I have a French ex-girlfriend," he said.

Darla wasn't sure what to say. He didn't seem comfortable talking about it.

"Do you still love her?"

"No!" he said quickly. But she didn't believe him. A stab of jealousy clutched her heart. She knew it was irrational to be jealous of someone in the past. She had no claim to him, and anyway, she was leaving in a few days. She changed the subject and talked about wanting to study Italian. André spoke Italian too.

"Wait. How many languages do you speak?"

He held up his hand and began counting on his fingers.

"Portuguese, Spanish, English, French, Italian. Five."

"Whoa!"

She wanted that so bad that she could feel it in her ribs. To speak several languages with ease. When she'd studied French at university, she'd had a knack for mimicking. She liked to think she could pronounce anything if she heard it a few times. Maybe someday. Maybe she could take some language classes back in Boulder or start using an app to learn.

After dinner, he led her up to his mezzanine. Crouched on the mattress, he rolled a spliff. She watched him scatter the tobacco and crush crumbs off a nubbin of dark hash. He sprinkled them over the tangle of tobacco. He lifted the delicate taco to his lips, licking the edge of the rolling paper. Darla was entranced, mesmerized by his every move. He deftly rolled the spliff and twisted the end. Snatching a lighter from his desk, he said, "Let's go!"

"Where?"

He winked and grabbed her hand, pulling her off the steps. He pointed to a door in the ceiling she hadn't noticed. Stepping on a small ladder, he opened the hatch. She followed him up and onto the roof. The sky blanketed Lisbon in dark blue. She could see the Tejo. She shivered.

"Cold?" he said. She shook her head. More like exhilarated, she thought. He sat down on the rough rooftop and pulled her next to him. He lit the joint, the flame flaring as it burnt the tip. He took a puff and handed it to her. She inhaled gently. It hit the back of her throat like a sandpaper kiss. She coughed, rolling back onto the roof. He took the spliff back.

"*Tudo bem?*"

She nodded and coughed out a yes. They passed the spliff back and forth. Within minutes, Darla's whole body relaxed. Being high dimmed and gentled the lights inside her and turned up everything else. Lisbon pulsed extra gold that night.

The air was just cool enough to keep them alert. She traced the shape of the city against the sky in her mind, imagining her pen moving along its terra-cotta roofs and wrought-iron balconies. The lit Tivoli dome showed off its curves. They perched above it all. The magic that had been hinting around the corners of Lisbon displayed its full glow now. Together, they rode the city sky as if on a fairy tale magic carpet. She smiled. She had forgotten how good being high felt.

She looked at André. He smiled, warm and mischievous, leaning over to kiss her. Their faces close, his lips touching hers was suddenly too much. A wave of dizziness overcame her. She pulled back. Somehow, André seemed different. Still handsome, still astonishingly young, now she saw something else. It startled her. She glanced away, up to the stars. He made a joke about being "high" up. She laughed, and the spell was broken. It was him again, the person she had only just met but already loved. How was she going to leave him in just two days?

They chatted about nothing much. He pointed out things in the city. She flashed back to that moment when he'd been so close to her ear, pointing something out at sea. Sintra had seemed so long ago.

Somehow, the topic of his parents came up.

"How old are they?"

He hesitated. "My mom is forty-four. My dad, forty-eight."

She constricted. His mom was only a few years older than her? That was a buzzkill. André seemed defensive.

"I've always had older friends. It's not like I am still living with my parents. I have my own life. I'm an adult."

"Sure, you're an adult. Of course you are. But doesn't it seem weird that your mom is almost my age?"

"Only if you think it's weird."

"What does she do?"

"She's a social worker."

Darla didn't know what to think. The good feeling of the hash lingered in her body, relaxing her limbs. But her mind was ricocheting off the rooftops around them, looking for a place that felt as good as her body. Sure, he was mature. Sophisticated. On track with his life and career. But she had some experience with younger men. She enjoyed the fun and playfulness. She didn't have children, and her lifestyle was like that of a younger person: no one else to be responsible for and freedom to travel. But did she need to repeat the part where they weren't able to commit long term? People usually want children, and the men she'd dated had gone on to marry and have kids. She shook her head, looking back at André. This was just a week-long fling, she reminded herself. She leaned in to kiss him. She didn't have to make lifelong plans. Just this week. Just this last time with a younger man. She shivered.

The cold closed in on them, so they descended the ladder. His mezzanine room seemed extra cozy, a small bedside lamp glowing. It was the storybook setting for lovemaking. Darla tried not to think about how this was going to end soon. She tried to be present, to enjoy the flow, the delicious emptiness and fullness sex brought. They'd been having sex all week, hot and intense. But nothing came close to that total surrender she'd felt in the hammock in Odeceixe. Was it the sea air? Being outside? She wanted to have sex with André everywhere. She imagined revisiting Monserrate and getting all her parts lubed up and exposed. All the flowers, the sex organs of plants, waving in the breeze. All the green soft spots where she could imagine them lying, sucking and licking each other. She giggled at the thought of them both in the giant banyan tree. She didn't tell him these fantasies, just let them play in her mind to help coax along her orgasm.

Later, she told André about talking with her mom. He left the bed and got a package from his desk.

"What?!" She hadn't gotten him a gift. Inside was a square tile. Painted in blue, it featured a cherub on it playing a flute.

"Thank you!" She was thrilled to get a Portuguese tile. She hadn't bought one at the museum or in any of the shops she'd visited.

"My dad painted this," André told her.

"Your dad is an artist?"

He nodded. "He paints tiles like this."

"Wow, that's cool." She got quiet. Her dad could be an artist, for all she knew. A twinge of envy gripped her. André had a relationship with his dad. What was that like?

He leaned closer and she hugged him. She breathed in his aftershave mixed with the fresh air and a lingering whiff of hash. She wanted to bottle this moment up and keep it forever.

Chapter Nineteen

Darla found the shop on Rua Dom Pedro V. She wove her way through the cool objects on display. She wanted to stop and touch everything, but she had a date in the tea garden. Out back, she found Julie and her friend, Inês. They stood and cheek kissed each other. Julie introduced Inês, who smiled brightly.

"Great to meet you," she said. "Welcome to Lisbon."

"Thank you! But I'm not staying." Darla took a seat in the low-slung chair. The garden was empty but for them. A platform with a few chairs and small tables scattered on it. The shopgirl came out and offered them the tea of the day—*chá do dia*. Darla didn't catch what it was, but they ordered a pot to share. She was flush with sex and love and open for anything.

"I love your dress," Julie said.

"*Obrigada!* I call this my Anaïs Nin dress."

The black lace dress clung to every curve. She'd gotten it at Lauren's giveaway party that Stephen had hosted. It wasn't something she would buy, but when she saw it on the padded hanger at Lauren's, she succumbed to its elegance.

"I'm going to an erotic literature discussion tonight."

"You're really getting into the spirit of Lisbon," Inês said.

"What do you mean?"

Inês and Julie exchanged glances.

"Well, you're not going to read this in the guidebooks, but Lisbon has a sexy reputation."

"Sexy how?"

"Lots of sex here. During World War II, a lot of people ended up here when they tried to flee the continent. Lots of affairs started and ended here," Inês explained.

"Thinking you could die really ramps up the rutting impulse," Julie said.

They laughed. The shopgirl brought out a silver platter, with an ornate silver teapot and three china cups on saucers. A plate of small, sweet bites accompanied the tea.

"How lovely," Darla exclaimed. She felt like she was in a secret garden being treated like a princess. Maybe she should dress up more often.

Inês poured tea around.

"What are you up to in Lisbon?" Darla asked Inês.

"I'm waiting for big news," she replied. "I applied for graduate school in New York, and I am waiting to hear if I got in."

"Ooo, that's exciting! What are you studying?"

"Behavioral psychology."

"Interesting! When do you find out?"

"Soon, hopefully. I'd move in August."

Darla refrained from complimenting Inês on her English. All the Portuguese people she'd met through Globalkin were fluent in English, and most seemed to have advanced degrees. They chatted, and soon Julie confronted Darla.

"I haven't seen you much at home. Nothing wrong with that," she rushed to assure Darla. "How's it going with your paramour?"

Darla blushed. She sipped her tea, trying to figure out how much to tell.

"Well, I have fallen into the Lisbon lover cliché," she confessed.

Inês leaned in. "Do tell!" She nibbled a cookie.

Darla recounted her first date with André and everything that had happened afterward.

"Ooo la la!"

"I know. This is totally not like me, hooking up with someone like this. But it's been fun. He's so sexy. And sweet." She gushed for a few minutes, then realized she was going on and on.

"But is it just sex?" Julie asked. "It sounds like you really like this guy."

Darla was dreading leaving Lisbon. Leaving André. She hadn't wanted to think that this connection could be more than just a fling. Perhaps it was more, but she didn't want a long-distance relationship. She shook her head.

"I guess it is just sex. But can you be close to someone for a short, intense time and then poof! It's over? Can you have a lot of short, great relationships?"

Inês frowned. "I've never had that experience. I don't want to get attached then suffer the pain of ending it."

"Now you know what I am dreading," Darla said. "I want to go to Paris, but I don't want to leave André."

"That's what I mean," Inês said. "It doesn't seem possible to not get attached."

"Men seem to do it," Julie added. "Why do women get so attached right away? The minute you have sex with someone, you're planning your kids' names with them. It doesn't seem to help us out very much."

Darla smirked. "Someone should invent a vitamin to help women have sex without attachment. Maybe quinoa has some special nutrient that can help us out with this?"

They laughed. Darla felt the warm glow of connection, different from the connection she felt with André. It seemed so easy to make friends here. People in Lisbon had been so kind. The Globalkins who'd given her such good recommendations, Margarida who'd put her up in Sintra, and of course, André. She couldn't help but wonder if he was just in it for the abundant and great sex, or if he too felt a deeper connection with Darla. She didn't make a lot of new friends in Boulder. She'd had her book group and a few close friends like Cat. Now she realized that she could develop friendships easily, but they weren't necessarily meant to last. Would she ever see Julie or Inês again? Or André after she left?

"You've got to check out this new guidebook," Julie told her. "You will love it!"

"What's it called?"

"*Le Cool Lisbon*. You can get it at this shop in Bairro Alto. It's upstairs above the Queen of Hearts."

"What's the Queen of Hearts?"

"Tattoo shop. I hear it's great. Maybe you should get a tattoo. To remember Lisbon."

Darla laughed. "Never. I've never wanted a tattoo."

"Well, anyway, this guidebook is super cool."

"Thank you. But I don't know that I need a Lisbon guidebook."

"Just check it out. I think it will inspire you."

They wrapped up. Julie was going to a work meeting, and Darla had time before her evening plans with André. She said goodbye to Inês, whom she'd warmed to immediately.

After tea, she went to pick up *Le Cool Lisbon* on Rua da Rosa. Julie was right; it was a truly unique guidebook. Compiled by artists, writers, designers, it was colorful and funky, spotlighing Lisbon's cool places. Darla pored through the fat book with its mysterious green cover, feeling cool that she knew of many of the places. Feeling sad she wouldn't get to explore the new ones.

She lingered on the sidewalk, flipping through the pages. A voice nearby startled her.

"We're in there."

She turned. A woman with rings in her nose and eyebrow and lots of tattoos pointed at the book, saying the title. She drew out the oos like a French person would.

"I just got this upstairs," Darla replied.

"And now for a tattoo." The woman smiled, and Darla saw a flicker of mischief cross her face. Here was someone who seemed to be living full ass. "Or a piercing?"

"I've never wanted a tattoo."

"Maybe you've changed. Maybe it's time."

The woman could seem pushy, but for some reason, she didn't. It was true; Darla had changed. She couldn't describe how, but she was different.

"Come in, have a look?"

Darla shook her head. "I have a date. But thanks!"

"Next time!" the woman called after Darla.

Back at Julie's, Darla checked her email. Nothing much. She was leaving soon and needed to check on her Paris plans. A friend date, a class at a cooking school. It was hard to imagine leaving Lisbon. Crazy how she'd known nothing about this city, and now she couldn't bear going. She closed her laptop and soaked in the bright colors of Julie's apartment. How had

Julie done it, managed to set up this great life in Lisbon? A sound at the door announced Julie keying in.

"Hey!" Darla called out from the living room. In just a few days, she and Julie had found an easy roommate rhythm. Even while Darla felt the temporary nature of her visit to Lisbon, she also felt quite at home here.

Julie joined her in the living room, tossing her bag down and plopping on a chair.

"How's it going?" Darla set her laptop aside.

"Oof," Julie exhaled.

"What's up?"

"Work. We're shorthanded, so I've been tasked with something impossible."

"Impossible how?"

"I have to write a report as part of a grant proposal. Report writing is not my forte."

"Can I help? That's my job back in Boulder."

"That's right, I forgot. But I don't know if annual reports are the same as what I need."

"I'm happy to help if you want. I'm not doing anything now."

"Would you? Oh my god, that would be so great."

They moved to the dining table, where Julie set up her laptop. She showed Darla the materials and told her what she needed.

"May I?"

Darla took control of the computer and read the brief. Before long, she was typing away, immersed in the project. Julie sat with her for a few minutes before getting up to make tea. Darla was in a work trance for who knew how long. The tea next to her had grown cold. It was dark outside. Julie was in the other room. Darla easily finished the report. Julie wandered back in when Darla stood to stretch. She sipped the cold tea while Julie read what she had written. Before long, Julie broke into a grin and gave a loud whoop.

"Wow, you're a whiz at this!"

"I don't know about that. But I do this for a living, so yes, it's easy for me."

"Thank you ever so much. How can I repay you?"

"Psh! Are you kidding? You saved me from that awful Angel. You're my good angel."

"Likewise. This is going to make my life so much better."

"I'm glad. I've never worked in such a sexy dress."

Julie winked. "Maybe it's got extra magic."

"It's so comfy!" Darla checked her phone. "Gotta go."

Instead of the cheek kissing, Julie gave her a hug. Darla hugged her back, so glad to have a friend in Lisbon.

Chapter Twenty

She walked through Lisbon like the city was her lover, completely alight, loving everything and everybody. In her Anaïs Nin dress, she felt like she fit in better. She met André at the Kamasutra Bar for the erotica discussion hosted by a Globalkin member. A group of them settled around a low table in the dark bar, sipping fussy drinks. She drank a Bodice Ripper, something frothy with rum that tasted of coconut.

Anita started the conversation, asking what books they found to be erotic. Ricardo brought up Fernando Pessoa, and several people objected, saying he wasn't known for his erotica. Ricardo wagged a finger and read. Darla didn't understand the Portuguese but enjoyed the sound of the language and the way the others leaned in to listen carefully. André whispered to her that it was a homoerotic passage. They discussed how brave it was for him to write about that in his era.

Darla was conscious the whole time of sitting next to André, of being in an erotic relationship with him. Of leaving him for Paris. She wondered what the others thought about them being "together." But were they together? This was a passing thing. She was passing through. Coming back from the restroom, she saw her new friends talking, laughing, comfortable discussing sex. She wanted to hurry back and be part of the fun. She wanted this kind of social life. Back in Boulder, she hadn't imagined anything like this.

Afterward, Darla and André wove their way through the throngs in the streets clustered outside bars, stopping to kiss along the way. She was in an erotic story. She felt they were the pawns of Dionysus and Aphrodite. This notion of being out of control, of being merely an expression of an archetype, appealed to her. In Boulder she would never have wanted to feel like she wasn't fully in control. But here, away from her culture and outside this one, this perspective somehow fit.

Back at Julie's apartment, she made tea. She brought the tray into her room and set it on the desk. André sat at her desk, rolling a spliff. The candlelight illuminated his face, and the rest of the room faded behind him. She caught herself staring. He was so handsome. She hadn't gotten used to it. Every time she saw him, that attraction tugged from deep inside. He smiled at her, holding up the spliff. He had a mischievous look on his face that made her melt.

"*Queres isto?*" She was getting used to understanding the meaning of something without understanding the words. She nodded and went to the open window. She wanted him more than the spliff, but she was incapable of saying no to anything he offered. They smoked standing at the open French window. Leaning out, they could see the moon hovering above. They chatted about sex. The erotic literature discussion and the spliff made it easy to ask and answer.

"Do you like anal sex?" he asked.

She hesitated. If she said yes, did that mean it had to happen later?

"Not sure," she giggled. "But I don't know about with you. You're so big, I can't imagine it fitting."

"We can try," he said. They kissed and smoked some more. "What else?" he asked.

She paused. The year before, while hiking in Colorado, her relationship with Gregory went off the rails. They were walking through fields and back roads and hadn't seen anyone all morning. They stopped for a picnic and afterward, lazy and hot with the sun, feeling alive and vibrant even at forty, Darla tried to seduce Gregory. Right there in the field, under a giant evergreen. But he refused the call. He fended her off. When she tried to masturbate and find some pleasure in the moment anyway, he called her disgusting. She had given him the silent treatment on the way home, hours without speaking.

But André wouldn't leave her hanging for sex. The moon was shining on his face, and he looked just so adorable. All the sex talk and the loose limbs that come from toking up made her need to have him.

"I like to have sex outside," she confessed.

"Like in the hammock?"

"That was hot," she said.

"*Também.*" They kissed some more. They kissed like there was a limited supply of oxygen and they needed to get as much as they could now. They kissed like they had on the bus earlier that week, as if their kissing was both limited and infinite. He pulled away and smiled at her. She was ready for what was next.

"What's that smell?"

He leaned out the window. Darla laughed and pulled him back in.

"You're high!"

"No," he said, "do you smell that?"

"Smell what?" She sniffed the air. She saw the moon, fat and steady, and also, a whiff of butter.

"I know that! Let's go!"

They put their shoes on, and he grabbed Darla's hand and pulled her down the stairs. Around and around they circled in the stairwell, laughing. Outside, they continued the spiral pattern, winding around the block again and again.

"Where are we going?"

He laughed and shushed her, taking one last turn. On the street behind her building a line of people huddled at an open door. Light spilled out onto the sidewalk. It was the only awake spot on the street. They joined the line. She couldn't believe there were so many people out after midnight. He said something in Portuguese. She tilted her head.

"Smells good, smells like Lisbon. *Cheira bem, cheira Lisboa.*"

His smile was big, his love of Lisbon beaming. They stood close, his arm around her. They inched their way to a gate with a window. Rows and rows of baked goods lined up on racks. Inside, they were ensconced in the yeasty, cozy smell of baking bread, sugar, and pastries. It was a dream out of time, the bright lights, the people in line laughing and talking loudly, the hair-netted lady behind the counter tonging pastries. They giggled and couldn't decide. André took charge and ordered two chocolate croissants.

They strolled, stuffing pastries in their mouths. The chocolate croissants were crispy flaky. In that moment, high with André, they were perfect. She couldn't believe she hadn't known about this until she was leaving.

Back in her room, they fell into bed to try new things. Darla was awash in the things she was letting herself have: sex, laughter, surprises, conversation about books, discoveries, and that rare feeling of being in love.

Chapter Twenty-One

André got ready for work the next morning. She watched him, sleepy. How could he work after a night like that? Dressed, he sat on the bed next to her.

"I'll see you after lunch. Just a half day today."

"My last day! I want all of it. All of you."

He leaned down to kiss her. *"Até ja."*

"Até ja," she repeated. She listened to him leave and stretched on the bed. Memories of the night before floated by. Her body, her very being was electrified, eroticized, and alive to life. She really liked him. She liked how he liked her. Here was everything she wanted. It had happened so easily and so soon. She wanted to stay in this joyful, fun place with André forever. Lisbon had enchanted her in the most delicious way. But she had other plans. A couple weeks in Paris to finally experience her dream city. Yet she couldn't help her melancholy heart. Leaving was always going to be hard. She reluctantly packed her toiletries. She wanted to enjoy her last day in Portugal.

She got out the door and across Lisbon in time for the meeting at the Martim Moniz plaza. A young woman named Véronica stood with a medium-sized black dog. A group huddled around them. Darla slipped in.

"This is Hector," Véronica was saying. "He keeps me from going on too long!"

Darla and a group of others laughed. The dog yawned,

bored with his role as icebreaker. Véronica gave an overview of the company and their mission. The tours were a way to include visitors in the ever-changing landscape of street art in Lisbon.

They walked for hours up the back stairs and through the side streets. Véronica wove story after story about the artists who'd made the enormous works of art on billboards, walls, and doorways. The city's history was tucked into the present-day issues about urban planning and art. Darla got fired up hearing Véronica end the tour with a call to people to enact their own creative dreams. On the way to André's, she couldn't help but wonder which of her creative dreams she could bring to life. She hadn't gotten any answers about her life after Lisbon. Maybe Paris would help. After the tour, she and André met near his place.

"What shall we do with this last precious day?"

He grabbed her around the waist and pulled her close.

"Whatever the lady wants."

"Let's get lunch and find some fun places to explore in here." She waved her Lisbon *Le Cool*.

"*Otimo.*"

They had lunch down by the river. Afterward, looking for a café from *Le Cool*, they found an art market in a giant old warehouse.

"Let's go in," André suggested. She couldn't imagine Gregory asking her to go to something like this. Every day, André seemed a better and better match for her. She shook her curls. She had to let go of a future with André. This was it. Today was the day. She was going to enjoy it.

The market was in a large room with a soaring ceiling buzzing with creativity and commerce. The painted terra-cotta walls made for a warm, inviting space despite the scale. Tables lined the perimeter of the room. They strolled through, checking out local artists' cards, knitted items, and pottery. They stopped to visit with a glass jeweler. The colorful beads glistened like candy. She tried on a purple-and-green bracelet. Darla looked at everything while André chatted in Portuguese. At another table, she found the coin purse she had been wanting. Europeans carried more coins than she did in the US, and she needed something small for them. Stitched with purple beads, the tiny purse was exquisite.

On their way out, André went to the bathroom. Darla waited outside, absorbing the Alfama air. A mixture of sea salt and smoky grilled sardines rose up. She tried to remember everything, snapping a photo. When André came out, she took a we-fie of them together. In his beret and striped shirt, his dark hair, and serious expression, he looked French. They spent the rest of the day exploring new places they read about in *Le Cool.*

That night, they sat in a restaurant courtyard that glowed with twinkly lights strung along the walls and in the trees. Gentle jazz drifted from inside. André chose a bottle of wine. They ordered an arugula salad and a giant pizza with mushrooms and onions. It was perfect. They talked about their summer plans. André might go to some climbing festivals, one in Portugal and one in Spain. Darla didn't want to think about going back to Boulder. Her mind couldn't go further than her trip to Paris.

Over cannoli and espresso, André gave her a look she hadn't seen yet.

"What?" she said. He paused. Sipped his coffee.

"I've been waiting and looking for someone like you, Darla." Did he have tears in his eyes? In the evening light, she couldn't tell. "I've been looking for you."

Darla realized she was holding her breath. She couldn't believe he was saying this. It was exactly what she had felt. She had wanted this kind of love forever. Someone fun, engaging, smart, and playful. Someone who was a deep thinker and a deep feeler too. She appreciated his mind, the way he thought, and how he was endlessly interested in everything. She had never felt this kind of reciprocated love.

"Me too," she admitted.

He reached across the empty plates for her hand. She locked onto his eyes and never wanted to look away. How could she have finally found who she wanted to be with—but was leaving?

"I don't want to leave you," she said.

He pulled her close and kissed her. She kissed him back, putting all her feelings about him and Lisbon and leaving into his lips.

She didn't know how long they sat there like that. Finally, they paid the bill and left. Full from dinner and wine, they walked through the streets. The yellow glow of the streetlamps worked its magic, framing their last moments in a golden hug.

At Julie's, they got her suitcase and satchel. She and Julie had said goodbye earlier. Darla picked up her tiny pillow.

"I couldn't fit this in my bag," she said. "I don't want to leave it behind."

"Take it! Take it everywhere," he encouraged.

She gave the apartment one last sweep, making sure she hadn't left anything behind.

"Goodbye, gorgeous apartment," she said. "I loved you so much!"

André watched from the front door, smiling. He'd seen her say goodbye to many places: their room in Odeceixe and the picnic spot in Sintra. She left the keys in the living room along with a card she'd made of a watercolor illustration of Julie's special tea set.

"Thank you, Julie."

She closed the door. André took charge of her suitcase and toted it easily down the stairs. Out on the street, she clutched her tiny pillow, feeling conspicuous. But André refused to let her indulge in this.

"No," he told her. "This means you had a life here. You have lived in this special place. Take it! Take it! *Travesseiro!*"

Darla laughed. She remembered that first pastry they'd shared in Sintra. *Travesseiro.* She had lived in this special place. She would miss Lisbon's grittiness and grandeur. This was why she left the idyll of Boulder. To experience the rub and itch of urban life, to see people who weren't like her, and to dare hope that she could belong everywhere in the world.

They stopped at the late-night bakery and picked up treats for the morning. Walking down Avenida da Liberdade, she knew she would miss the classy avenue with its black-and-white cobbled patterns. Back at his place, she left her suitcase downstairs. They got ready for bed. André flipped onto his side and promptly fell asleep. Darla stared at his muscular back. She couldn't believe he'd conked out. Maybe all their late nights had finally caught up to him. She had hoped for some lovemaking, some sweet conversation, a grand finale. She tried to wake him, but he was gone.

Before dawn, she showered, dressed, and gave his apartment one last look. It was a spacious, cool place, and she had enjoyed being there with him. He came up behind her in the kitchen.

"*Tudo bem?*"

She turned. She hoped he didn't see the tears in her eyes.

"I'm going to miss your apartment."

They laughed.

"I will miss you, too, Darla. This has been a special time."

They kissed, and then they had to go. They took a taxi from the Avenida. Driving out of Lisbon was much faster than driving in. Sunday morning, no traffic, André at her side. At the airport, people surged around them. They couldn't help but walk slowly. She wasn't sure what she was feeling, whether it was exhaustion or sadness. She had to check in without him—an excruciating thirty minutes while he waited beyond the checkpoint.

"I'll be out there waiting for you," he said. When she rejoined him, she relaxed into his arms. How would she stand being away from him? How could it be that this was the end of it? At the airport café, they had coffee with milk and the pastries from last night. He ate a yellow-filled donut thing, and Darla had the chocolate croissant. After that, the nervous jangling in her veins slowed down.

"Darla, you are priceless."

Her eyes grew hot. She hated goodbyes, especially when it was the last goodbye. She wanted to flee. He was still talking, but she hardly heard what he said. She didn't have any speech planned. She was better at writing. She'd send him an email.

He leaned in to kiss her again. Kissing André. They had kissed all over Portugal. On her doorstep, the first time. Waiting for the #15 at Praça de Comércio. Walking in Bairro Alto. In his room at the top of a building, with a window peeking onto the botanical garden. In her room, on the mattress, and at the window. In his kitchen while making curry. Along the sea in Cascais and in the town square in Odeceixe. On the beach and now here in line to go to the gates at the Lisboa airport. They pulled apart, and the spell was broken. He got something out of his backpack.

"Here," he said. "For you."

He handed her a small package, wrapped in green tissue paper. She was caught off guard. Another present! She didn't have anything for him.

"André! What?"

She had admired it at the market. The green-and-purple glass bead bracelet. She slid it onto her wrist.

"I love it! When did you get this?"

He smiled. He seemed happy that she liked it.

"When I went to the *casa de banho*."

"Thank you." Now she couldn't hold back the tears. "That's so sweet."

"That's your flight being announced," he said. They hugged, and she tried to not cling to him.

"Have fun in Paris," he said with a look she couldn't translate.

"I will." She snuggled up against him, not wanting to be anywhere but with him.

Chapter Twenty-Two

Darla took the train into the city, then the metro to Bastille. It took a while to figure it out, but she felt like she was getting the hang of traveling in Europe. It was Sunday, and the city was tucked under a gentle, steady rain. Her heart clicked along with the train sound, mimicking its urgency. The excitement of finally being in Paris had lit in her the minute the plane touched down in France. She checked her phone for anything from André. Nothing.

Her rented apartment near the Bastille was tiny, or "cozy," according to the description. A longing for André crowded in with her. If he were here, they would of course surrender to the bed, and each other, immediately. She brushed the thought aside. It was over. She'd moved on. She was in Paris, for god's sake.

She set up her paints at the tiny desk. She got caught up in the view out her window. The rain pooled in the courtyard, green moss on a pipe, the orderliness of the windows framing a picture of Paris intimacy. She couldn't help herself; she texted André the view from her window. He hearted the photo and sent a note in Portuguese. She translated it and wrote back. *I miss you too.* Oh, she just wanted to curl up in the bed with André next to her. She unpacked a few other things, then bundled into her jacket to greet the city.

The rain had let up. Majestic buildings were reflected in the water on the pavement. She strode along, trying to warm up, energized by the cool air. She had planned for her weeks in Paris. Her list of must-do experiences mostly revolved around food and art supplies. Sennelier was a must, as was the Red Wheelbarrow bookshop. She had a list of pastry shops to explore and insisted on at least one *pain au chocolat* per day. And, of course, she had to eat as many macarons as possible and paint them too. All the colors! She had some dates with Constance, a friend from her New York days. Constance had booked them for a cooking class. Reviewing her to-do list, she wondered if she'd have time for it all.

Darla was eager to try Vélib', the bike-share system. She set up an account and found a bike dock near her apartment. Before long, she was floating down Boulevard Richard-Lenoir. Nothing matched the freedom a bike gave her. She hadn't biked much since she was a girl. Her mom had given her a banana-seat bike, and it had become her ally in finding the freedom she desperately craved.

Now, zooming past the elegant buildings along the boulevard, she tried to let go of obsessing over André. It was just a fling. There would be others. She imagined a shred of her obsession flying off and landing in a gutter along with the losses of others.

She rode for the limit of the bike's rental time, then walked for a bit. At a café, Darla sketched her coffee cup with the café's logo on the rim. A bike dock was outside the café, so she sketched that too. Another bike ride was in order. She pedaled along the wide boulevards and wound her way through the narrow, quiet streets of the Marais. The joy of being a *flâneur*, albeit on a bike, thrilled her.

Darla found herself close to the Pompidou, so she docked her bike. Her body was electrified from the ride. She murmured a silent *thank you* to the bike and entered a line to get into the museum and cultural space. She lost hours wandering the modern art exhibits. Discovering the library, she soaked in the essence of focused study, envying, for a moment, the people and their place in Paris. In the giant bookstore, she chose a journal. She picked out postcards for Cat and her mom.

She sat on the sloping plane outside the Pompidou and texted Cat. He responded right away.

In Paris! Croissant and heart emojis.

Having fun?

Sure . . . I miss André though.

Dude, you have been wanting to go to Paris your whole life.

And now you're there mooning over some Portuguese hottie?

I know. It's embarrassing.

It's love!

Well, it's something. I am probably suffering from sex with-drawal.

That shit's real.

Sad emoji. Baguette emoji.

Hope you're having some fun. Guess what?

What!?

I got my Sprinter!

Squeeee!!!

Van emoji.

Yea, it's all kitted out. I got an incredible deal.

Congratulations! That means . . .

I'm leaving soon.

Sad emoji.

But you'll be there when I get back.

When do you get home?

She texted him the date.

Yep, I'll be here for a few weeks after that.

They texted for a few more minutes, but it just made Darla feel lonely. She'd no longer have Cat in Boulder. What was left for her there? Returning to her job felt impossible. Now she couldn't imagine all the dull hours ahead of her in the office. The freedom she'd had in Lisbon and now Paris, all the time spent making art in her sketchbook, was not going to go back into the box so easily. *She* wouldn't go back into the box so easily. But what were her options?

It would have been easy to walk past the shop on the quai had it not been for the alluring window displays. An abundance of color and shapes, but orderly, giant sets of watercolor paints, stacks of blank notebooks, rows of pens. She let herself be wooed, swaying in a gentle joy before going into the shop.

Sennelier had been serving artists since Monet's time. The wooden floors creaked under Darla's step. Quiet murmurs of people browsing and chatting with staff gave the art supply shop a library feel. The shelves were stocked with bottles of color, racks of crayons to be bought singly, stacks of paper, and sketchbooks to be riffled through. She took her time, glad she was alone.

Despite the abundance of supplies, she didn't see the pens. Markers and brushes and crayons, yes, but no pens. A smocked employee pointed upstairs when she asked for *les stylos*. She climbed the spiral staircase. Upstairs, she found herself in a small room packed with pens. Display cases of pens and a case in the corner held more of the rectangular watercolor pans.

A man with a graying 'fro and kind eyes manned the pen

counter. Darla said, "Bonjour." She wanted a pen for lettering. She opened her sketchbook to show the pen man what she was working with. He oohed and complimented her. Startled, she tried to see her art with his eyes. Maybe it was already good? She only saw the ways she wanted it to be better. She jotted notes about what he said in her sketchbook with one of the new pens. She bought a collection of specially chosen pens and a few watercolors pans. Darla emerged with her new supplies, elated. The way the employee had taken her needs seriously and complimented her work made her feel like a real artist. Darla couldn't keep the smile off her face.

Later, she visited the Red Wheelbarrow. The books on the display table were mostly new to her. This was exciting, and she picked up a few novels to take home. She explored all the shelves. She ended up with a pile of books, some cards, and two blank notebooks. Who knew when she'd be back? This stack was a source for her. A life source. A creative source. Darla tucked everything in her bag.

She made her way back toward the Seine. A crowd of tourists flocked in front of Notre-Dame cathedral, homing in on the heart of Paris, Kilometer Zero. Darla strolled in the garden along the Seine side of the cathedral. At the back, she lingered on a bench in the garden. The shade of the plane trees, the effusion of the garden, and the lack of tourists made this a lovely resting spot. A few moments in a hidden green pocket made it easier to slip back into the buzz and whirl of the city. She let her attention settle on the few people who strolled by, on a couple eating slices of quiche on the next bench, on the gentle breeze that stirred the leaves and nudged them off their branches. Now she was up close with herself, feeling all the contours of her life's shape. She reached for her sketchbook to capture this moment. Before that, she checked her phone. A message from André. It was a picture of his hand coiled in a rope.

Sexy, she texted back.

The rope, his hand, a confidence radiating off the image. They had a long text chat. It wasn't the same as being in Lisbon, but still, she felt connected to him.

She lined up her new pens and books on the green bench. She managed to keep talking while taking a photo. She was about to hit send when André told her his roommate was moving out. He'd taken a job in London.

Oh wow, she texted.

She thought about how big and cool his apartment was. She'd love to live there with him. But how? How would she make a living in Lisbon? She didn't share any of these thoughts with André. She sent him the photo of her Paris stash.

He replied with a string of emojis. Then a picture of him in his cubicle. He didn't seem bothered by his nine-to-five. But he was younger and just starting his career climb. Darla certainly wasn't done working. She had twenty or more years of work ahead. She'd never considered it that way. How could she do it? What would she do if she didn't have her job in Boulder?

I have to find a new roommate, he texted.

I'm sure you will, she replied.

Chapter Twenty-Three

She joined her friend Constance at the cooking school on the quai of the Seine. Constance and her husband had retired and bought an apartment in Paris. Darla had always wanted to visit her, and now here she finally was.

After quickly catching up in the lounge, they donned aprons and met the other students. Darla sketched the setup while the teacher welcomed the class. Darla made the page look like an old-fashioned recipe card, with illustrations of the ingredients. Ten students fluffed flour, made dough, grated cheese, and chatted while they waited for the gougères to bake. The teacher, Suzanne, came over to see her drawings.

"Wow," she said. "Fantastic."

Darla's heart leaped at the praise. Aloud, she demurred.

"It's not painted yet. It's just notes I took during class."

"No, it's lovely. I think the owner would love to see this. Can you send it to us?"

"Sure," Darla said. "I'll send it after I paint it. The class was great!"

Suzanne offered her contact info. They sampled the cheesy gougères with a flute of champagne. The students shared a fun, celebratory vibe. Creating something together felt good to Darla, and she chatted easily with the others. Sipping bubbly before noon felt daring, and the alcohol gave Darla the thrill she'd always loved when doing something naughty. She'd had precious few of these unconventional moments until now. So many of her experiences in Lisbon and Paris were completely new; what else was possible?

Darla drew the finished cheesy puffs alongside the champagne. She and Constance chatted outside after class. Darla was high on life. The feedback from the teacher glowed all over. Her joy was like a freshly baked croissant, all crunchy and golden and to be savored immediately. They walked along the quai.

"You should definitely send that to her," Constance said. "This could lead to other things."

"Like what?"

"There's a trend of people drawing events now," Constance said. "Graphic recording. For businesses and conferences. But why not smaller events like this cooking class?"

"I like that," Darla said. It would give her a chance to be with people but also have a job, something to do. Sketching objects and lettering was fun. Little notes accompanying the food completed a page, turned it into a story, drew people in when she showed them her sketchbook. Later, she emailed Suzanne the image with some notes about other things she could illustrate. She'd never had this feeling with anything work-related—thrilling, daunting, daring. She sent André another photo, the view of Louvre across the river from the upstairs window at Sennelier.

Later that day, she ran out of steam. She'd been walking everywhere. After lounging in the Luxembourg Garden, sketching and people-watching, she decided to try the metro. At the ticket kiosk in the Vavin metro station, a surge of heat overtook her, sweat accumulating everywhere. A rushy flow of foot traffic surged past her. People nimbly swiped cards and whooshed through the turnstiles, disappearing into the white-tiled depths of the metro. But she was stuck there, unable to join the metro ballet. She couldn't figure out how to buy a set of tickets. She didn't have a pass and didn't want one. Usually, she would have done all this research ahead of time. Instead, she'd spent her time with André. She tried to slow down but couldn't calm her urge to get through this quickly.

Suddenly, a boy was next to her. She sized him up to be around thirteen. He was short and pudgy, smiling at her.

"You need help?" he said. "Here." He touched the screen, pushing buttons so quickly Darla couldn't follow. A flush of irritation rose up.

"*Non, merci.*"

But it was done. He'd gotten her to the final screen, and she saw how to make the payment. Clutching her credit card, she finished the purchase.

"Merci," she said, turning to thank him. But he was gone. The station was now empty. A tile mosaic caught her eye. The map of the city in symbols was so cool, she had to grab a photo. She reached for her phone, but it wasn't in her pocket.

"What?! Fuck!" She searched her pockets and bag. No phone. The kid. Where had he gone?

"Fuck, fuck!" She looked for a metro employee. No one was there. No one was anywhere. She used one of her tickets and ran down the steps. The platform was nearly empty, but for the "helpful" boy. He stood at the far end of the platform looking at a phone. A surge of adrenaline pushed her toward him. Her phone case flashed in his hand. She was at his side, shouting.

"Donnes-le!"

He backed away, pushing the phone into his back pocket. He let loose a loud string of French she couldn't understand. Darla got in his face and pushed him to the tiled wall. He scrunched up his shoulders.

She shouted again, *"Donnes-le!"*

He shook his head. Before she could think, her hand was at his throat, pressing him against the wall.

"C'est mon portable!"

His eyes bulged. He shook his head. She pressed harder and got closer to his face. Reaching around, she pulled the phone from his pocket. It was indeed hers. She still had her hand on his throat. She pushed the phone into her pocket. She was huffing now, shot through with adrenaline. She didn't know what to do, so she slapped his face.

"Don't steal people's phones, you little shit!"

She released her hand. His mouth was open, no words rushing out now. She turned and ran down the platform before he could think. Up in the light, she rushed toward the Luxembourg Garden. Adrenaline coursed through her veins, pushing her quickly down the side streets of Montparnasse. Her good feelings about Paris vanished. Now she just wanted to leave.

"I can't believe that just happened. I can't believe that just happened," she muttered to herself.

At the garden, she paused near the apiary. The boy had not followed her. She checked her phone. It seemed okay. Her hands shook as she texted André, describing what had happened. None of it seemed real. She couldn't believe it was her who had done that brave thing. But she had.

A minute after she sent the text, André called.

"You okay?"

Relief coursed through her, tempering the stress she felt.

"Yes! I'm fine. Still shaking. I can't believe that happened."

"People get pickpocketed all the time at Paris."

"No, I can't believe I got my phone back! I didn't even think. I just went after him."

"I'm glad you are okay. That could be dangerous."

She nodded, gazing at his face. Just seeing him calmed her down.

"Thank you. Thanks for being here for me."

"I miss you."

"Miss you too."

They ended the call. Darla snapped a photo of the garden and texted it to him. He sent a smile emoji and a picture of his hand, curled on his lap. She didn't know if it was an accident or meant to be sexy. She sat in the garden for a long time, mindlessly people watching. What was she doing here? She just wanted to be back in Lisbon. To be with André. But in a few days, she would head back to Boulder. To work. To routine. The only thing she looked forward to was seeing Cat. But he'd be leaving soon, off on his own adventure. What was the point? A gloom settled over Darla. Suddenly imagining herself back in Boulder was impossible. It was a picture she couldn't reset. To be so sad in Paris! It was a crime. She tried to shake it off. *Amorino*, she thought. The gelato shop was on her list. Pistachio and coffee would cheer her up, and it was nearby.

Chapter Twenty-Four

Darla found herself taking more pictures. Suddenly everything was interesting to send to André or capture to draw
later. She kept at it, going out every day, all day, soaking up
Paris. There was so much to devour. She didn't think she could
stop. But one rainy morning, on a side street near her place,
she found herself peeking into a large streetside window. The
space inside was cozy and lit in such a way Darla couldn't stop
staring. Inside, a woman sat at a long table piled with things—
pots, brushes, pens, stacks of paper. Darla wanted to be in that
studio with that artist. She wanted to be that artist. The rain
picked up. She headed toward her place, stopping at the patis-
serie for a treat. Back at her apartment, she shed her wet jacket
and boots. In the kitchen, she fired up the tea kettle.

Then it struck her—she could have that cozy studio right
here. With her tea and pistachio "escargot" pastry. And her
own art. The idea lit in her. Darla set up the kitchen table with
her art supplies. She found a podcast with conversation about
design and art and life. She binged it, hours passing while she
painted on blank cards she'd bought. A rainy morning series:
the "escargot" nestled on its turquoise and gold bag. She nibbled at it while drawing. She drew her teacup, the teapot and
kettle, the cute glass yogurt cup. The rain never let up. She
never let up. Until, suddenly, she felt the absence of the rain's
rhythm. No sound.

She stood, stretched, jiggled everything. She lined her paintings up on the table. At a glance, they had the look of tarot cards or seed packets. She swooned a little when she saw them. This surprised her. While she'd been enjoying her art for months, this was the first time she'd let herself appreciate her work. A new recognition filled her. She snapped a photo.

It was early evening now. Outside, she shook with the chill. She walked and walked, pumped up by all the time she'd spent focused, drawing, painting, hearing artists talk about their lives and what they were creating. It was the most fun she'd ever had. She had felt guilty, or something, that she wasn't out enjoying Paris. Doing something, seeing something. But she'd been doing the thing she'd wanted to do. She felt both rested and energized by the time she'd spent in her "studio." When she got back and saw the paintings from the doorway, they seemed like a coherent *Rainy Paris Day* set. She took a photo and texted André the shot of her Paris art studio, a table full and scattered with watercolor supplies.

One night, over a bottle of red wine at Les Philosophes with Constance, Darla moaned about having to go home.

"Maybe I shouldn't have taken so much time away. Four weeks! Now I don't want to go back to Boulder."

"So don't! Go somewhere else."

"I have to get back to work. I've used up all my vacation time." A desperate, pushy feeling rose up inside Darla. She tried to fend it off by talking more. "It will be another year before I can take off again, and only for two weeks. You're lucky."

"Well, I'm old and retired. That's different than being lucky."

Darla fiddled with her wine, her fingers twisting the stem of the glass. What would her life be like in twenty years? She couldn't even imagine the next month back in Boulder.

"I actually *am* lucky," she confessed. She told Constance about Lauren's bequest.

"I'm sorry your friend died."

Darla nodded. She still missed Lauren. It had been easier while she was away. But knowing Lauren wouldn't be there when she got back made Boulder seem ever bleaker.

"But to get that inheritance—that's super cool!"

"I know. It was supposed to be Thrill Money. I still have most of it. Lisbon was so cheap."

Their dinner arrived—French onion soup for Darla and steak frites for Constance. They dove in, Darla nipping some of the fries while they were hot. Constance asked about Lisbon.

"Only if you want to talk about it," she said. "I know it can be hard."

Darla shrugged. "It's okay. I don't want to talk about it all night. It was just a fling. But we are still in touch."

"Oo la la! Maybe it's not over?"

Darla laughed. "No, it's over. I don't think either of us is interested in a long-distance thing."

Constance poured more wine for them.

"Did you like Lisbon?"

Darla struggled to get a decent bite of soup. The cheese refused to yield, spooling around and around her spoon.

"Lisbon was great! I loved it. Now that I have Paris to compare it to . . . I think I prefer Lisbon."

She told Constance about her favorite walks, about the miradors, and about how she'd soaked up so much more of it because of André and the other people she'd met there. It had never been so easy to connect with people. She could tell Constance was happy for her. They chatted about Paris and were eating *île flottante* when Constance asked about Darla's art.

"The sketches you did at the cooking class were phenomenal."

Darla brightened.

"Yes, the art! I can't believe how great it's been for me. I never would have thought I'd come this far. I guess being on vacation has given me more time for it."

"Seems like more than just a hobby," Constance said. "It really expresses a part of you I am happy to see. It's magical how your drawings seem to illuminate the real you."

Darla couldn't stop the unwelcome tears. Constance was right—making her art restored something she hadn't known was missing.

"Thanks. Thanks, Constance. That means a lot."

"You could do something with some of those pieces. I see a whole Darla design line." She moved her hand in the air in front of them like underlining words on a marquee. Darla perked up.

"Wow, I hadn't thought of it that way. But I do have ideas for different series of cards. I love cards! I could see making greeting cards and recipe cards."

She pulled out her sketchbook and shared some of her ideas for illustrations. She'd already done some of the Journey Blessings. She could practice her language and lettering skills by using words in French or Portuguese. She'd almost finished a series of *Lisbon Treats* and had begun a *Paris Treats* series. Constance mirrored her excitement.

"These could also be calendars and stand-alone prints."

Darla jotted notes to capture Constance's encouragement and ideas.

"You might have a career here."

For the first time, Darla let that idea land in the giant field of possibilities. Could she make a living as an artist? The time away from work had greatly diminished her interest in her old job. Maybe it was time to think of what she could do next. She didn't have to be like her mom, working her whole life at one job, saving all the good stuff for retirement.

Darla basked in the connection with Constance. It felt good to be with someone who knew her. She wanted people to feel happy for her. Later that night, she and André FaceTimed. She showed him the illustrations from the cooking class. He gave her two thumbs up.

"Really good, Darla!"

"*Obrigada.*" She smiled and listened while André caught her up on what was happening at the climbing gym. He'd been spending more time there since Darla left. The brightness in his eyes told her how much climbing meant to him. But she couldn't chase away the question that had been itching at the edge of her mind this whole time.

"What are we doing here, André?"

He tilted his head.

"What do you mean?"

"I mean . . . I love talking with you. It's been great to be connected with you while I'm here in Paris. But what's going to happen next? I'm going home, and I won't be anywhere near your time zone."

He nodded, pushing his glasses up his nose. "Do you not want to talk?"

"No, I do. I do. But are we just prolonging the inevitable? The end?"

"I don't see harm in talking. I miss you."

"I miss you too."

She dropped it, glad to soak in the beauty of his face and

the reassuring quality of his voice. They talked about nothing much, sharing silly moments from their days. She wanted so badly to crawl through the phone and kiss his face. He was so close and so far away. Trying to prepare herself for the inevitable end wasn't working.

Chapter Twenty-Five

The night before she left, she bent over her sink, splashing water on her face. Naked, she felt André's absence, a thousand tiny prickles on her bare skin. How being naked with him had been so primal and joyful. She hadn't known how lonely she was until she wasn't. But patting her face with a towel, she experienced her loneliness in a new light. The familiarity of her emptiness comforted her. Instead of the usual prickly, painful feeling, the loneliness settled into place. Just accept the familiar. Go back to Boulder. She slept badly, wrestling with the duvet, flinging it off when she got hot, tucking it around her when the air chilled her. Why didn't European beds have a top sheet?

Darla got to the airport hours before her flight. She didn't want to be this early. She didn't want to be here at all. She wanted to be in Lisbon, with André. When they'd spoken the night before, she felt all the things together: connection, fun, joy, and a need for more time with him.

She resented the long lines at check-in and security. Dragging her carry-on and schlepping her daypack, she trudged through the airport, getting hot. Her purple jacket really needed a wash. Once through security, she found a café for a macchiato and a pain au chocolat. In her sketchbook, she outlined the moment, adding words to describe how she felt. Her life in Boulder still felt like an enigma. She'd met more people since she left home than she'd met in all her years in

Colorado. Life was just more interesting—exactly what Lauren had wanted for her. Thinking about Boulder weighed her down. Filling in more spreadsheets at work. Her boring apartment. Maybe she could paint it brightly like Julie's place. The idea of showing Cara her sketchbooks was the only thing that roused her. She'd filled three of them, plus made a few postcards.

She sighed. If only she had more time. She snort laughed. When planning this, she'd been afraid a month was too long. She should have taken the whole summer. She'd have to plan another trip for next year. But even that didn't cheer her up. Where would André be in a year? Probably not in Portugal. And what was this, anyway? An adult "gap month"? Casual sex? She laughed again. Never had she thought of herself as someone who easily had sex with strangers. Could she travel, form connections, and have fun flings? Maybe that would make life in Boulder bearable.

She checked her phone. It was almost noon in Lisbon. She still had thirty minutes before she had to be at her gate. She messaged André.

I miss you!

Também. Heart breaking emoji.

Wanna video call?

Sim.

Let me find a quiet spot.

She found a chair in a quietish corner where she could park her stuff and talk privately with André. She initiated the call.

His face filled her tiny screen. His grin lit her heart. She smiled back, and for a minute, they just grinned at each other.

"I had the best airport pain au chocolat," she reported.

"Only in Paris!"

"*Oui oui*. Despite the great pastries here, I am not sad to leave Paris. Not like I was leaving Lisbon."

"Paris wasn't what you thought it was to be."

"No, but neither was Lisbon!"

"You have to go to find out."

"Right?! All the ideas we have in our mind about how things will be can be so wrong."

He glanced around, and she saw that he was still in his cubicle at work.

"Do you have to go?

"No, no. I am at lunch now."

"Do you have to go eat?"

"I can eat something later. This is our last chance to be on the same continent."

She grimaced. Her stomach flipped around the coffee and pastry. There would be food on the plane. The thought of a transatlantic flight made her stomach even more twisted.

"I don't want to go."

"I know," he said. "I don't want that either."

There was a long pause. They gazed at each other. Boarding announcements wouldn't let Darla forget where she was. Clusters of people rushed past, toting duty-free bags full of airport gifts: boxes of macarons, alcohol, scarves, and perfume. Darla's Paris souvenirs filled the pages of her sketchbook. She had a few things from Lisbon for her mom, like *flor da sal* in a cute ceramic container.

"Getting on a plane feels so wrong now."

"It's a long flight."

"Not just that . . . flying away from you."

"Do you think you'll be able to come back soon?"

She shrugged. "I just used all my vacation time."

"If only you didn't have that stupid job!"

She'd told him how bored she was at work and how much she didn't connect with her clients or her boss. She had one friend with whom she complained about the tight deadlines and unrealistic client expectations. Her brain couldn't calculate going back to making boring statistics into engaging stories that would inspire shareholders. She teared up just thinking about how different life in Lisbon had been.

She shook it off. It wasn't real life. It had been just a vacation. Just a fling. Be practical. Right when she heard that voice, she also felt a sense of Lauren. She still had more than $20K of the inheritance money. She could use some of it for art classes, maybe a retreat somewhere cool. The boarding announcement for her flight broke through. She was in Group 7, so she didn't have to rush. She took a deep breath and spoke what she'd been thinking since she arrived in Paris.

"I would love to never go back there again."

André laughed. "I was thinking the same thing. Well, don't!"

"Don't what?"

"Don't go back. Stay here."

"In Paris?"

"No, Lisboa. Come back to Lisboa. I need a roommate."

She reeled back. "A roommate?"

"No, no, I didn't mean that. I can find a roommate anywhere. It's you I want."

She placed her fingers on her neck. Her pulse raced and jumped. Was she having a heart attack?

"I want you, too, André, but I have to go back." She squirmed, her heart continuing its gallop.

"Why?"

Asked so bluntly, she was hard-pressed to find a real answer. Her job—she had reached the limit of what she wanted to do there and now recognized that she was bored shitless. Her apartment—it was fine, but she didn't love it. Cat, she'd miss Cat, but he was going on the road in his Sprinter van soon enough. A jolt pulsed through her. Was her life really that disposable?

"Fuck, I can't think of any reason to go back. I mean, I have this plane ticket . . . and we're about to board."

He gave her that naughty smile that made her pulse race even more. She couldn't sit any longer, jumping up, jiggling her video on the small screen. His smile broke into a laugh—a laugh that thrilled her.

"Oh my god, what if I did come back to Lisbon?"

"I would love that," he said.

"Me too." Her grin got bigger and felt permanent. Like she would always be this giddy with possibility.

"But how . . . how would I stay?"

"Don't worry about that now. We can figure it out. Together."

"But what—"

"You're at an airport. There's going to be a flight to Lisboa soon. Hold on."

His face angled away from the phone while he typed. She stared at his jaw, his head, his hair longer and curlier than when they'd met four weeks ago. He was so damn sexy. God, she loved him. At their last dinner, he said he'd been looking for her for a long time. What if André was a bigger part of her future than she'd thought? What if despite their age difference and different cultures, *they* were another perfect couple?

"There is a TAP flight direct to Lisboa leaving in two hours. There is ticket available."

"OMG, OMG!"

He laughed.

"Don't let me pressure you. Do you want to come back?"

"Oh, I so want to come back. I want to come and stay, and there's so much more I want to do with you."

"Camping!"

"I was thinking of more hot sex."

"Of course, that is what I meant." They laughed.

"Okay, okay, I have to get a ticket."

"I emailed you the link."

She propped the phone on her suitcase, leaning it against the open handle. She fired up her laptop and found the link from him. Within minutes, she had bought a one-way ticket to Lisbon.

"Done! I'll be there for dinner." Her whole body fizzed, waves of disbelief crashing around her. What was happening? Was she really doing this? She wanted to dance, to dance with André, to dance with the world.

"I'll cook for us. In our home."

Her heart leapt.

Her phone pinged. It was a link from André.

"A song for the flight here. I'll see you at the airport."

An explosion of emotion overcame her. She was crying and laughing. Passersby glanced at her and hurried on. She tried to steer herself more toward laughter. She didn't know why she was crying. She put away her laptop and gathered her phone.

"Okay, I have to switch gears here. Au revoir, Boulder; hello, Lisbon!"

He said something in Portuguese, a huge grin on his face. She hadn't seen him look so happy. A recognition flooded through her, warming, relaxing. Finally, someone was mirroring how she felt inside. They reluctantly signed off.

At the gate, she pushed her boarding pass across the counter.

"I won't be getting on this flight."

The employee looked startled.

"I'm moving to Lisbon instead! I'm not going home. Lisbon is my new home."

"Okay . . ." he said. Of course he didn't need to know that. But announcing it aloud to someone made it real.

"Where is Terminal 3?"

He pointed, and she took off, rushing past travelers going too slow, going home, going back to their jobs and lives. She ran, dodging travelers, her suitcase bumping and tilting behind her. She ran down a narrow hallway and then down a longer hallway and outside and through yet another long hallway. She didn't stop running, even when she didn't have to. She didn't know why, and she didn't care. It felt good, to be running like this, straight toward her new life.

She was oddly light, free, doing something she was sure Lauren would definitely call full ass. Her gate was crowded with a group of gray-haired travelers wearing bright, sporty jackets and backpacks. They chattered loudly and self-assuredly. They were living full ass, going somewhere with friends, doing something active.

Darla situated her stuff in the overhead bin and took her seat. She put her earphones on and cued up the song he'd sent, "To Build a Home."

Chapter Twenty-Six

At the Lisbon airport, there was André, his glasses, his smile, his arms open to her.

"Olá!"

"André! I can't believe I'm back." They kissed, her chin instantly rubbed raw. Holding him close, Darla relaxed, finally.

Back home, Darla parked her luggage upstairs. Looking at the apartment in the bright daylight, she sighed. She'd made it. "To Build a Home" played in her mind, a haunting, melancholic, and beautiful song. André called out from downstairs, suggesting the beach.

"*Sim! Por favor!*"

She zipped open her suitcase. She found her beach stuff, including her fouta. She searched for her purple jacket, but it wasn't there. Huh, she thought. Then it came to her: she had stuffed the jacket in the overhead bin along with her carry-on. A rush of emotion pushed her back onto the bean bag.

"No!" Anger followed a gush of angst. She needed Lauren's purple jacket. She felt like she had some of Lauren's magic around her when she wore it. Now it was gone.

André rushed upstairs. "What is?"

She couldn't speak. She couldn't stop crying. Finally, she caught her breath and told him. He grimaced dismissively.

She put her hands over her face. She hated him seeing her this way. At the edge of her mind was the accusation that she had been careless to leave the jacket on the plane. André cleared his throat, but no words came out.

"Beach?" he finally offered with a hopeful smile.

She shrugged. She didn't really want to go anywhere, but it was not yet noon. They got ready for the day trip. Sunscreen, swimsuit, towel. André told her they'd buy picnic food when they got there. She freshened up. In the living room, André pulled her close for a kiss. There was the connection she'd been craving in Paris. His lips against hers, he said, "*Vamos!*"

They left the apartment, bouncing single file down the four floors of winding stairs, their footsteps tapping a rhythm of vitality that filled the narrow stairwell. Emerging onto Rua São José, they caught the metro on the Avenida. A short ride, then onto a giant bus. Without André, Darla would never have known this route. The bus rolled out of the city and into a green landscape. She pushed away the loneliness she'd felt when he hadn't understood why she was so upset about the lost jacket. It felt real and right to be sharing a home with André. They snuggled in the seat together. The bus rocked around the curves in the road. She liked being pressed up against him. The weeks without this physical touch had seemed unbearable at times. They made a plan to go to IKEA later that week.

"What should we call our home?"

"It needs a name?"

"Why not?"

"I want to host all kinds of dinners and fun gatherings," she said. "Think of all the people we'll have over. The Globalkins."

"It's like an embassy," he said.

"Yes! A Love Embassy!"

"That's it—we call it the Love Embassy."

They sealed it with a kiss. She took a photo of him, then

one of them together. Collecting evidence for what she could hardly believe was happening. She didn't *try* to go for younger men. Maybe the young men were attracted to her beauty, to her eyes, or to her wavy hair. She suspected they mistakenly thought she was a woman who wouldn't need them much, who had her act together so much that they would be relieved of the emotional tending relationships required. She snapped back to the present, soaking up his gentleness and his appreciation of beautiful things, including her.

It was early afternoon when they alighted in Sesimbra. The beach town clung to the edge of the continent. The sun pounded the whitewashed, low-slung buildings around them. She'd have to get a hat. Her skin didn't tan; first, it burned. They headed toward the beach, strolling through town. She didn't need to know where she was going. She liked being in control and knowing things. But now, with André, she surrendered knowing anything. She was surprised that she relished turning the reins over to someone else.

Sesimbra reminded her of Odeceixe, a small village near the sea. They found their way to an open market. They wandered past stalls offering the usual Portuguese garden fare: mountainous heaps of greens, piles of tomatoes, onions, and carrots. She was ravenous and wanted everything. André selected a few tomatoes, a hunk of pungent cheese, and a small loaf of bread. He tucked the goods in his backpack. She paused at a hat stall and tried a few on. She bought a cute orange one she thought would go with her swimsuit.

They passed through town and emerged onto the boardwalk. A group of old men perched on the wall facing the sea, chatting and smoking. Their caps shaded their faces. Darla wondered if they were retired fishermen. She snapped a photo of them lined up like birds on a wire.

On the far end of the beach, near some large rocks, they set up their spot. Darla inhaled the fresh air and soaked up the bright light. She stripped off her shirt. Underneath was her Target bathing suit, a cute maroon skirt, and the top that draped over her belly. André stood up from laying his towel down and caught sight of her. He had stripped off his T-shirt and shorts and was wearing his tight black underwear. Darla caught her breath; he was so fit and hot. His smile faded.

"What?" She pulled down the skirt of her cute new suit. André looked uncomfortable. He glanced around.

"Nada, nada, nothing. Let's have fun."

She fiddled with the straps of her suit. She took in the other people dotting the beach. Immediately, she noticed the range of bodies. Small bodies, skinny bodies, fat bodies . . . everyone was there. Everyone let it all hang out. No one else had her same cute, skirted suit with the top that draped the belly. But Darla liked her two-piece. It covered what she considered her bad parts. But everyone else was letting all their parts—good and bad—hang out all over. Everyone seemed completely comfortable just as they were.

They arranged their stuff and tucked into the picnic food. The tastes of Portugal were different than what she had eaten in Paris. She couldn't describe it, but the cheese was different and the bread had a texture unlike French breads. With food in her tummy, she felt her whole body relax. After lunch, André rustled in his backpack and pulled out a spliff. He held it up with a smile. Darla hesitated. She hadn't smoked since she'd left Lisbon. Was this an everyday habit with him? She wanted to be healthy. Smoking and drinking didn't fit the picture she'd had of a healthy Darla. But the sunlight glinted on the sea, André was smiling, and it was her first day of her new life in Lisbon.

They passed the joint. The tension over the bathing suit melted away. Her critical thoughts drifted off. The sting of losing her jacket dimmed. She stretched, feeling her body finally arrive in Portugal. She was about to get her sketchbook out when André stood.

"Let's go in," he said, holding out his hand.

"Is it okay to leave our stuff?"

He nodded. They dashed into the water. Bobbing around together on the waves, they hugged and kissed. A wave of joy overtook her. She was so glad she had left Paris. There was no beach there. No André. Boulder, her life there, her job, seemed like another planet. She could hardly recall the faces of her people there.

She lay back and floated up and over the waves, cresting and ebbing toward shore. This floating feeling anchored her to herself. She was transported back to the Michigan lake where she'd pass the summer waterskiing, swimming, and loafing on the raft with Cat and their friends. She could float on an inner tube for hours, but for the giant horseflies. Nights they'd build a fire down by the water, drink beer, and tell stupid jokes and silly stories. Cat's parents seemed to have room for everyone and believed that their kids' friends, for the weekend, were their kids too.

It was so different from her apartment with just her and her mom. The raucousness of it. And she always felt a bit of relief when she got back to their quiet home with no one but her most of the time. She bobbed in the memories, the water cradling her, the sum warming her.

André broke in, swimming close and calling her name.

She came to, his face merging into focus. He looked super hot, all wet, drops of water beading on his face, his head sleek. Walking out of the sea, following his tight, tan, muscular body, Darla couldn't believe that she was with this beautiful man. This gorgeous younger man.

Back on their towels, they shared the picnic, then dozed briefly. When she woke up, André was still asleep. She pulled her hat back on and got out her sketchbook. She drew the shore of the other side of the small inlet. Watching the families and children playing, she moved her pen across the page without looking down. She liked the gestural drawings of the figures on the beach. She added color with her portable watercolor kit. The splash of colors she used. She liked this moment she depicted, despite André's reaction to her swimsuit.

Leaving the beach at the end of the day, she took a picture. The moon rose over the rocks on the beach. Moon, water, beach, this was the stuff of her dreams. She looked back to their spot, the sand all pressed down in the shape they'd made.

"Thank you, spot," she said.

They stopped at one of the clubs along the shore where they ordered tiny beers. A small beer cost only a euro, which they accompanied with the Portuguese bar snack, *tremoços*. He told her he loved hanging out at these old men's clubs. She respected how well he spoke English. Hearing him say almost any word warmed her deep inside. His great body, his gorgeous hazel eyes with long lashes, his confidence, his charm. Every testimonial on his Globalkin page talked about how easy he was to talk to, how he could talk about any subject. Sipping beer, slipping the skins off the beans and munching their bland, pithy skin, Darla could almost convince herself she belonged in this scene.

Chapter Twenty-Seven

"Bom dia," **he said,** snuggling in. She relaxed, parting her lips for a kiss. The low, slanted ceiling cradled the bed. Light filtered in through the tiny window. She had no idea what time it was—she'd have to get a bedside clock. The cheesy poster phrase popped into her mind: today is the first day of the rest of your life. It felt like a totally new life. Exactly what she had left Boulder to find. Darla had woken in the night confused about where she was. André had slept away next to her, as if sleeping alongside a new partner was perfectly natural.

Now, he kissed her and held her close. Some fondling ensued, but André needed to get to work. Down in the kitchen, he passed her a yogurt. She prepared coffee in his stovetop espresso machine. Spooning in the yogurt—coconut, a new flavor for her—she scanned the apartment.

"We need a dining table," she said, leaning against the counter.

"Big enough for friends. We will get that in IKEA."

"I've never been there," she said. She considered herself more of a quality furniture person. She perceived IKEA to be cheap with a factory feel. But she was willing to check it out with André.

"You'll love it. We can get table and chairs there. And things for your studio."

They'd discussed turning the mezzanine into her studio and his office.

"I don't need much. Just good light." But she thought about a way to hang the cards she'd started making in Paris. Maybe a corkboard? Their list was getting long; she'd need to write it all down. She liked making lists and always had. André had got out cups for the coffee. She'd force it down black today but had to get some milk right away.

"You need space for your art," André said. "I love what you have shown me."

"Thanks, me too."

She handed him the coffee. André was already dressed for work. How clean and tidy he looked in his dress pants and shirt, open at the neck, no tie. He was peeking at his phone. He didn't realize how important that was to her—that he cared about her art. She was ready to return to the kind of focus and productivity she thrived on. She had no idea what that would look like with her art. But now that she was taking it more seriously, she sensed she needed structure. But Portuguese-style. Not too much work. Time for the beach and playing with André.

"Okay." He downed the espresso. "I go." He grabbed her for a long kiss. She relished the blend of two favorite things: the taste of coffee and the feel of André's lips.

After he left, Darla soaked in the quiet. High up at the top of the building, the noise from the street was barely perceptible. She washed up the coffee cups, looking out the window. Their kitchen overlooked the roofs of the neighboring buildings. André called it a village. Was that a lemon tree? She'd dreamed of having a lemon tree in her yard. But this tree wasn't theirs, and it was just out of reach.

She had to call her mom, and Cat, and also deal with work. Was she just going to quit? Right now, here in her new Lisbon home, she felt bold and free. The idea of her job and being tethered to Terry's demands and schedule was just a big fat *no*. But easier said than done. While she was resolved—she had made the leap to living here—she wasn't quite ready to let the world know. Later. Luckily, the time difference worked in her favor. It would be hours before anyone would be awake at home.

She took stock of André's supplies. A range of bottles ruled a shelf high above the stove. Some olive oils, some vinegar, tall jars of spaghetti, and a few things she didn't recognize. She pulled open drawers and cupboards. He had a set of dull knives. Maybe they could buy a nice knife together. She pulled out a heavy pan. It looked like a stovetop grill. This could be good for vegetables, she thought. All the things they could cook together rushed into her mind. Roasted vegetable galettes, grilled cheese, quesadillas, if she could find or make tortillas.

The fridge was bare though. A couple bags of produce— tomatoes and onions. Who kept tomatoes and onions in the refrigerator? A battalion of yogurt cups lined up. She didn't usually eat much yogurt, but the coconut yogurt had been yummy. She'd go shopping today.

She explored their future bedroom. It was huge and empty except for a bed against the wall. Two French doors opened onto pocket balconies. She stepped out and leaned against the railing. From there she could see all the action along Rua São José. Ahead was the Avenida, sheltered by big trees. The Louis Vuitton store ruled the corner; she doubted she'd shop there. Opposite Louis was a domed building. Sunlight struck the dome in a way that made her want to get her paints. Back in the room, she tried to imagine what they would change. There was no closet, just the open space with incredibly high ceilings. A nook by the bed held a few shelves. She could use that for her cards and jewelry.

Up in the mezzanine, she surveyed her suitcase. Everything seemed to explode out of it. The new pants she'd bought in Paris, a funky green, ruffled at the cuffs, with strings to pull that raised or lowered the pants. The bag of cards and books from the bookshop. She looked around. There wasn't anywhere to hang her stuff. No closets up here either. Darla imagined herself sitting here in the mornings, painting the view. An idea came to her—she could paint a series of postcards of her life in Lisbon. Perhaps someday she could sell them. She felt full and energized with this idea. And by the time she had written it all down, the logistics of how she would print and sell them, how would that be profitable . . . all the logic flooded in to overtake the joy. She shook her head. She didn't need to figure any of that out now. Just make the paintings. She made a few notes.

Darla breathed in deeply, the breeze ruffling her hair, a feeling of freshness in the morning air. Here she was, in her new life. The day felt open and full of possibility. She closed her eyes to savor the feeling. This was what she had left her comfortable home for—a sense that life was open and exciting.

She did laundry. It took forever to figure out the washing machine. Darla didn't consider herself stupid, but the machine somehow got the better of her. Finally, she pushed the correct sequence of buttons, and the washer churned to life. The timer said 3:50. Could that be accurate? A four-hour wash cycle? No matter. She wasn't waiting for the clothes to start her day.

She unpacked her art supplies, arranging her sketchbooks, watercolors, and pens. A shelf for the *Le Cool* guidebook along with her new books. She put her toiletries on the few empty shelves in the bathroom. The washer whirred away, accelerating its spin with a noise that sounded like an airplane taking off. Setting herself up in her new home felt great. Having only a few things was new and welcome.

But soon she was hungry. Yogurt and coffee wouldn't cut it for a real breakfast. She decided to go out for lunch. She was upstairs getting ready when her phone pinged. It was André. She let him know she was headed out to get groceries and lunch. He dropped a pin to show her where to shop and included a nearby lunch spot.

Tonight we set up our new bedroom.

Yes!

She added sexy emojis. He replied with a few of his own.

We can clean everything and make it ready for us.

Spring cleaning!

Darla wasn't into cleaning, but the idea of doing it with André, of making the place theirs, felt good. Really building a beautiful home. She felt full and happy with the idea of it. Finally, home with someone else. Gregory had been evasive about not wanting to live together. It had frustrated her. And then when he had presented the key, she had realized she couldn't trust him. She hadn't believed he really wanted what she wanted. She had been so sure they'd get married, but he hadn't wanted to live together or marry. They'd seemed like the perfect couple, but if he hadn't wanted to step further into the relationship, that wasn't true. Darla always had the sense that there was something missing in her. That while he liked her in his own way, Gregory never wanted to be with her fully. Even after three years. Perhaps this was why they'd been together so long—neither wanted to hurt the other's feelings.

We can have lunch at home some days. I sometimes go with my colleagues but also take lunch at home.

Darla already felt comfortable in their apartment, its spaciousness, the bright bigness of the bedroom. As a girl, she regularly rearranged her room. She had fun putting things in order, and she enjoyed the feel of a freshly reorganized space. It would be fun to do this with André. She took her time getting ready to leave. A parade of diversions tried to convince her that lingering was of utmost priority. How many ways were there to avoid the world? She saw them as a storyboard illustrated simply.

Change your outfit.

Check your makeup.

Write one last email.

Lean out the window to double-check the temperature.

Grab something out of the freezer to thaw.

Forget your wallet and go back. Forget your sketchbook and go back up. Forget your map and circle all the way back to the top.

This list made her laugh. At the kitchen table, she sketched them quickly. It was time to leave her tower and join the party on the street. By the time she got out the door, down the stairs, and onto the street, she'd exhausted her interest in her delay tactics. A cluster of people kibitzed on the sidewalk by the café. The minute she was out, the city energized her. How could she ever have delayed this joy, this urban vibrancy waiting for her?

She walked on the street parallel to Avenida da Liberdade. A blind man tapped his way along Rua São José. He carried a cascading sheet of lottery tickets and yelled their price. Rua São José was lined with practical places like the hardware store and the shop that only sold lightbulbs. She passed an abandoned lot deteriorating behind a crumbling brick wall. A pack of feral cats lived there, eating from the takeout trash people threw out. The skinny cats lurked on the sidewalk, dodging between parked cars when she approached. Darla stopped to watch a kitten claw her way laterally up the brick wall.

She stopped at a pasteleria for a quick lunch. At the grocery store, she stocked up. It took a long time, but she didn't mind. It felt good to be buying groceries, to have a kitchen to cook in. She had to study every package, deciphering the Portuguese, making sure she was buying sugar-free almond milk. All the new things felt like a fun challenge. At another market flush with fresh produce, she marveled at the choices—heaps of fresh greens, mounds of tomatoes and potatoes. She bought the most gorgeous green figs.

She got as much as she could carry in her string bag. Navigating the uneven sidewalks in her neighborhood, carrying more groceries than she could really manage, was an urban survival test. She did it, though, arriving hot and sweaty at her front door. Keying in, she felt proud that she lived here. Huffing up all four flights made her rethink her shopping ways. No loading up a lot at once like in the US. She put everything away and went upstairs to imagine her studio. She could put a desk against the wall, and the light from the mansard window would give her enough light to work on her painting. They'd keep the beanbag chair.

She texted Cat even though it was too early for it in Boulder. She had to let him know. She prepared a coffee and set a few figs on a small plate. It took a few minutes, but he responded.

OMG you wild thing!

Stack of emojis showing all the feels.

I'm going to quit my job.

She sat at the couch with her coffee, phone, and figs. Opening her sketchbook, she eyed the figs.

About time!

I hope I am not completely screwing up my life.

Her pen swooped, replaying the curve of the figs on the page.

How could you screw up your life? You're in love! You're in Lisbon!

Feels so much better than Paris. Shocking.

What are you going to do with your apartment?

I have to sublet my apartment.

She finished a clump of fig shapes and added in her coffee cup.

I might want to move in. I gave notice on my place when I bought the Sprinter van, but it needs some work before I'll be able to go anywhere in it.

Darla put Cat in her apartment as a thought experiment. She could see it. That could work.

Yes! Why not! That could be great. I'd love you to stay there.

They discussed details, and Cat said he'd think about it. She hoped it worked out. So far it had been all too easy to erase herself even further from her Boulder life. But she shrugged it off. She was where she was meant to be now, here in Lisbon with André.

In her work portal, she filled out some paperwork and sent them to Mel in HR. That was the easy part. She still couldn't face the tough call, and luckily it was too early in Boulder to reach anyone anyway. It was finally a decent time in Michigan to reach out. Her mom would be pinging her to ask how it went. She wanted to get ahead of that with the news she'd decided to stay in Lisbon.

She scanned the apartment for a background that would not give away that she was in Lisbon. It would be best if she broke the news slowly. But the rough stone walls, the half-timber beams, upstairs the low ceilings and mansard window . . . Nothing here looked anything like her home in Boulder. She settled onto a cushion in the big bedroom, the white wall behind her giving nothing away. After a lot of ringing, her mom picked up.

"You made it home!"

Darla's throat clenched. She had made it home, after all these years.

"How's it going there?"

Her mom glanced around, then refocused on Darla. "It's fine." She sighed.

"Doesn't sound fine."

Her mom's lips pursed. She shook her head slightly. Was she tearing up?

"Mom?"

It took a moment for her mom to be able to speak. When she did, she whispered.

"It's Henry."

"Is he okay?"

Mom shrugged. "Well, yes and no. Most of the time, he seems fine. But I wonder if he's getting a little . . ." She made a gesture next to her head.

Darla shifted. She worried about this. Sometimes, her mom seemed a little out of it. Maybe it was normal. Not everyone was "sharp as a tack," as only someone in their eighties was referred to. But Darla's mom was not close to eighty.

They chatted for a while. Darla hedged when it came to her to talk. She gushed about her trip to Lisbon and Paris, filling her mom in on fun anecdotes and showing pages from her sketchbook.

"Well, you're back at work now. I hope it was all worth it."

"*So* worth it." Darla thought of André and couldn't stop grinning. Now was the time to tell her about him. About staying in Lisbon.

"You look happy." Darla's mom's shoulders dropped a smidge. "Okay, gotta run."

They signed off. Darla huffed out a sigh of relief. She wanted to tell her mom, she did. But maybe not quite yet. She flopped down on the wood floor and stretched. This was her home now. The ceiling was high, high above her. A breeze ruffled the gauzy drape at the French door. It was so chill here. She'd thought Boulder was mellow, but Lisbon was another story. Lying there, she felt her whole body relax. She texted Cat, telling him the news. She sent the picture of her and André from the day before. An emoji explosion came back. He was thrilled for her.

Now for the hard one. She'd procrastinated enough. She checked the time and got a fresh glass of water. Taking a deep breath, she punched the number into her phone.

"Terry here."

"Hey, Terry, it's Darla."

"Hey there! Looking forward to seeing you today. Hope you had a great trip."

"I did; it's been great. Life-changing." She took another deep breath.

"Well, we missed you. Lots to catch up on. See you this morning?"

"Uh, well, no. That's why I'm calling."

"What happened? Delayed flight?" She could tell they were on speakerphone and could hear his keyboard clacking.

He never did just one thing and expected everyone else to multitask too.

"Um, well . . . I'm not coming back. I filled out the forms. Mel knows."

"Mel knows? What the hell."

Darla rushed on.

"It's been great, and you've been a great boss. But, well, I'm not coming back to Boulder. I moved to Lisbon."

"What kind of cockamamie move is that?!"

One I'd never thought I'd make, Darla thought.

"My move," she said. "I'm sorry to leave you in the lurch without notice."

"Yea, you are. You won't get any severance, and your benefits will be cut off immediately."

Darla knew this wasn't true. Mel in HR had run her through it all, and she had six weeks before she had to find new health insurance. But the severance—she'd never had that and didn't expect it. She still had most of Lauren's gift to float her until she figured out her finances. If she had to, she could pull from her 401K, but she didn't want to do that. Right now, she just wanted to get this done and get away from Terry.

"Sorry, Terry. It's just that—"

There was a click, and she realized he'd hung up on her. What a dick. All that angst about quitting, and this was the response. Good riddance, she thought.

Chapter Twenty-Eight

André got home around 8:00.

"*Olá*," he called. Darla was in the bedroom sweeping. By that time in Boulder, she would be finishing dinner. She was near the door and leaned over to kiss him.

"Wow," he said, noticing the clean room. "You didn't wait for me."

"I had some time, so figured I would get us closer to having our bedroom."

"*Obrigado,*" he said, kissing her longer. They swayed, their bodies pressed together.

In the living room, he saw the clothes-drying rack with her clothes draped on it.

"You washed clothes too?"

"I did. A regular *hausfrau* today," she said.

"You can't wash clothes during the day," he said.

She laughed. "It's okay. I still got some stuff done." She wanted to tell him about the call with Terry, and the one with her mom.

"No, it's not allowed to run the dishwasher and clothes washer during the day. Portugal law—we have set times for that."

Darla had never heard of such a thing. The thought of someone mandating when you could do housework seemed archaic. André explained that it was because of the cost of electricity. It was cheaper if you ran the appliances at night.

"That makes sense now," she said. But she still felt chastised. The drying rack in the middle of the living room made her feel silly. But how would she have known? She was learning something new every day. That's what she wanted. That's why she'd left home.

Darla's stomach growled.

"*Olá*," André said, nuzzling her tummy.

"I'm starving," she said. "I got groceries, but I haven't made anything for dinner."

André offered to cook. He changed out of his work clothes and put on some music. She hung out nearby with her sketchbook. Soon she noticed that he was narrating everything. She wasn't sure if he was talking to her or just speaking aloud. At the window, he said, "Now I'm going to open the window. Now I'm going to make coffee. Now I'm making dinner."

Darla smiled and murmured, "Okay."

He opened the fridge.

"Darla, now I am going to make some cheese and tomato."

"For an appetizer?"

"Yes."

Darla was grateful. He carefully laid out rounds of sliced tomato, basil, and fresh white cheese on a plate. He sprinkled the cheese with ground pepper and salt. He laid out a bowl of olives he'd marinated and seasoned with lemon zest. Darla wandered over to the kitchen. Having someone else cook for her was the ultimate. She traced the shapes of the caprese and olives in her sketchbook. Later, she'd add the red and green that made this dish pop. But she enjoyed making simple drawings, quickly capturing the moment in one continuous line. She was starving and growing impatient.

"Now I am going to taste the wine." André poured wine

and picked up a layer of tomato and cheese. He offered it to her. She opened her mouth and took it, licking his finger as she did. She savored it slowly. A few sips of wine and nibbles of the appetizer took the edge off her appetite. She drew the items he was chopping. He leaned over the cutting board, getting close to the food. He did the same when stirring the coconut sauce.

Darla wanted to tell him this was terrible posture. But she knew better. He looked so handsome to her, so young and bright. She didn't feel old next to him per se, but she did notice that she had ideas about when it was ideal to eat and sleep. So far that had been tossed out the window here in Lisbon. What did it matter? She had left Boulder to have a different life, she had to keep reminding herself. What did she really need to hang onto? Maybe the better version of herself ate dinner at midnight and slept till nine.

Despite the appetizer, her stomach pinched in on itself. Waves of anxiety frizzled through her. Drawing helped distract her, but she couldn't deny her hunger. She was about to say something when around 10:30 André announced dinner. The pasta with red peppers, tomatoes, mushrooms, and tofu was delicious. She inhaled the fragrant steam. After several bites and sips of wine, Darla's tension dialed down a notch. She hadn't realized how on edge she'd been. Glancing at her sketchbook, she liked the spread with André's recipe. After she'd eaten, she got her sketchbook again. This time she drew André's hands, big and sure in their movements. Hands were hard to capture, but Darla was relaxed, and the drawing flowed.

Darla got a second wind. She told him about quitting her job while they set up their bedroom. Both French doors were open, a breeze adding to the fresh feeling. They wrestled the sheets into submission, waving the sheet in a billowing sail above their bed. Finally, it was all tucked in and ready. They flopped on the bed, laughing and sweating. It wasn't long before their clothes were off and they were making love.

Afterward, they lay watching the sky out the French door. The Tivoli dome was lit from below.

"We christened it," André said.

"Our room," Darla added. "I am starting to feel at home here."

"Me too," André said. They hadn't said it yet to each other. Darla was holding back, waiting for André to say it first. This felt like game playing, which she abhorred. She was about to doze off when André spoke.

"Do you want to go climbing Sunday?"

"I don't climb," Darla murmured. "Despite coming from Boulder."

"What's Boulder like?"

"It's right up against a mountain range," she said, making a wall in the air with her arm. "It's really pretty. Everyone is überathletic. You either hike, run, climb, or do a lot of yoga."

"Do you want to climb with me?"

"I never wanted to, really. But when you add 'with me,' it feels irresistible."

"*Vamos!* Now is the time to try." He smiled.

She hesitated. She truly didn't want to. But why not? She'd tried so many new things already: fish, going out with a group of strangers, moving in with André. Why not try climbing?

"I have everything you need," he said. His confidence! She laughed at the irony that she left Boulder, Colorado, the rock-climbing capital of the US to come to Portugal and fall for a climber. In all her years in Boulder, surrounded by gear-toting, Prana-sporting, microbrew-guzzling, Subaru-driving, software engineer-by-day dudes, she had to come all the way to Portugal to become a climber. She never had an invitation to climb in Boulder. Would she have accepted? But then she thought about all the classic movies she'd sat through with Gregory. They'd bored her, and she spent more time thinking about where they would eat afterward.

"You go," she said. "I will stay home and make some art."

He didn't say anything, but she felt a touch of disappointment come from his side of the bed. Before she could think of anything to say, sleep overtook her.

Chapter Twenty-Nine

———

She let Julie know she had moved to Lisbon. Julie had responded with a series of enthusiastic emojis and a lunch suggestion. They met outside a pasteleria, where Julie greeted Darla with European cheek kissing and a big smile.

"Wow," she said. "This is a welcome surprise."

"Right?! It all happened so quickly. While I was at the Paris airport!"

They ordered salads and fresh juice and found a table near the window. Darla had a fleeting sense of the quotidian, the simple but pleasurable daily acts that make the fabric of a life. Lunch with a friend. What was new was this spaciousness, the feeling of her time being hers and not solely devoted to her job. Julie smiled as they settled in.

They ate their salads, chatting about upcoming events in Lisbon Julie was part of. Darla made notes in her notebook. She sketched their tiny pingado cups. Finally, she braved the subject she had been avoiding.

"Remember our tea date with Inês when we talked about sex?"

Julie nodded, smiling.

"Now I need your help."

"Uh-oh," Julie said.

"No, nothing's wrong. I'm hoping to prevent any kind of 'oops' here. I'm thinking of going on the pill."

"Not a bad idea."

"I have no idea where to start."

"Well, with a gynecologist. I can recommend mine. She's fantastic."

"Does she speak English?"

"She does, and her office staff is also bilingual and really helpful."

Darla wrote down their info.

"So, things are going well with André?"

"Yes," Darla enthused. "Our apartment is great! You and Inês should come for lunch someday."

"Sure," Julie said. "But you two are getting along well?"

"Of course. Why the doubt?"

"No doubt, just checking. It's a big adjustment to move in with someone. I know when I came here there was a sort of transition from dating to cohabitating. Little issues that needed to be resolved."

Darla nodded. "You're right. It is an adjustment. I don't know if I will get used to eating dinner so late. Ten thirty the other night! We stay up so late. But it doesn't matter if I sleep in. No nine-to-five to get to!"

Julie laughed. "You'll adjust to Portuguese time. Late nights. And things going slower than in the US."

"It's great not having a job, but I will have to find work at some point."

"How long is your runway?"

"I gave myself to the end of this year, but I think I'll have money to cover myself for longer than that if I don't go crazy buying stuff or taking trips. I'm more worried about how to stay here legally. I was kinda crazy, just taking a leap to come here, thinking I'd figure it out when I got here."

"Yea, maybe not the best plan," Julie said. Darla felt a slight shiver of doom.

"How are you here legally?" It felt intrusive to ask, but they'd already crossed some politeness barrier. Darla appreciated that. She needed friends here, not just polite acquaintances.

"I got a work visa through my job. I have to renew it annually, but it doesn't have a limit."

"Do you see yourself staying here forever?"

Julie shrugged. "Who knows. I try not to think about 'forever.' I'm just going with it, and whenever it stops working, I'll change."

Darla nodded. She wished she could be so easygoing. From the outside, it might seem like she was just rolling with it. But inside, she still wished for more certainty about what her future held.

The next night was Darla's birthday. She and André planned to celebrate with dinner out. Up in the mezzanine, she dressed in her Italian linen dress, a long, drapey thing in a gentle lavender color. It wasn't really her size, but she thought it was feminine and pretty. She was putting on jewelry when André came up the stairs. He froze, half of his body out of sight.

"What?" she said. He had grown pale. "What is it?"

"That dress," he said.

"Isn't it pretty?" She twirled around. The skirt made a swirling bell around her legs. He swallowed. She could tell he was deciding whether to give his opinion or not.

"It's, well, it turns me cold," he said.

She recoiled, shocked that a dress that seemed so benign could have such a dampening effect. Darla said nothing. But she didn't take it off. She moved aside for him to change out of his work clothes.

That day, while grocery shopping, she'd felt a twinge of acute discomfort over their age difference. She piled several bunches of greens into her basket at the market. It didn't seem to matter when they were together, but adding another year between them made her self-conscious.

Her last birthday with Gregory had been such a painful disaster. This relationship felt like a better match sexually. She was determined that this one would be better.

At the register, she'd loaded all the greens and tomatoes into her string bag. She might have bought too much but figured it would last.

Now, down in the bathroom, she fluffed her hair. She was shocked by how tan and relaxed she looked. She didn't look old, and the dress was fine. She raised her chin, determined not to let André's comment ruin her special day.

Out on the street, they headed toward the water. Darla had always walked when it was possible in Boulder. Here, she didn't even have a car. The ease of it, the liberation, felt good. They held hands, and Darla pretended she'd forgotten the moment with the dress. Hardly any cars came down Rua São José. Soon the street was lined with gaudy restaurants with hawkers outside. They waved menus at passersby but not at them. Being with André was a signal that she belonged. She was here for good, not just passing through. She liked having André as a passport of sorts.

Coming upon a plaza, André gestured toward a brightly lit storefront window. A sign over the door said Ginjinha Sem Rival Eduardino (exclusivo) Marca Registada. A group of people had gathered there, and others dotted the plaza.

"Want a Ginjinha?" he asked.

"What's that?"

"Vamos," he said, smiling.

Inside the tiny shop, an older man served customers. She heard only one thing "*Com o sem?*" André ordered *com*.

He paid with a couple of coins and handed Darla a tiny plastic shot glass. Outside in the plaza, he explained. "Ginjinha is a cherry liqueur, with a preserved cherry to suck and nibble on." He winked.

She was impatient to try it. They toasted, nudging the plastic cups together and gazing into each other's eyes.

"Let's take a picture," she said. Fumbling in her bag, she pulled out her phone. She wanted to capture all these moments. All the flashes of experience that she had a hard time believing were happening. She wanted proof for herself. She didn't draw and paint people very much, but maybe she would. They looked into the camera, toasting and smiling, the dark sky behind them, the intensity of their connection filling the frame. She especially liked the one where he kissed the side of her face like someone inhaling pure love.

She sipped the sweet and sour liquid, letting it pour over her tongue.

"You like?" he asked.

It tasted a bit like cough syrup, but she knew that when someone shared something special, a cultural icon of the nation, to be diplomatic.

"Sure!" she said, hoping she sounded convincing.

"I'll add this to my Portuguese beverages series."

She made it up on the spot, but once she said it, she liked the idea—an illustrated article of the drinks she'd had in Portugal. They downed the shots. Walking to dinner, she added drinks to the to-illustrate list in her mind.

Over pizza, salad, and a bottle of red, they talked about hosting dinner parties. Getting buzzed, they stoked the dream of their life together. The waitress came and said something to André. It broke their rhythm. Darla was frustrated not to understand.

"I want to learn Portuguese," she said.

"It's hard," he said, finishing off his wine.

"So I've heard."

Julie had told her that even she, who had become fairly fluent, struggled with people's response to her.

"Portuguese people will pretend not to understand you and will revert to English. They like showing off that they can speak it fluently."

Darla was optimistic. Words were easy. In an Italian class she'd taken in Boulder, Darla had a great time learning Italian words and matching them to their English counterparts. It was like being a child again, acquiring language and sounds for every little thing. Like discovering the world all over again. But after a few weeks, they accelerated into the grammar lane. Rules came into play. Matching genders. Memorizing tenses, cases, and pronouns. Fitting them all together and trying not to sound like an idiot. Real effort and thinking were required. Like stepping away from play and into work. Her brain had slowed down, and learning became less of a game and more of another way to prove she could conquer anything.

Still, she wanted to attempt to learn Portuguese. And André helped her believe it was possible.

"Portuguese is a gateway language. Once you have Portuguese, you can have *all* the Latin languages."

"Like a giveaway—buy one, get five free."

They laughed.

"With Portuguese, Spanish is a given." He snapped his fingers when he said that. The idea that learning this challenging language had a bonus motivated her.

The waitress returned, holding a plate aloft, lit with a sparkler. She and André sang "Happy Birthday" to her in Portuguese. Darla blushed, delighted by his thoughtfulness. A crepe oozed chocolate, a ball of ice cream holding the sparkler. Darla made a wish and blew it out.

"What did you wish?"

"You know I can't tell! But hopefully, it's something you want too." She had let herself hope that this was going to work out, that she would learn Portuguese, that she and André would have a great, long life together, and that she would finally feel like she belonged somewhere. Then he ruined the hopeful moment.

"Maybe I buy you a dress for your birthday?"

She pulled back from the crepe, the ice cream melting on the plate in a chocolate puddle.

"Because you don't like this dress?"

"Because I want to buy you a dress. You deserve something new and pretty." She wasn't sure how she felt about it. A gift was nice, but this felt like he had a different agenda. To change her. She didn't want to talk about it. It was easier to go along with him.

"Sure. Would you pick it out?" She was curious what he would dress her in. He obviously thought a lot more about clothes than she did. In Boulder, he would look dressed up all the time. In Lisbon, she looked like she was headed to the park every day.

"No, you pick it out. But I buy, for your birthday," he smiled.

"Okay." She finished the last puddle of ice cream and chocolate.

That night, André offered Darla a massage. He spread sheets on the floor in the bedroom. He lit candles and queued up some soft music. She lay down on the massage zone. Soon, she relaxed. His big hands, strong from climbing, also knew how to loosen her muscles. Afterward, sleepy, noodley, she massaged him. He couldn't believe she knew how to give a massage. He groaned and sighed under her hands.

"Your touch!" André said with incredulity.

"What?"

"You have such a great touch. And how do you know how to massage like that?"

She shrugged. "I don't know. Getting massages, I guess."

They vowed to give each other massages regularly. A Love Embassy special. She thought it was cool that André was into massage. But it signaled something that she suspected wasn't really there—a sort of esotericism or spiritual sensibility.

The touching turned into lovemaking. Their oily bodies flowed together. Darla forgot all about the dress, all about clothes or anything to do with the world. It was just her and André, the flickering candles, movement that felt like an easy dance, and pleasure. Pure pleasure. They paused to put on a condom. She loved watching his hands move over his cock. Their bodies melded together, slipping with the oil. She moved into a new position. André came quickly, and Darla did not. She didn't mind; it had been fun. He pulled out and she flopped onto her back.

"Oh no," he said.

"It's okay. I don't have to have an orgasm every time."

He held up the condom. Fluid dripped from the tip.

"I think it broke."

She sat up, the pleasure replaced by dread.

"What? Are you sure?"

He stood and rushed out. She sat there, stunned, her breasts getting cold. This had never happened in all her years using condoms. She followed André into the bathroom. He held the condom under the faucet. Water sprang out from more than one hole.

"*Merda.*"

"Fuck."

He laughed but then saw her face.

"I don't want to have a baby," she said. She had friends who'd been desperate for children and who'd gone to extreme measures to have children. At forty. It was possible to get pregnant at her age. But while she felt love for André and what she hoped to build with him, she didn't want children. They hadn't discussed it.

"Do you?"

He left the bathroom, and she trailed him back to the bedroom. He gathered up the sheets and shrugged.

"I guess I haven't thought about it."

She guffawed. How could you not think about that? As a woman, it was always part of the equation. Sex wasn't just sex but was a potential life-changer. And for her, someone wanting a child was a relationship deal-breaker. She'd just gotten to Lisbon, had just cast her lot with this guy, and he hadn't thought about having children?

He came back from putting the massage sheets in the laundry. She was in bed, her body alight with the fear of being pregnant.

"Maybe you go with birth control?"

"Maybe you get a vasectomy?"

He drew back, his face screwed up in a clear no.

"I think it easier to go with birth control."

"Easier for you." Darla's stomach gripped. She hated being at odds with him. When André got into bed, she drew closer.

"I'm sorry. That was scary. Now I have this stress of waiting for my period."

André was listening, but she could tell by his tense neck muscles that he didn't want to be having the conversation.

"I'll think about the pill," she said. She'd make an appointment with Julie's OB/GYN right away.

Chapter Thirty

On the city bus to IKEA, they reviewed their list. Dining table and chairs. A desk for Darla and some rugs. They rode standing, holding onto the yellow poles. Darla wore her black pants and her flowered linen top. She liked having a limited wardrobe. Come fall, she'd need to buy some clothes for cold weather. But now, in early July, she soaked up the happy illusion of endless summer. The bus passed through a vast green space, and André told her it was the Monsanto Forest.

"We'll come here sometime," he said.

They began making plans about how they'd they'd divide up the housework. André made lists in his little notebook. His handwriting was small and cramped. Darla had a hard time reading it. These plans satisfied the engineer in him and the dreamer in Darla. They discussed how they'd handle their mutual expenses like the furniture, food, and anything else they'd buy for the Love Embassy. They agreed to contribute a monthly amount to a shared account—an account André would manage. Darla would pay him rent. It was way cheaper than what she'd paid in Boulder. She had never shared a home or expenses with a lover. Neither had André, so they were making it up as they went along. So far Lisbon was cheap, so her money could go further. But she didn't want to go crazy buying too much new stuff.

They entered the maze at IKEA, filing past setting after

setting. André pushed through until they got to showrooms with lots of options. After surveying an endless sea of tables, they chose a black dining set with six chairs. André bent down to inspect a number on the card and wrote it in his tiny notebook. Darla peeked over his shoulder.

"What's happening?"

"You write down the number and then pick it up later."

"Fine." Darla was starting to get hungry. She was ready for the shopping spree to be over. She'd looked forward to this outing, and now she just wanted to get back home and eat. It would be late before they'd have dinner. Why hadn't she thought about this and had a snack before she'd left?

They found a simple desk for her. After testing several chairs, she chose one with a cushy back. In the marketplace downstairs, they picked out some silverware and a few dish towels. Darla got a special coffee cup with a saucer for her coffee ritual. André paused when they got to the rugs.

"We should get these for camping," he said, pointing at a stack of simple cotton rugs the size of doormats.

"Sure," Darla said. It was easy to go off list and get things they hadn't thought of. But now she wondered how much this was all going to cost. André didn't seem to mind the expenses adding up. She hadn't asked him about his finances, how much he made, how much he saved. It hadn't come up, even when they talked about sharing expenses.

André had compiled everything they wanted on a list.

"How do we get these things?"

"Come," he said. They emerged from the marketplace into a large warehouse. Rows upon rows of inventory were shelved in boxes.

"We look for the codes I've written down. Then we pay."

"But how are we going to get this home? We can't carry all this on the bus."

André frowned.

"We will do it. We will find a way." A look of intense determination crossed his face. "Let's go to the front."

There, they learned that IKEA could deliver the items. But André thought this was too expensive. The other, cheaper option was to rent a small truck and drive the items home.

"But then you have to return the truck," Darla pointed out. "Isn't it easier to just have it delivered?"

"Darla," André said, grabbing her arm, "listen. I am a ranked rock climber in Portugal. Nothing is too hard for me."

She didn't know what his climbing status had to do with renting an IKEA van, but she let it go. Her stomach was starting to growl, and now that they'd chosen their stuff, she was ready to go home. They paid, and after André rented a van, they loaded everything in the back. He drove them back to the center of the city. Darla hadn't been in a car much since she'd arrived in Lisbon. She enjoyed being in the passenger seat while André was joyous. They talked about the summer they'd have together.

They pulled up in front of their apartment. André hit the hazard lights.

"Can we carry this all up together?" she asked.

"Of course!"

They wrangled the long and slim boxes upstairs. The table, chair, and desk. A giant blue bag full of candles, rugs, and dish towels. They filled the living room with giant slender boxes.

"Now I go return the truck," André said.

"But it's late! What about dinner?" She couldn't wait any longer to eat.

He grabbed an apple. "Eat without me."

"Do you want me to go with you?" She felt she should offer.

"No," he said, fervent and geared up. "I will go." He pulled Darla close and planted a hard kiss on her mouth. He put his beret back on.

"I'll be back soon. Don't worry," he said, heading downstairs on a wind of virile enthusiasm.

"I'm not worried," Darla muttered. "I'm starving."

She opened a bottle of wine and had some bread and cheese. After a few sips, she wondered if she had been too practical. André was so gung ho, anything possible. She saw only the clock. But after a few bites of cheese and bread, her anxiety retreated, the urgent pinging for her attention fading away. She chopped some vegetables and cooked rice. By the time André made it home, it was past midnight. She was in bed reading. André popped his head into the bedroom. He seemed triumphant, hardly tired.

"You made it!" she said.

"Of course I made it," he replied. "Did you doubt it?"

"Of course I didn't doubt you," Darla said. She eyed his intense, victorious face; his breath coming sharp and fast; his jaw locked in triumph. She was ready for sleep and not interested in assessing his abilities. She got up and went into the kitchen. "I made some dinner." He followed her.

"Dinner? No. No dinner." He pulled her to the couch. They tugged off their clothes and writhed against the black leather. The IKEA boxes sat silent, witnessing their coupling. André's body, so strong. Her body, so open. She relished the coziness of having a lover, the cuddling, the feeling that she wasn't alone. In bed, they snuggled, the sound of a garbage truck downstairs clattering cans and spilling trash into the truck. She checked her bedside clock. 1:30. Garbage trucks after midnight? She tried to recall ever hearing garbage trucks in Boulder. Nothing came to her. Thoughts of home were getting further away. This was her home now.

The next night, when André got home from work, they smoked a spliff. She was getting used to getting high together. She didn't love the tobacco and hash mix, but letting go of overthinking felt good. Letting go of worry. Just being present in the moment with what and who was right there. Darla had eaten some nuts so she wouldn't get into the red zone of hunger and fatigue. André applied his Portuguese determination to putting the furniture together. He showed her how to read wordless directions and how not to get confused by extra, unnamed parts. They assembled the table and chairs quickly. They put her desk together in no time. Well, they worked together easily if she just handed him the tools. They carried her desk upstairs. She was excited to set up her first art studio.

At the dining table, André laid out the new placemats and cloth napkins. She set a candle alight in the middle of the table. She was in love with this table. It represented home, the bounty and beauty of their food, the possibility of sharing with others. Darla imagined lots of shared meals and conversation here.

"You are no more an IKEA virgin!" André exclaimed.

"Oh the things you've done to me," she flirted.

"I'll do many more things," he promised, coming to kiss her.

After dinner, they sat at the open window in their room in chairs they'd dragged in from the living room. The night breeze cleared away the day's heat. André had a notebook on his lap, rolling a spliff. He sparked the lighter again and again, heating a dark nub of hash, rolling bits of it into a rolling paper. The bits of hash nestled in a tangle of tobacco. Darla imagined drawing the lines, the blobs of hash, the paper. What colors would she use? Tobacco would be tough—not brown, not yellow, somewhere in between. She doodled it in her sketchbook, wondering if they needed another joint.

"You mentioned camping. I'd love to camp. It's been years." Gregory hadn't been outdoorsy, and she didn't have gear and wouldn't have gone camping on her own.

André set the lighter down to roll the joint. "I live for camping. I have camped everywhere. On the side of a mountain."

"What? Like, tucked into the rocks?"

"There's a special tent for climbers. It hangs on the side of rock." He licked the paper, tightening it into a roll. Darla wanted to draw his big hands, manipulating the delicate paper. She envisioned him nesting in rock, like a caterpillar in a cocoon. She got images like this and imagined drawing them. Typically, she felt like she was an artist who drew from life, but every once in a while, an idea would come from nowhere, and she'd see it in her mind. She pulled her sketchbook over and began doodling while they chatted. He passed her the joint and lighter.

"I can show you some special places," André said.

"What kind of special places?"

"I've camped in some of the most beautiful places in Portugal. There are many places to climb here."

"I love camping," Darla said. "But do we have gear? Do you have a tent?" She lit the joint and inhaled deeply.

"We can go to Decathlon and get gear. A tent, some sleeping bags. I have a small stove."

"Okay, but I can't spend too much." She wanted to have a more thorough conversation about their spending. But not now. She passed the spliff to André. She wanted to go camping, and it seemed worth investing in a sleeping bag and tent. She'd spent a lot of time outdoors at Cat's family cottage, hearing the wind in the trees, feeling close to the earth. She believed she was a wild child, even now. All this had been trained out of her by the need to make a living. She didn't make as much time for fun. The only mountain she had climbed was the career ladder. It had paid off until it hadn't.

"Let's do it," she said. Now, high, anything seemed possible. She took another toke, her energy picking up, her heart beating faster, her connection to André feeling stronger.

"I tell you something," he said, eagerly turning toward her. "I love to shit outside."

She laughed. "Okay, I love to pee outside, but pooping? Not on my list of peak experiences."

"Oh, me, yes. It feels so good to be out in nature and to just let go."

"Where should we go first?"

He told her about Gerês, a national park in northern Portugal at the Spanish border. They dreamed and planned. She sketched the Tivoli dome, again. Clouds drifted across the night sky, catching in the trees sheltering the Avenida. She wanted to frame this moment, the view from their home, them sitting together, planning fun things for the future. She sipped her water. Being high was fun, but not the dry mouth. How had she managed to not get high all her life? It was so much more relaxing than wine. Her friends were drinkers. That seemed more socially acceptable. She hadn't gotten where she was by being a stoner. But now she was free floating from her career, and it was time to try all the things.

The doodle of André in a sleeping bag looked more like a nondescript cocoon. Maybe drawing from her imagination wasn't her jam. She closed her sketchbook. She cleared the table, put the dishes in the sink, and got ready for bed. André stayed upstairs, watching YouTube videos on his computer. He was learning new knots for his ropes and practiced along with the videos. Naked in bed, she heard sounds from the street through the open windows. Water hitting pavement—someone hosing off the sidewalk? A few shouts and laughter from below. Her place in Boulder had been so quiet. But she liked the sounds. She liked living in a bigger city. Somehow it made her feel like she was living more full ass. Could Lauren see her now? She still hadn't spent much of Lauren's money, other than the plane ticket to move to Lisbon.

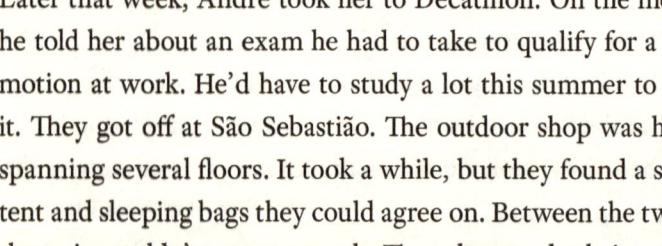

Later that week, André took her to Decathlon. On the metro, he told her about an exam he had to take to qualify for a promotion at work. He'd have to study a lot this summer to pass it. They got off at São Sebastião. The outdoor shop was huge, spanning several floors. It took a while, but they found a small tent and sleeping bags they could agree on. Between the two of them, it wouldn't cost too much. Then they made their way to the basement to look for clothes. She tried on a cool hoodie. It was long and loose and could be dressed up or down. He had the same brand, which she took as a sign of quality. She was deciding when she felt it. That familiar feeling in her underwear. She found the restroom, and there it was—a blotch of blood.

"Oh, thank god," she murmured.

Chapter Thirty-One

Her days in Lisbon were spacious. For the first time ever, her life didn't revolve around the nine-to-five cycle. She liked the slow pace of mornings with André. They'd wake late. André always greeted her with a kiss and a *bom dia*. After snuggling, he got ready for work while she languished in bed. Sometimes, he'd get up and putter around. He wouldn't eat much for breakfast. He was a yogurt freak. Darla adopted the yogurt habit too. One of them would get the coffee going in their Italian stovetop espresso maker. Darla liked to put dishes away while waiting for the coffee.

But one day, André complained about the noise. So, she stopped. They would have coffee and plan their evening. Then he'd suit up and go to work. The door would click shut, and his feet echoing down the circular stairwell cued Darla's loneliness. She'd eat her yogurt, fruit, and muesli and wonder what to do with her day. The "vacation" feel had worn off, and now Darla needed something to focus her attention on. Now that she'd set up her studio and the rest of the apartment, she needed something to work on. She could wander around the city only so much.

Back in Boulder, which had its own brand of mellow, she was a speedy, focused, get-it-done kind of woman. Here, she couldn't imagine being like that. Maybe the sun or ocean breezes chilled her out. Or all the sex. She liked to think it was because she was finally where she belonged. She didn't miss Boulder at all, with the exception of Cat and a few friends. She liked not having to snap to for anyone else's agenda. Not having to get dressed and go into the office. Not having to prepare for endlessly boring meetings. She gradually slowed down, not starting the day at the laptop. She got in the habit of taking a second coffee upstairs to her studio. A daily ritual of sketching her cup as a warm-up took root. She was growing used to the quiet high up in her studio punctuated by the sounds that reached her through the tiny open window. Scooters beeping as they buzzed by. The barking of the dog downstairs. A parrot eking out a few repetitive whistles. Some days, another whistle, followed by a phrase she couldn't catch. Maybe she could learn some Portuguese from it.

She prepared another coffee and lit the fire under it. She wanted to be like André, a polyglot. She dreamed of speaking five languages. She wanted to be able to connect with anyone, anywhere, on their own terms. Speaking another language was a way to play with words. But she had surrendered that dream. Back in Boulder, she would have thought she was too old to take on a new language. But now she was determined to do it. She had an ear. She could mimic anyone and pick up languages. She'd studied French and Italian. How different could Portuguese be?

She hoped that one month of Portuguese lessons would do the job. But at some of the Globalkin events, listening to the Lisboetas speaking together, she understood nothing. In French, she could pick out words, get a sense of context, and understand at least 20 percent of what was going on. But Portuguese? Nada. A wave of consonants *shushing* past, mimicking the lick of the ocean against the coast. A blur of sound, no words distinguishable from any other.

While waiting for the coffee, she researched language schools in Lisbon. Apparently, there were a bunch of other tongue-tied fools like Darla who thought they could breach the shore of this language. She found something a short metro ride away. Classes were Monday through Friday mornings. She could do this! She could learn Portuguese.

She brought the coffee pot and cup to the studio. The shape of the Bialetti coffee maker was always a drawing challenge. Putting on some music, she set to sketching the pot and cup. Before long, she had a complete and somewhat decent drawing of the pair. She took a bathroom break, and when she came back, she was surprised by the painting. She'd really captured it. Not in a photorealistic way but in a wonky, playful way. Seeing the painting made her think it could be an illustration in a magazine. She compared it to the other pieces she'd done. The Tivoli dome with a background of trees at the botanic gardens. A set of stairs with potted plants at the side. She could see a style developing. She could see her illustrations getting more confident, her lines more sure, the colors vibrant and fun. She was finding her true colors, her Lisbon colors.

She took the coffee pot downstairs. Hungry, she cooked an egg and steamed some leafy greens. She toasted one of the little buns from Dolce Real. This suited her stomach much more than a sugary yogurt. She ground salt and pepper over the meal. Eyeing the shapes of the grinders while she ate, her mind traced them as if drawing them. Another perfect couple, she thought. She laughed, imagining a story about how salt and pepper met and became an iconic couple. Her fork clattered to the plate.

She rushed upstairs and grabbed a notebook she'd been using for art ideas. A series bloomed: *Another Perfect Couple.*

Fork and knife. Bread and butter. Bialetti and cup. She scribbled notes and made quick sketches and lists. Animating objects and giving them stories made her chuckle. Back downstairs, washing up, she wondered if she and André were a perfect couple. What did people think when they say them together? She didn't think she looked old, and certainly didn't feel old, but André was clearly younger than her. Did people think she was a cougar? The name made her cringe.

Finishing up, she tucked the tea towel onto the oven door handle. She could hear Lauren poo-pooing her insecurity. "What others think of you is not your business." And it was true. She'd never know what "people" thought anyway. What mattered was what she and André thought. And they were in love, having fun, and building a life together. Adjusting the tea towel, she saw an opportunity: *Another Perfect Couple* tea towels. Or cocktail napkins for speed dating events. Writing it down in her notebook, she wondered where these ideas came from.

One afternoon, Darla walked to a nearby office building. It was a gorgeous summer day in Lisbon. The breeze from the river kept the heat off her brow. The chorus of raucous children at play floated over the wall of an elementary school. Nothing dispelled the dread she felt about the appointment. In the waiting room, she checked in, filling out a form. She could read most of it in Portuguese but used her mini dictionary for the rest.

Inside the examining room, she undressed and put on the paper robe. She hated gynecological exams. So exposed. But when the doctor breezed in with a smile and a confident air, Darla relaxed immediately. The pre-exam interview went smoothly.

Why was she here? She wanted a prescription for birth control. Yes, she was sexually active. Just one partner. No, she hadn't been tested for STDs lately. Did she have health insurance?

She did have insurance but wasn't sure if it would work in Portugal. Another thing she had glossed over when she took the leap to move to Europe. At the time, it had seemed bold to not take care of these adult details of life. Now she felt foolish, like she should have known better. But the doctor didn't seem phased, just typing Darla's answers into her laptop.

After the exam, she declared that everything looked good. She wrote out a prescription and directed Darla to a nearby pharmacy. Darla dressed and paid an astonishingly small fee for the doctor's visit. She took the card for the doctor in case she needed a follow-up appointment. Outside, she relished the freedom only a post-doctor visit gave her. Relief. Freedom. The kind of exuberance you see with dogs after they've taken a poo, their whole bodies free and alive as they kick back their feet, clawing up dirt. She smiled inside, thinking of dogs. Did André like dogs like she did? They'd never talked about it. Maybe they'd get a dog together.

Today, she would let herself explore, maybe treat herself somehow. She wore her new sun hat. She wandered the shops in Chiado. She came upon a thrift store selling vintage clothes. Inside, she riffled through a rack of dresses. She took a few into the dressing room. The best one was a style she wouldn't have thought suited her. But it was perfect, a brown dress with a flower pattern that fit tightly around the bodice. It was flattering and comfortable, with a wide skirt that flared wide when she twirled in the mirror.

She wondered if André would like it. The saleswoman smiled and said a few words that Darla took to mean, "That looks great on you." She got it, shocked at the low price. Nearby, she found a shop selling bathing suits. Trying on bikini tops took forever, but she finally found something she thought would go with her bathing suit skirt. After a tosta in a pasteleria, she headed home.

The sidewalks on the Avenida da Liberdade sprawled out with cobblestones adorned with patterns swirled by black stones. She spotted a shoe shop. The display showed shoes both classic and funky. She let herself be lured in. It was a brand called Fly London. She loved the classic styling with a high rubber wedge. She hadn't planned on buying shoes, but a red pair with a strap and a teardrop cutout on top called to her. She tried them on. She adored them, but they were expensive. Walking around the shop in them, she felt a confidence and swagger she'd never experienced. She could hear Lauren egging her on. She'd get them. Use some of Lauren's money for them. Her money. They'd go great with her new dress.

She wore them out of the store. She was shocked to find heels that were actually comfortable. Maybe this was the beginning of starting to look more like André wanted. She strutted home along the Avenida, swinging her shopping bag and feeling like a new person.

"I have a surprise," she told André after dinner.

In the bedroom, she put the dress and shoes on. She added a choker necklace and some lipstick. With her lingerie underneath.

"Close your eyes!" she shouted.

Out in the living room, André was sprawled on the sofa, eyes closed. She strutted toward him, clicking her fingers. He opened his eyes.

"Wow." A smile took over his face. He said something in Portuguese she didn't catch.

"You like?" She twirled around, the skirt flaring up over her knees.

"*Eu gusto*," he said, gesturing for her to come over. She stood over him, putting one of her new shoes up on the couch next to his thigh. He stroked her calf, moving his hand up to her thigh. He pulled her down and she straddled him, the dress flared around them. He slipped his fingers past her panties. Leaning forward, she kissed him. Before long, the dress was off, the sexy lingerie was off, and all she wore were the red shoes. They moved into the bedroom where the condoms were. She wasn't going to take any chances.

Chapter Thirty-Two

That Monday, she, too, had somewhere to go in the morning. She changed outfits three times before settling on her comfy capri pants. For a three-hour class, she'd need to be comfortable. On the subway, she had that New York feeling of being part of a place, not just skimming the surface as a visitor. She was doing something.

The language class took place in an office building near Marquês de Pombal. A young woman, Tania, welcomed her into a nondescript meeting room. They sat at tables circled around a room. She invited them to share why they wanted to learn Portuguese. Darla, two young Norwegian men, a Canadian woman, and a Hungarian woman introduced themselves in turn. Everyone's reason for being there was different. Darla took pride in having moved to Portugal to be with a lover. Tania responded slowly to each person in Portuguese. Darla didn't get everything, but she started to pick up words that Tania repeated.

Finally, she passed out their textbooks and a workbook. Darla eagerly opened hers. The book was a gorgeous visual dictionary. Darla couldn't stop staring at the illustrations, especially the food section. The book wasn't big, and it wasn't textbook-like. It inspired her to learn and to draw more.

On that first day, Tania outlined the structure of the class. Because they only had four weeks together, it would be an immersion. She'd speak mostly in Portuguese. As she said all this, she wrote words on the board. If only there were subtitles, Darla thought.

In the beginning, the exercises were easy. Tania started with the important stuff: where are you from, how to order food in a restaurant, and how to make plans with friends. Darla hoped to have Portuguese friends. She could practice, perhaps, with Inês. Throughout the course, Tania wrote endless vocabulary words on the board. She recounted stories about Portuguese culture. She waited patiently while they stumbled through the sea of shh sounds and bad usage. Progress was painstaking. Basics like telling time took forever. At least two minutes were required to spit out the correct time. It was humbling. But no one seemed better than anyone else, and Darla took comfort in being with people all bumbling along.

Learning built slowly. Tania added verbs, nouns, adjectives. Conjugating verbs forced Darla to memorize. It was still hard to understand what people were saying. When André had the news on at night, she could make out a word here or there. She dutifully did her homework in the workbook. Her tiny Portuguese-English dictionary was her new best friend. She could get lost looking up words. She thumbed through it on the metro to class, fantasizing that she could commit all the words to memory.

Her at-the-ready tutor, André, taught her something new. Her new sentence was *"Estou a aprender Português."* I am learning Portuguese. She liked this better than "I don't speak Portuguese." The former was an open door, an invitation for people to help her learn. She mastered the numbers, the days of the week, and a few phrases. André insisted that she ask him the names of things and spoke to her in Portuguese. The first full sentence she understood in Portuguese was a sexual one.

This was not something she could brag about in class. People said that having a lover teach one a language was the best way to learn, and now Darla saw why.

She was getting better at fixing her face, a big part of learning Portuguese. When André was talking to someone, asking directions or who knows what, she tried to assume an "I completely understand everything that's going on" expression. But Portuguese didn't take root right away. Going from the cute language book to real life presented a learning curve as steep as Lisbon's hills. Picking up Portuguese was nowhere near as easy as picking up a Portuguese man. But she had committed to Portugal and to André. People talking to each other across the narrow streets and in the shops added to her language lessons. Darla realized that the goal was not to do the exercises as quickly as possible but to do them slowly so she could understand and remember.

She laughed at herself. She didn't know why she thought that doing the lessons quickly was a sign of intelligence or aptitude. Her tendency to speed was revealed here in Portugal, where things moved more slowly. André was always asking her to *acalmar*. And she wanted to calm down, she did. What was the point of living in a Latin culture if she was speeding through it all the time?

Julie and Inês came over for lunch. Darla had grilled an assortment of vegetables and halloumi cheese, sprinkled with fresh herbs and accompanied by salad and small bread rolls from Dolce Real. She poured lemon water around while they gushed over the apartment.

"This is fabulous," Julie said.

"*Otimo!*"

She showed them around. Inês seemed reluctant to go into the bedroom.

"We don't really give people tours of our homes here in Portugal," she finally admitted.

"Wow, that's the first thing we do in the US," Julie said. Darla nodded.

"May I ask why not?" Darla said.

Inês shrugged.

"I don't know. It's just not done. I'd say it's something to do with not wanting to show off. We don't flaunt our wealth."

"That's all Americans want to do," Darla said. She'd never felt great about showing her tiny apartment in Boulder. Most of the people she knew in Boulder had giant, well-appointed homes filled with children and a spouse. Her solo lifestyle didn't need all that space and opulence. And honestly, she didn't want that much space. The Lisbon apartment was pretty big, and cleaning it for her guests had taken most of the morning.

Up in her studio, they oohed and aahed.

"This is fabulous!" Julie cried out.

"I love your art." Inês was looking at an open sketchbook and some partially done watercolor postcards.

"Thanks!"

"You're really into it," Julie said. "You've gotten better since you were staying with me."

Darla nodded. "I think things are starting to come together. I'm excited to see what happens."

They caught up over lunch downstairs. Julie vented about how busy it was at work.

"We're shorthanded too. We need more staff. I think we're going to hire someone soon, but we have to get funding for that."

"I get it," Darla said. "Some of my clients were NGOs. Always needing funding."

"We've been lucky so far, backed mostly by a major organization I cannot name."

"Oh, now I want to know. A hint?" Darla teased.

"Mum's the word," Julie said. "But I can tell you they believe in the power of art to make a positive, global impact."

"Sounds like a line from one of my reports."

"Well, they've put their money where their mouth is. But now that we're expanding, we need more funding sources. And someone to help us find them."

Darla passed around the salad bowl.

"What about you, Inês? What's up?"

"I'm going crazy waiting to hear if I got into NYU. I don't know what my life will look like in two months," she said, folding lettuce onto her fork.

The idea of New York presented an immediate turnoff in Darla. Lisbon was so much more her speed. But she could be happy and hopeful for Inês.

"You'll love New York. So much to do," she said.

"If I get in!" Inês looked worried.

"You'll get in," Julie reassured her. "Believe that New York is where you'll be soon."

Inês chewed, and Darla could tell she was unconvinced by this "believe it" approach.

"I know the feeling," Darla said. "I feel pretty uncertain about my future too."

"But you just moved here. You're all settled," Julie said.

"Kinda not really. I don't have a visa and am basically illegal here. And work? I don't know how I'm going to make money." She stared at her salad. "This has been a great adventure, but I need to get out of vacation mode and figure that out."

"You told me you have plenty of runway," Julie said. "And the inheritance."

Darla poked some errant vegetables back into her sandwich. She dipped it into a puddle of salad dressing on her plate.

"That's true. I guess it's not just the money. It's wanting to know what I am going to do with myself now that I'm not an annual report writer."

"*É isso!*" Inês said. "That's what I want too. To be engaged in my studies. If I don't get into school, I don't know what I'll do."

Julie poured herself more water and passed the pitcher around.

"You could start a blog, writing about things you love."

Darla could tell that Inês wasn't into that. She was set on grad school. Inês shrugged.

"Who would read my work? It's not really for the public."

"You never know," Darla and Julie said at once.

"You Americans!" Inês laughed. "Always so optimistic."

Chapter Thirty-Three

————

One day after class, she sat in a park. She made quick sketches of children kicking a ball nearby. The doctor had said the pill would take effect in three weeks, so they had to use protection in the meantime. Darla relished the idea of unprotected sex with André. So free. So sexy to not have to worry about getting pregnant. She turned to the other thing she worried over: telling her mom she'd moved to Lisbon.

Darla checked the time, then dialed. The interminable ringing before her mom finally answered.

"Hello! It's early. You must be calling before work."

"Hi, Mom, how's it going?"

"Oh, you know, the usual. About to play bridge."

"How's Henry?"

"He's out for his morning walk. What about you, how's it going? Happy to be back in Boulder?"

Darla wanted to follow up about Henry, but she might as well rip the Band-Aid off.

"I'm not in Boulder, Mom. I'm in Lisbon."

"What? Lisbon?"

"Yea, I, well, I didn't come home. I stayed here."

"When are you coming back?"

"I don't know . . . I, I met someone."

A beat, then her mom cleared her throat.

"That's unexpected. I thought a break from Gregory would

bring you to your senses."

One of the kids' balls bounced over to Darla. She kicked it back, waving at the little boy who ignored her and resumed playing. She took a deep breath, glad for the pause.

"Mom, I'm happy here. Happier than I have ever been. I never felt this way about Gregory."

There was a long pause. She heard her mom muffled, talking to someone on her end. Henry must be back from his walk. Darla's enthusiasm drained away. She sat on the bench, limp with her mom's disinterest in her life. The kids' shouting intensified. It didn't seem like an adult was attending them. Her mom came back on the line.

"Sorry, that was a delivery." She sighed. "Well, I don't know how to take this news. You already were so far away in Boulder."

"Maybe you'll come visit me and André."

"Who's André? A Frenchman you met in Paris?"

"No, Mom, he's my boyfriend. He's Portuguese, and we live together in Lisbon. I'm not coming back."

She stood, hoping to end the call and escape the shouting kids.

"Okay . . . well, I'm glad you're happy."

She reached the edge of the park and entered the city.

"Mom, I wanted to ask you about my father."

"Mmm?"

"What was he like? How did you meet?"

There was a pause. The suspense was agony. Darla had never had the courage to ask about her father. She'd convinced herself that the unit she and her mom made was enough. Her mom hadn't seemed to need her father, so she wouldn't either. Her mom sighed.

"At a wedding. I was there with a friend, and he was solo. I saw him during dinner and couldn't help but notice his pink tie. It really stood out." She laughed, and the sound brought her mom straight into Darla's heart.

"Then he asked me to dance. He was so tall I wasn't sure how it would go. But we danced that first dance and never stopped. By the end of the night, I just wanted to be with him all the time. He had such charisma."

Darla could imagine her mom and some tall, handsome stranger getting together in the romantic glow of a wedding.

"How long were you together before I was born?"

Another pause.

"Not so long," she said. Darla was afraid to ask, but she suspected she'd been conceived at that wedding. She shifted gears.

"Am I like him?"

No answer. She pressed on.

"I mean personality-wise."

A deep sigh reached Darla, then her mom spoke.

"I think you are. He was so adventurous. I loved that about him. But that's why he couldn't stay around. He had to go find the next thing."

Darla could hear the pain in her mom's voice, even as she tried to sound breezy about it. How much it must have hurt her mom to lose him.

"Moi, adventurous?"

"Of course you are, silly. You lived in New York and then moved to Boulder. Now you're in Europe, which doesn't seem the wisest move to me, but hey, I'm not you."

Darla's eyes burned with sudden tears. She and her mom had been so self-reliant. She hadn't given much time to thinking about her father. She'd kept her curiosity locked up rather than face the pain of being abandoned. All the time she'd spent saving money, staying with a dull job, wanting a solid relationship she could rely on, she'd been following her mom's practical steps. Now it was time to dance to her dad's rhythm. It didn't make her less mad at him for abandoning her mom, but it somehow gave her courage.

"You know what, this is weird. I think your father's father was Portuguese. He grew up in California, and I remember something about his family being of Portuguese descent."

Darla considered this. "Maybe I'm in my fatherland, then. What was his name?"

"Tom Silva."

"But you weren't married, so you didn't take his name."

"I'd love to tell you more, Darla, but honestly, there isn't much to say."

"Mom, you were so brave to raise me on your own. I don't think I ever thanked you for all you did to make sure we were okay."

"Oh, Darla, that's what mothers do." Darla could hear the tears in her voice.

"Thanks, Mom. I gotta go now. I'll send you an email with my address."

They signed off. Darla's eyes stung. She knew her mom well and suspected the call would go like this. But still, every time, a twinkle of hope glimmered around the edges. Maybe her mom would see her for who she was and not a mini her.

The children's play cries now felt like something else to Darla—loud, desperate pleas for attention. It was too loud, much too loud, but Darla was pinned to the bench. Her breath came in fast and hard, like she was the one running around after a ball, screaming. Oh no, oh no, she thought. She put her head down, panting into her lap. Why had she asked about her father now? What good did that do? Her thoughts chased her heartbeat in a desperate race to right. She forced herself to take a few deep breaths. Finally, she calmed down. What had happened to her? Why so emotional all the time? Was this the cost of courage? Darla wasn't sure she could take it. The children had left the playground. Darla headed toward home.

In the Jardim do Torel, she paused under the shade of the giant trees. A Lisbon breeze washed over her. This was one of her favorite views. She took a bench and did a quick sketch. Savoring the view and settling into her sketchbook helped push away her disappointment from the call with her mom.

One night, they took the train to Cascais for dinner with one of André's friends. It was late when they alighted in the seaside town. Darla delighted in the narrow streets, the mellow beach feel. They walked along a row of upscale shops, and she realized Cascais was fancier than Lisbon. At a modern apartment building, André pressed one of the buzzers. A crackly voice came from the speaker. André responded, a big smile flushing his words with delight. The buzzer sounded, and they made their way inside and up the elevator.

A young man waited for them, holding the door open.

"André!"

The two embraced, sharing big smiles. André introduced her to Raoul. He gave Darla air kisses and welcomed her.

"Come, come," he said, stepping aside to let them in. Inside, they met his wife, Maria, and their baby, Rosa. They exchanged air kisses and hellos. Raoul welcomed them into the living room, and Maria took Rosa into the kitchen. She was making dinner for them. It smelled great, the familiar odor of garlic and onions. Darla offered to help, but Maria shooed her out of the kitchen. She joined André in the living room. The TV was on. Raoul brought drinks in—Negronis. André and Raoul chatted in Portuguese. She sipped her drink, sketched the orange slice in her glass, and occasionally glanced at the TV. It seemed to be a drama. Suddenly, the scene shifted to a sex scene. A rather graphic sex scene. She peeked at the guys, but they were chatting and didn't notice. She squirmed and sipped her drink. She didn't think of herself as a prude, but it wasn't what she'd expect on TV. She'd only seen the news at home with André and wondered what else she'd been missing on Portuguese television.

At dinner, André sat next to Rosa. He flirted with the toddler, winking and smiling and doing goofy little waves. She giggled and stared, entranced by his attention.

The age difference between Darla and André suddenly became super sharp. He wanted children, she thought. Of course he did. He hadn't admitted it when the condom broke. She didn't want children, certainly not after forty. But did André? The way he fawned over Rosa made it obvious. The ground under their relationship slid away, and she saw it for what it was—temporary. How could she think of making plans to live in Europe with André? Dinner passed in a numb blur as she tried to get past what she felt to be the truth. She pretended to smile and be engaged. She complimented Maria on the food, but the conversation stalled there.

After dinner, Maria went to tuck Rosa into bed. They stepped onto the balcony to have a spliff. She couldn't deny that the hash helped her in these social settings. It seemed that smoking together bonded her with others more easily. She was starting to wonder about all the smoking. She and André sometimes smoked just cigarettes together, rollies. She'd never been a smoker, never wanted to. But now it seemed right, necessary even.

They moved to the living room, where Raoul brought beers. Darla got out her sketchbook and drew the scene, André and Raoul caught up in Portuguese. In a high haze it was easy to tune them out and get sucked into her sketchbook.

Around midnight, they said goodbye to Raoul and headed back to Lisbon. At the station, waiting for the train back to Lisbon, Darla worked up her courage.

"They were nice," she said.

André nodded, distracted, looking at his phone.

"Are a lot of your friends having babies?"

She wasn't sure he heard her, but after a long, painful minute, he pulled his attention away from his phone. He looked at the sky instead of at her.

"I haven't counted."

"You don't need to count."

"Well, I guess, yes, people are having babies."

She wanted to talk about children but had no idea how. She didn't want to be a mother. The thought of having a child with André was like imagining life on another planet.

He shrugged. It was clear to Darla he didn't want to have this conversation.

"Well, we're on birth control, so that's not something we need to think about," she said.

She gave up and gazed out the window. Her eyes adjusted to the night sky. Her dad was out there in the world somewhere. Or maybe he wasn't. She hadn't told André or Julie about her father. She didn't feel the lack of a father. She'd lived with her mom as her sole anchor forever. Still, she had heard about people getting visas based on heritage, relatives from the country you wanted to relocate to. She shrugged. She was finally finding her own path. She didn't want to search for another man.

Chapter Thirty-Four

André studied for weeks for his exam, using a small book and doing practice tests. Darla felt like they were both students again. At the beach, he'd read the exam book while she moved through chapters of her language book. A few times a week, they'd meet after work for a drink. A plaza near the city center became their go-to. Lined with trees and filled with tables, this was an easy place to relax and connect before going home or out to dinner. André always looked so great when coming from work, his jacket open, his gait assured. Darla practiced her Portuguese. But the waitress got the same look on her face that many Portuguese people got when she spoke Portuguese—a look of pain. She hated this but bravely plunged on, repeating her order and insisting that this repetition would change their expression and bring clarity.

Darla ordered Vinho Verde and André an espresso.

"Doesn't that keep you awake at night?" She gestured to his coffee.

"Do you not sleep with me? Can't you tell I sleep all night?"

This both made sense and didn't. If she were asleep, how would she know if André was awake? But it was also true that he didn't seem to have any problem getting to sleep.

"I couldn't do that. I can't drink caffeine after noon, or I won't sleep as well." André shook his head. The concept of drinking or eating anything to alter a mood or generate energy seemed completely foreign to him. She pressed on.

"People drink coffee to get a high or a buzz, to energize themselves."

André shrugged. "I drink it for the pleasure of it."

After they finished their drinks, she got ready to bring up birth control. Before she could, André rustled in his bag and handed her a wrapped package. A surprise! She bounced a bit in her chair. The label was from a fancy pen shop. She peeled away the wrapping. In the box nestled a fountain pen. An even better pen than the one she'd lost in Sintra. Tears flooded her eyes. Why was he so thoughtful sometimes? She gave him a quick hug.

Later at home, he put out some *queijo*. Darla put her hand on his arm. "I need to dial back the dairy," she said.

"What's that?"

"What's what?"

"Dairy?"

Darla pulled back in disbelief.

"Milk products, like cheese or milk or yogurt. From cows or sheep or goats."

He still didn't get it. Darla finally had to drop it. The concept of focusing on a healthy diet was completely foreign to him. He seemed more prickly than usual. In the kitchen, she checked in.

"Is something wrong?"

He didn't look at her, bent over the cutting board with the knife.

"Nothing is wrong."

She tried to give him space and did her homework on the couch. But while making dinner, he pulled open the silverware drawer.

"What's this? Darla!"

"What?" She approached him.

"The forks. Line them up. They're just in there all messy."

Darla saw the chaos in the silverware drawer for the first time. She wasn't a slob, but she wasn't a neatnik either. Apparently, André was.

"Okay," she said, "I didn't know that mattered."

"Everything matters," he asserted, as if confident that his way to move through the world was the best way. She tried not to take it personally. She was learning the ways of the Portuguese and the ways of André. This was normal relationship stuff. But she couldn't help but feel that everything she did was just a touch not right for André.

Later, in bed, after perfunctory sex, he opened up.

"I did not pass the exam."

"What?" She hadn't known he'd taken it. Darla wanted to press for details, but she knew he'd tell her in his own way. "What happened?"

He shook his head.

"Well, that sucks."

"I will get it. I can retake it, but I have to learn a new program."

"You can do it!" she said, squeezing his arm.

He sat up in bed, the light from the French doors highlighting his chest.

"I don't need you to cheer me on," he said. "I don't like that."

Darla was confused. Who didn't like being encouraged? She was glad he couldn't see her face.

He jumped out of bed, striding around the room. His cock waved back and forth, tapping against his thighs.

"Listen," he said, "at university I studied engineering. The teachers shouted at us, told us we were shit. They swore at us. They pushed us—pushed us hard. They never said 'yay' or 'good job.' It wasn't like that. We didn't need soft encouragement; we needed toughness."

"Wow," Darla said, "that sucks. That sounds rough."

"It was. But that's normal," he said. "Teachers are tough here. They don't give praise. They think that's weak."

Darla believed in the sandwich method of feedback. First, you say something encouraging and positive about the work. Then you share what you think could improve. You finish with encouragement. She had tested this many times, also trying the opposite. The "bread" of the sandwich—the encouragement—allowed the other feedback to be received more easily. She knew that people tend to focus on the negative, and that could end up dissuading someone from going forward. She'd seen the difference a few kind words made. She explained this to him, but André blew it off.

"My teachers at engineering school would never say something like that. It was only telling us what was wrong with our thinking and how we needed to be better."

Darla felt something harden in her stomach. This kind of critical teaching seemed so wrong to her. Who would thrive under those conditions? She imagined that was what it would be like to be in the military—any individualism or sense of pride in progress knocked aside for the sake of toughening you up. But she had some experience with that kind of rigor.

"I get it," she said. "The nuns were tough on us too." But she'd hated it. And what had it gotten her? A lifetime of jobs she hadn't really wanted. The ability to sustain some level of sanity in near-abusive work environments. Even if she didn't know what she was going to do for her career, she had to believe that she was in a better place now. And that was because of love, and kindness, and generosity. Because of Lauren and her love for life and for Darla. But André didn't want any of that soft stuff.

"*Tudo bem*," André said. "I am me because of that. I am succeeding because of that."

He seemed to take this rigor as a matter of pride. Like kindness or encouragement were weak, something only soft Americans needed. She tried not to take it personally. She found these cultural disparities interesting. If every country were the same, the world would be boring. She had moved to Europe to have a different experience than in the US, but that didn't mean she had to adopt all of what was offered.

"Come back to bed," she said. But he was pulling on his tight undies.

"I come back." He went upstairs, and Darla heard him boot up his computer. She smelled smoke coming through the French doors. She rolled onto her stomach, hugging the pillow.

⁂

One Saturday, after a swim, they lay on the beach, and he drilled her. His method was to repeat the words close to her ear so she really heard them.

"Twowla." He pointed to the beach towel.

"Twowla," she repeated. The tickle of his lips sent a shiver across her bare skin.

"Twoowla."

"Twoowla."

He shook his head. Reshaped his mouth.

"Twowla."

"Twowla."

After ten versions, Darla wanted to slap him. With each repetition, André tore a thread of her confidence away and tossed it to the sea wind. She sat up and pulled on her cover up.

"Listen, André, 100 percent accuracy in pronunciation isn't possible. I will always have an accent, and that's okay."

He frowned. "You can do it. You have to try."

"It's not that I'm not trying," she insisted, getting tripped up in her double negatives. "Striving for perfection is just shutting me down. It's making me not want to learn."

André shrugged and picked up his book. She took his silence as a reproach. That she was being a weak and spoiled American. She shrugged. They were different in this way. It was okay; they had plenty in common.

They were on the bus home when André made an announcement. Night had fallen, and she was sleepy, content.

"I will go home this weekend," he said, glancing at her.

"Home?" She sat up.

"To Aveiro. I'm going to see my parents."

Of course he would invite her along. They'd been together every night since she'd arrived in Lisbon, and she was used to his company.

"That's great!"

She wasn't sure what was so great about it, but she couldn't help but try to be positive.

"I have some things to get from home," he said.

A lump in her throat made it hard to talk. Her face flushed, and she was grateful he had his back turned. She squawked out, "Okay. When?"

"I leave Friday after work. I'll be back Sunday night."

She wished she had her pen, but what fool can draw in

the dark? She took a deep breath. She couldn't ask. She didn't want to ask. But why wouldn't he invite her? What would she do without him? This was the first time she couldn't look at André. He didn't seem to notice that she'd shut down, and when they got back to their apartment, it was as if nothing had happened. She tucked the pain away and pretended it hadn't stabbed her. She tried to look on the bright side. She liked spending time alone. She was perfectly self-sufficient. She could do more painting and catch up with Cat.

On Friday afternoon, she sat in her studio while André packed. It wasn't too late for him to change his mind and ask her along. She worked up the nerve to say something.

"What will you do in Aveiro?"

He avoided her eyes. "Eat my mom's cooking. See some friends."

"That sounds fun. Maybe someday I'll meet your parents." She couldn't help it. She hated having to invite herself. It seemed obvious that she would meet his parents. Maybe they didn't speak English as well as André. Maybe they didn't know he was with someone almost their age. Maybe they didn't know about her at all.

"Someday," he said.

He finished packing and tucked his phones into his jeans pockets.

"I will text you. I will let you know when I will be home Sunday."

"Sure," Darla said.

They kissed goodbye. She closed the door behind him, its heavy lock clicking. His steps faded down the spiral staircase. Soon it was totally silent, completely still. Drifting into the living room, relief flooded in. Something unhooked, and she felt more herself than since she left home. Pausing by the window, she let the view in. She hadn't noticed how tense she was around André. Like she was going to mess up somehow. She turned on music. "Everyone Needs an Editor" blasted through the apartment while she cleaned. A basket near the bathroom held a load of clothes André had washed but not dried. Darla was tempted to hang them to dry, but she knew better than to touch his clothes. They would molder there until he got home on Sunday. Now she knew why, though he was always impeccably clean, a whiff of mildew followed him around. Later, she ate dinner at the little table in their room, reading her book. Soon, loneliness invaded the empty flat. She roamed around, turning off lights and closing the home down for the day. She lingered in their spots—by the French doors, the bed, the mezzanine beanbag.

At the kitchen window in the dark, she brushed her teeth. She felt particularly alone, removed not just from André's company but from the world. Boulder and all her friends were far, far away. But this wasn't a new experience for Darla. Even in Boulder, this loneliness had been part of her everyday life. Friday nights were particularly tough. Darla imagined everyone else was out doing something fun to celebrate the end of the week. Her loneliness shadowed her as she rinsed and washed her face, bent over the sink.

She crawled into bed with her novel. The bedside light cast an embrace that kept the rest of the room in shadow. The ceiling seemed to soar higher without André.

Chapter Thirty-Five

——

The bright Saturday morning chased away the night's gloom. Sunlight blanketed her where she sprawled in the bed. She lingered, soaking up the feeling of no time, no schedule.

With a fresh coffee in her studio, she noodled in her sketchbook. She got into making a series of her coffee pot and her new IKEA coffee cup and saucer. Each one had a little story accompanying it. A few hours passed before she realized she was hungry and stiff from sitting in the chair so long.

Downstairs, she gobbled a yogurt with muesli. She had to get out. It was so cozy here at home, quiet and peaceful. Taking up all the space, with no one watching or judging, felt so splendid. It occurred to her that she was finally feeling okay with a day that had no agenda, no tasks, no purpose. But the city called her too.

Discovering new things in Lisbon was exhilarating. Her gait had changed, adapting to the uneven terrain of the cobblestone sidewalks. Even in her Fly London shoes, she could navigate the paths that regularly tossed tourists to the ground. She put on some music and got ready to go. "All I Need" by Radiohead fit the mellow morning, and she crooned along as she got dressed. She'd hit up the organic market. Bring her sketchbook.

Lisbon was quiet on a Saturday morning. The Avenida offered a cool, shady haven. Up a few hills and into the park at Príncipe Real, farmers set up organic fruits and vegetables. Shoppers strolled through the market, pulling trolleys and chatting. The air was cool, and birds sang in the tree canopy. Darla soaked up the mellow vibe, happy to be part of it all. She cruised the row, taking note of prices, who had what, and what she wanted to buy. Bunches of buxom, wavy chard. Adorable yellow patty pan squash. Fat bundles of parsley, mint, basil. A few stalls sold prepared foods like bread and jars of preserves and pickles. A second pass brought her into contact with the vendors. She practiced her Portuguese, but most communication was done by pointing. Before long, her string bag bulged with fresh produce. She hauled it to the café in the park.

At a table outside, she ordered coffee and set up to sketch. All of the produce she bought looked abundant when laid out on the table. Across a spread in her sketchbook, she drew each item. Cucumber. Basil. Lettuce. She got out her mini palette and water brush and brought the line drawings to life with color. She added the Portuguese words: *pepino, manjericão, alface*, checking her mini dictionary for accurate spelling.

Someone passed by. She sensed them stop behind her. Glancing up, she caught the eye of a man smiling at her pages.

"*Muito legal*," he said in Portuguese. She had no idea what that meant. Legal? Did he know she was here illegally? Darla swallowed, wishing she and her sketchbook could disappear. How to respond? He was smiling, so she smiled back.

"*Muito obrigada*." She tried to see her pages from his perspective. The vegetables did have a life with shadows under each item that gave depth to the page. Before leaving, she treated herself to a bouquet of mixed wildflowers.

Back home, she put the market booty away. She arranged the flowers and put fresh herbs in ceramic cups on the counter.

She didn't feel like doing housework. Maybe more art time? She did a few breezy sketches of her kitchen, with the fresh herbs and gorgeous flower bouquet. The scent of basil and mint and chives stimulated her in more ways than one. Soon she was hungry. She took a light lunch up to her studio.

Flipping through her sketchbook, she liked the way her drawings were taking shape. Today's market illustration startled her with how professional it looked. She made some notes on each one. An idea struck her. She pulled out one of her blank postcards made from watercolor paper. She dove in. She painted the bench at the mirador and wrote a fun little description of it. "If by chance you find an empty mirador bench, befriend it immediately. What you lose in time will be gained in a priceless Lisbon moment."

It was getting too hot to be in the mezzanine. Downstairs, she slathered on sunscreen, grabbed her bag, and headed out. Walking down Rua São José, she wondered about selling the cards. Originals or prints? She had no idea how to get the cards printed. Mostly she relished the idea of having a specific project, something alongside the sketchbook.

Wandering around, she honored only her impulses. She followed her instinct around the city, stopping here and there to sketch. A set of stairs with twinkly lights draped over them. A wall of street art. Her sketchbook was peppered with graffiti imitations. Copying the funky lettering gave her ideas for her own lettering style. The letters were usually angular and architectural. Every other page in her sketchbook had at least a thumbnail drawing of a street mural. She liked copying the style of layers, colors, and shapes that people adorned Lisbon with. She liked tracing the image of a stencil art into her white page with a black charcoal pencil. They mussed up the page a bit with black soot, but she had finally accepted that. Her sketchbook was messy, of the moment, in response to the world around her. It was a place where she didn't have to be good or in control. It took a couple of months to realize that, but when she did, she knew that sketching was an everyday part of her sanity.

She noticed everything, all the patterns and colors filling her with desire to put it all in her art. The electric lines of the trams crisscrossing the space above the sidewalks. She hopped on the less-popular #13 tram, enjoying the rocking and swaying along the city's curves and hills. Suddenly, the driver had stopped at the bottom of a hill. He stepped out, and Darla groaned. Craning back, she saw the driver behind the tram, taking a hold of the line connecting the tram to the line above. Oh no, she thought, we've lost connection to our power. Suddenly, an idea came to mind, and she quickly tucked it into her sketchbook. The driver just shook the line a couple of times and got back in the tram. He turned the crank, released the brake, and they set off again up the hill.

A text came in from Julie.

Wanna get a drink?

Sure!

They made plans to meet. The feeling of having a friend, the pleasure of an unexpected date, gave her the sense that she was living a good life here in Lisbon. Back in Boulder, everything had to be scheduled so far in advance. Her friends had to arrange childcare; everyone had their workouts they needed to get in; and life just felt so overcomplicated and overscheduled. It was really working out for her here in Lisbon, and she sent a cosmic wink to Lauren, thanking her for the nudge toward Portugal.

She made her way to Chiado, where she found Casa Ferreira. The sign outside boasted art supplies and classes. Inside, the store was small but cozy. Brushes and pens neatly lined the shelves, and the smell of paper filled the air. She bought some watercolor cards and splurged on a couple of new paint tubes. Art supplies would be a write-off if she started selling things. She kept the receipt.

Abuzz with the particular joy that comes from buying art supplies, Darla stopped at a tiny café near the Santa Catarina mirador. The outdoor space of the restaurant formed a pointy space that jutted out from the door of the restaurant. Straddling two streets, the little patio was packed with tables, chairs, and umbrellas. Waiting for Julie, Darla sipped Vinho Verde and drew in her sketchbook. Sitting there was like being on the prow of a ship. Popular in her pages were drawings of a wineglass and their decanter. She was just getting the radical curve of it, the color of the wine lining the bodacious bottom. And coffee cups! Sitting in Lisbon's cafés and *pastelerias* gave her and her sketchbook plenty of time and space to capture cups. When she flipped through this sketchbook, she liked what she saw. Her style was emerging. Using Lisbon's color palette almost exclusively had given her colors an order, a meaning. She was a much better artist than when she had left Boulder. Being in Lisbon was good for that at least.

"*Olá chica!*" Julie squeezed through the tables and chairs. Darla stood for a cheek kissing.

"*Tudo bem?*" She had her pat Portuguese phrases, but they slipped to English right away. Julie sat, and Darla poured her some wine.

"Ahhh," she said. "It's been a day."

"What are you up to?"

"It's been a great weekend," she said. "André is away visiting his family, so I've enjoyed having time to myself. Thanks for the invite—it's great to be spontaneous."

She didn't tell Julie about the relief she'd felt when André left. She didn't like to admit to herself that being alone now felt better than being with him. She couldn't open that curtain of what that might mean for their relationship.

Julie asked about André, where he was from, and what he was doing back home. Darla felt a distinct suspicion under her queries.

"What are you thinking?"

Julie shrugged, stalled by sipping her wine.

"Have you met his parents?"

"No, I want to. He seems a little squirrely about it."

"Hm," Julie said. All the tables around them were now full, and a liveliness sprung up on the terrace. Glasses clinked; Portuguese formed a soundscape around them. The waiter moved deftly through the crowded space, his tray held aloft.

"You? Of course you've met Rui's parents."

"Yes, right away. I think he wanted to convince them he could find a professional woman and not just another hippy." She did air quotes around professional.

"Did they like you?"

"Not immediately. You know how people are with their children. No one is good enough. But soon enough they saw that Rui and I are great together. They saw how happy he is with me."

Darla wondered what André's parents were like. She didn't think that he looked so happy with her. Not like in the early days. Not like when they'd first met.

"Do you plan to get married?"

Julie looked away, as if losing herself in the scene around them.

"Who knows? We have only been together for a year."

Darla wanted more certainty. She wanted someone for whom it was working out. It was working out with André, she insisted to herself. Julie spoke up.

"I don't mean to be a jerk, but I am surprised André didn't bring you home with him."

A sting of doubt pricked Darla's consciousness, supporting what she had thought.

"Right? I thought so too."

"What did he say?"

"Nothing! He acted like it was perfectly normal for him to go without me. And it is," Darla insisted. "It's good to have time apart. My ex and I didn't even live in the same city. It worked great to get together a couple times a week."

"How'd that work out for you?"

Darla winced.

"Sorry, I didn't mean it like that," Julie said.

"Honestly, I was pretty bummed when he didn't invite me. I made up all kinds of reasons he didn't want to bring me into his home world. But when he left, I started to enjoy the solitude."

"Damn straight," Julie said. "Enjoy some girl time."

Darla nodded, wanting to be reassured, but she wasn't.

"Anything planned for tonight?"

"Nothing at all," Darla replied.

"Want to come to a concert? We're sponsoring a live painting event during the show. One of our visiting artists does this all around the world. I can't wait to see her in action."

Darla perked up. "That sounds cool!"

"It is cool. She's cool. Aria. She's a muralist who has painted so many spots all over the world. She also does these live events. I've never seen her in action but have heard great things."

"Wow. I can't imagine painting a mural—or painting live in front of a crowd."

"You should come! I can get you on the guest list." Julie gave her the details.

Chapter Thirty-Six

Darla showed up at the venue around sunset. A crowd was gathering at the barrier of the park. She joined the group funneling toward the gate. She gave her name to the woman checking tickets, who waved her over to a guy holding a clipboard.

Inside, she texted Julie, who'd be working but had said she could get her a good spot near the stage. The park was crowded, people gathering on the lawn in front of the stage. The buzz coursed through Darla. She couldn't remember the last concert she'd been to. Outside like this, it felt easier to bear the crowd. Plumes of smoke from spliffs floated above the crowd.

After milling about for a few, she found Julie. They cheek kissed. Julie was flushed, excited and distracted. She was using a walkie-talkie to coordinate with her coworkers. The live painting experience was only one of the things Paint the World was hosting. Seeing Julie in action inspired Darla. This was no desk job. She couldn't imagine ever being bored.

The crowd got denser as it grew darker. Julie led Darla to a hilly spot near the stage.

"This is where you'll best see the artist. There she is now, setting up."

Behind the roadies checking the instruments on stage was a woman also setting up. She wore light blue coveralls and a white tank top, with a baseball cap turned backward. The artist had a rack of paint cans she was opening. An array of brushes hung on a peg board to the side.

"Hey, Rui is here! Do you want to hang out with him and his friend Tiago? I will be mostly backstage and working the interactive event."

"What interactive event?"

"We have a group art project where people can paint a giant canvas. It's over by the food trucks."

"Wow, you're doing cool things here, Julie!"

Julie smiled.

"Thanks! I gotta run now. Can I give Rui your number so you can connect with him?"

"Sure."

Darla watched while the artist set up. A giant canvas stretched behind the band. The night air was cool on Darla's neck. She saw the artist off to the side of the stage, getting ready, stretching, bouncing on her toes like a boxer. Then she stilled and closed her eyes. Darla could see her chest moving up and down as if she were breathing deeply. Her lips moved. Was she meditating? Chanting? Darla was transfixed, absorbed in the artist's process.

Her phone pinged. Rui. He was near. Soon Darla was meeting two young Portuguese men. They cheek kissed. She warmed to Rui right away, glad to finally meet Julie's lover. Darla lost track of the artist while chatting with Tiago and Rui. Someone passed a spliff. She almost took a puff before she realized she didn't want it. She was more than happy as she was. Before long, a guy took the mic and riled up the crowd. In Portuguese he introduced the artist, who ran on stage, waving. She took up her paintbrush and stood near the canvas. The musicians came on in a spray of colored lights. A moment of quiet, the sky above holding it all, the crowd now packing the space in front of the stage, Darla in the middle of it all.

The music started, a power blast of sound and energy. Instantly the crowd was moving along with the music. The artist also sprang into action. She dipped her brush in a paint can and gestured along the canvas. A sploosh of turquoise fanned across the white space. She bent and twisted, adding more paint, using so many brushes and colors. With every song, the painting developed. Darla danced with Tiago and Rui but kept watching the art unfold. She lost track of time and thought. At one point she closed her eyes, moving with the sound, happily lost in the rhythm. When she opened her eyes, the painting behind the band seemed complete. While watching it she hadn't been able to track what it was. But coming to it with fresh eyes, she saw it was an ocean scene. Sea life flowing along a blue background. Coral, starfish, octopi, and eels. How had she done that?

The band finished with an enormous crescendo. The crowd lost it, arms in the air, waving, dancing, cheering. Darla joined in, blissed out. Tiago and Rui both had huge grins. She caught Tiago's eye. He smiled and bent down to speak near her ear.

"Amazing, isn't she?"

She shook her head in disbelief. "How did she do that?! I was watching the whole time but now . . ."

"She's a magician," Tiago said. "And she does a loose drawing on the canvas before painting."

"Ahhhhh . . ." Darla now understood the rough sketch that Aria had filled in during the show. Rui leaned over.

"Want to go backstage and meet the artist?"

Darla both wanted to and didn't. What would she say?

"*Vamos*," Tiago said.

She followed them through the dispersing crowd. The roadies were on the stage, winding cords and dissembling the equipment. Aria tended her materials, putting her brushes in a big bucket and snapping lids on the paint cans. She exuded positivity. Darla gazed at the canvas up close. She could only say, "Wow, wow, wow," to herself. Several people lingered, and she talked while she worked. Darla and her friends approached. Aria noticed them and flashed a big smile.

"Tiago!"

She gave him a big American embrace, no formal cheek kissing. Tiago hugged her back, then introduced her to Darla.

"That was . . . wow. Amazing." Darla wished she had better words. But also, what she'd experienced was beyond words. The blend of music and painting had transfixed her in a way she'd never experienced.

Aria shone, her face and chest glistening with sweat. But her eyes and smile were also lit up. Darla was certain she'd never seen anyone so alive, vibrating with life.

She mostly listened while Tiago and Aria chatted. She helped Aria carry her stuff off stage. Before they left, she got Aria's card.

"Follow me on Pinterest," she told Darla. For once, Darla had a real reason to spend time on Pinterest.

They connected with Julie and made a move for drinks. They ended up in a rooftop bar in Cais do Sodre. Darla was tired but also hopped up on the energy she'd felt at the concert. She scanned Aria's Instagram profile while waiting for drinks. So many murals. Such great, big beauty.

Drinks arrived, and they toasted with bubbly wine to celebrate the successful event. Darla asked how they found artists like Aria. Tiago explained their process.

"What a cool organization," she said. "How long have you worked there?"

"Since they opened the Lisbon office. I was one of the first ones on the team here. Then came Julie."

Darla asked questions about their work, and Tiago shared some of the initiatives Paint the World was planning. It all sounded so exciting, and Darla envied the camaraderie and creativity they found at work. Later, the women went to the bathroom. In line, Julie dropped some news.

"I don't want to announce it publicly yet, but Rui and I are engaged."

Darla squealed.

"That's fantastic! *Parabéns!*"

They hugged. News like this gave Darla hope. An international couple *could* work out. Rui and Julie were proof. Julie's eyes sparkled.

"I wonder if you would do the art for our wedding invitation."

Darla shook her head. Certainly she'd misunderstood.

"What?! That's crazy. This is your wedding. You can't have some janky sketch on your invite! You should find a pro."

"But we want you. We want your janky sketches. We both agree, your art will be perfect for our invitation."

Darla shook her head, eyes wide.

"I guess . . . I mean . . . you'll tell me what you want, right?"

"Of course, silly. It's going to be great."

They hugged. Back with the others, Darla felt completely lit up from inside, but different than when she'd first arrived in Lisbon and was alight with fear. They stayed for a while, longer than Darla would normally. It was easy to hang out, chat, and get to know Tiago and Rui. Mostly Tiago, who was also an artist. They showed each other their work on their phones, swapping stories and sharing their mini galleries.

On her walk home, Darla soaked up the feeling of connection. She was starting to make friends here. Keying into their apartment, she realized she hadn't thought about André for hours.

Chapter Thirty-Seven

Darla was up early on Sunday. Making coffee, she replayed the evening—Aria's breathtaking performance and art, how good it felt to dance, and then Tiago, fun to dance and chat with. She immersed herself in her studio, getting out her new supplies and setting up to experiment. It didn't take long to get lost in the exploration. She dove into the colors and shapes, all the tools and possibilities, a sort of out-of-time escape from her reality. She was far from André, far from home, in her own zone. She could decide what to do, for how long, and how. It was a welcome change from her time with André. A noticeable change. She was less confused when she was on her own. She wouldn't have noticed it if he hadn't been away for a few nights.

She took a break to check online. An email came in with a curious subject line. She skimmed past then scrolled back. Was this another spam? It was from the cooking school in Paris where she'd taken the *gougères* class. She read it twice. Patricia, the owner of the school, was following up on the illustration Darla had done during the class. Would she be interested in selling that to her and perhaps doing more?

Darla read through it twice, not believing what she was reading. Paid art commission? She surely wasn't ready for paid work, but here it was, knocking at her digital door. She pushed back from the desk, stunned and invigorated. Her nervous system pulsed with electric excitement. She ran down the stairs and paced the living room. She jumped into the air and let out a few involuntary yips. She didn't know what to do with all the energy pouring through her. She wanted another coffee, but that seemed like a good and bad idea.

She pinged Cat.

Guess what?!

No reply, so she typed out a brief note relaying Patricia's message. She prepared another coffee. Coffee belonged with every good moment. Even if she couldn't do the gig, she was flattered by the offer. She poured oat milk into a tiny pan and settled a flame under it.

The coffee was burbling out of the spout when her phone pinged.

Cat with an explosion emoji.

Darla sent an emoji chain back.

What should I say? I can't accept . . . not in Paris anymore.

Maybe other ways to do this? Maybe not related to specific events?

Darla pondered, pouring hot oat milk into her cup. Back upstairs in her studio, she found her sketchbook with the cooking class. She'd done a sketch of the cooking school kitchen before class started. Maybe she could play with that. She snapped a photo of that page and texted it to Cat along with her idea. Sipping her coffee, she watched the three dots from Cat pulse on her phone.

That's a great idea! You don't have to be there to do that.

I think I will do a sample to send her.

Send to me too.

Galvanized, Darla got out some of the larger paper she'd bought. She put on Feist and got to it. Pulling up a photo of the cooking school's façade, she sketched that out at the top. She had fun copying the lettering of the school's name and its logo. She emphasized the arches of the store. In the foreground, she placed the chalkboard. It was larger than it was in life, but if displaying the events was the main point, then it should be prominent. Finally, she loosened up and got it sorta right.

After a quick break, she came to the page with fresh eyes. It needed something, but she didn't know what. This was new to her—drawing a scene of sorts. But it somehow worked out. She hadn't been this energized about her art ever. The idea that someone else wanted it and would pay for it was completely new. She responded to Patricia, taking time to craft her counterproposal. She couldn't wait to share the news with André. She kept peeking at the illustration. It wasn't done yet. Maybe she could do this. But if she were going to be a pro artist, she had better learn how to draw people.

Her phone dinged. It was Julie.

Can you come over? Aria is here.

Darla perked up. She'd love the chance to talk with Aria more. And tell them about her new commission.

Darla rang the buzzer at Julie's. Her hand was warm from holding the box of cardamom twists she'd brought. She was hooked on them and thought she probably dropped by Julie's more than necessary just to get the treats from the bakery downstairs.

She arrived at Julie's door and heard the kettle screeching. Julie and Darla exchanged hugs at the door. In the kitchen, Aria stood at the stove, filling a teapot, steam rising around her like she was on stage and this was her big moment.

Light poured from the big window at the end of the narrow room. The smell of tea brewing. A small radio on the
counter played jazz. Darla took a seat at the table, the one with
the view of everything so she could draw it all. She got out her
sketchbook. Aria asked about it, and Darla was modest. She
changed the conversation to Aria's performance. They chatted
about how great the show was, how cool Aria's painting/per-
formance was, and where Aria was going next.

Aria asked what Darla was up to. Darla tried to be nonchalant about her big news.

"I got an art commission from a cooking school in Paris."

"Wow," Julie shouted. "Why didn't you tell me?"

"It just happened!"

"That's cool," Aria exclaimed. "How fun is that?"

Darla wanted it to be fun. She did. But right now, she was
starting to panic.

"I don't know if I can do it! Honestly, I'm freaking out."

"They obviously think you can do it, or they wouldn't have
hired you," Julie stated.

"I can't deny the logic of that." Darla nodded. She took
another pastry. They were small, the size of a walnut. She
could never stop at one.

"But everything doesn't have to be all logic," Aria said.
"Most of my life defies logic. If you had told me when I was in
high school that I would be traveling around the world painting and collaborating with other artists, I would have laughed
you right out of Oklahoma."

"Same," Julie chimed in. "I never imagined being in the
arts in Lisbon."

"But I don't mean just sit around and wait. I'm sure you
knew some of what you wanted, Julie. I always knew I wanted

to paint. But I never imagined that I would be a muralist. I just knew I wanted to make art and travel. And meet interesting people like you both."

They sipped their tea. Darla doodled, her mind following new trains of thought.

"But did you have a plan?"

Aria laughed. "I don't have a plan. I have a magic formula. It's way better."

"Do tell," Julie nudged.

"Three things," Aria said. She held up three fingers and touched each one as she recited her formula. "One. Know what you want. Two. Believe you can have it. Three. Ask for it."

"But what if I don't know what I want?" Darla lamented, circling the page, drawing the cardamom knots. In her sketchbook, she lettered Aria's formula, making the words "Know, Believe, Ask" big and vibrant.

"I think we all know what we want, under the surface. But we usually don't know what it's going to look like," Aria said, pouring more tea all around.

"Wait, how can we know but not know?" Darla asked.

"Like I said, I knew I wanted to be an artist. I knew I wanted to travel. But how was all that going to work out? I had no idea. But here I am, and honestly, my life is beyond what I could have imagined."

Darla was quiet, trying to absorb a philosophy of living that was nothing like her planned, practical life. Julie started tidying up the kitchen.

"Here's my card." Aria handed Darla a square, bright business card. "I've written all about this on my website."

"Cool, thanks." Darla tucked the card into her sketchbook.

"I've got to get to work," Julie announced.

Darla said her goodbyes, cheek kissing them both.

"Good luck with everything, Darla," Aria said. "I'm excited for you and your art."

"Thanks, Aria. I'm excited too. And scared."

"Better to scare yourself doing something you love than to bore yourself doing something you loathe." She winked at Darla.

Julie's phone pinged. Reading the screen, she let out a yelp.

"Inês got in!"

Darla felt a rush of excitement followed by a plummet of disappointment. She would miss her. She and Julie and Inês had a great thing going.

"That's great! So happy for her."

Julie texted. Darla and Aria finished clearing the table.

"We're celebrating with drinks at Noobai this afternoon. Wanna come?"

"I can't, but thanks for the invite," Aria said.

"Of course I'll be there!" Darla didn't know when André would return. But who said she needed to be there when he got home? She headed back to Avenida da Liberdade.

Walking through Lisbon, her body moved with a feeling she'd never experienced. With her red Fly London shoes and a new pair of black cargo pants, she felt invincible. She couldn't recall ever feeling this excited about life. The commission was beyond anything she'd expected when she took up art. Now, a glimmer of possibility grew. Seeing Aria and learning about her art business had given Darla some new ideas. Everything Darla passed she wanted to draw. The bodega with stacks of fruit crates in the doorway. The bottle of Vinho Verde and glasses she saw on a café table. Another idea surfaced; she could lead sketch crawls in Lisbon. She'd heard about groups that wandered around drawing together. Maybe she could lead one. Maybe one focused on foods and drinks.

Later, she met her friends on the rooftop at Noobai. The sun was giving its last blast of heat and light. Darla wished she could capture that light in her sketchbook. Someday. Darla hugged Inês.

"*Parabéns!* This is fantastic!"

Inês grinned. She looked so happy. All Darla's disappointment flew away on the Tejo. She felt cleaner with it gone.

"I can't believe it!"

"Believe it. You earned it, lady," Julie said.

Their Aperol spritzes arrived. They raised their glasses. The sunlight winked off the glass. Darla felt matched—the burst of golden light was exactly how she'd felt walking over.

"When do you leave?"

"In two weeks!"

"Wow, that's fast."

"What will you do with your gorgeous apartment?"

"My cousin Diogo is going to stay there. He just broke up with his girlfriend and needs a fresh start."

Inês told them everything: how she'd heard the news, how the department had helped her find lodging, how her family was both thrilled and dismayed to lose her to New York. Darla didn't feel so guilty now, having mixed feelings. She recognized the same full-body enthusiasm that Inês seemed to have at the thought of moving to another country. She'd settled in here and had lost some of that *zhuzh*. And now, with all the tension with André, she didn't know how long she'd be staying. Maybe this adventure she was on was less about finding her place and more about finding fluidity. She'd spent so long thinking she belonged somewhere else. Maybe she belonged nowhere. Maybe belonging wasn't about a place but about how you moved through the world.

She jotted this idea down in her sketchbook. Maybe another whisper from Lauren. She added the shapes of the Aperol glasses and the suggestion of a seagull dotting the sky over the river.

"We will miss you dearly," she told Inês.

"Come visit!"

Darla had to give a list of her favorite New York restaurants. Lisboetas had been generous with her, giving her tips on their favorite places. She was happy to return the favor to Inês. She made a quick audio note and sent it to Inês. They caught up and ordered food. Darla worked up the nerve to tell them something scary.

"I'm thinking about hosting a sketch crawl! I'm both excited and terrified."

"What's a sketch crawl?"

Darla explained that she'd be leading a two-hour walk through Lisbon for people who wanted to slow down, see more, and practice drawing in their notebooks.

"I would love to come," Julie said.

"That sounds cool!" Inês couldn't make it but wished her good luck.

"It's going to be great," Julie assured her.

She expected André to be back, but when she got home, the apartment was still. Though it was early, she did her bedtime ritual. Tucked into bed, she soaked in the pleasure of good company. It hadn't been easy to make friends in Boulder. She was grateful for their support of her art and the sketch crawl idea. While it seemed doable, she was also terrified. What if it didn't work out? How could she lead a sketch crawl—she'd never even been on one herself. She was trying things, seeing what fit in her new life. Moving to Lisbon had given her a sense of purpose, but that wasn't the whole picture. Just a sketch. She had to fill in the shape and colors of her new life. André wouldn't do that for her. No one could.

Chapter Thirty-Eight

When she told André about the commission, he seemed surprised. It took him a minute to congratulate her. She believed
him when he said he was happy for her. But when she told him
her idea for a sketch crawl, he just nodded and smiled. What
wasn't he saying? But she didn't press him, just kissed him and
waved him off to work.

She spent some time with coffee and Aria's website. Reading her manifesto and her posts about mindset and creative
risks got her so excited, she had to move. She put on Feist and
danced around to "I Feel It All." She loved being able to move
around the entire apartment with no one watching or wondering why she was flinging herself around or why she was dancing in the first place.

Later she borrowed Aria's enthusiasm to bolster her
courage. It didn't take long to set up a meetup on Globalkin.
She wrote a short description, identified a meeting point,
and set a date. She added a few photos of her sketchbook to
give people an idea of what to expect. The next day, Darla
was shocked to see that five people had signed up for the
sketch crawl. She started to get nervous. This was really happening, and André seemed to believe she could do this and
have fun too.

She began preparing. On the map, she traced a way they
might take.

Later that week, she walked the route, identifying spots where they could stop. Lisbon's wide and shallow staircases offered plenty of spots to sit and sketch. Assessing the city for sketch possibilities turned her visual sense up even more. The shapes of the buildings, the typography on signs and etched into cobblestone pavements, the patterns formed by the electric tram lines . . . There were an infinite number of interesting shapes to capture.

The day before the sketch crawl, she checked the event page. What?! Surely there was a mistake. Eighteen people had RSVP'd. Names she didn't recognize along with several she knew. Maybe there were more people like her, tired of spending so much time looking at their phones, hungry to see the world through a more creative lens. Lauren would totally have encouraged her to do this. Somehow, making her art and setting up the sketch crawl made her feel closer to Lauren.

On the day of the event, she couldn't leave the bathroom. André had gone climbing. Her stomach was twisted, and she feared she wouldn't make it to the sketch crawl. She SOS texted Julie.

I think I'm going to vomit.

That's normal.

Julie sent a panic emoji.

You will be great, Darla.

Hearing her name, even on a text, soothed her. If only Julie could be there with her. But she was doing this solo. Solo with eighteen people.

They met at one of her favorite spots, the park in Príncipe Real. She waited at the giant cypress tree, which she thought would be fun to draw. The tree was massive, supported by a circular frame. Underneath the frame, benches formed a ring.

She held open her sketchbook with Globalkin Sketch Crawl drawn in bright bubble letters.

Thank goodness André was climbing. She'd be more nervous if he were there. Soon, her people gathered around, holding their own sketchbooks. She counted fifteen people. She greeted several friends she saw regularly at Globalkin events, grateful to have some known people in the group. She got things underway, trying to hide her nerves.

"Hello, everybody. Olá. Welcome to the sketch crawl!" She introduced herself as a Globalkin fan and a new Lisboeta.

"I'm also a new artist, and I love wandering around a city with my sketchbook. Is this anyone's first time doing a sketch crawl?"

Almost everyone raised their hands.

"Great! You don't need to know much, but I wanted to start with a brief intro about why I'm doing this and what to expect. We'll end up at Rossio, where we can have a drink together."

She paused to take a sip from her water bottle. Peeking at her notes, she took a deep breath.

"I'm not here to teach you how to draw. Instead, our goal is to slow down, tune in to what's around us, and use our senses to capture things in our sketchbook. I hope we can relax, have some fun, and leave our inner critic behind."

A ripple of nervous laughs coursed through the group. She gave a few more guidelines and set everyone a task of sketching the cypress without looking at the page. She set a timer on her phone and started her line in her notebook. In a wink, the timer went off. She had filled her page with lines, forming an abstract rendering of the tree. It didn't really look like a tree, but she liked it. She invited everyone to gather and hold up their sketchbooks. They looked eagerly at others, shyly holding their own notebooks. Darla led a brief discussion, sharing other methods for getting out of thinking mode and into perceiving mode. Then they set out.

Their route led them along quiet side streets. They stopped at a vacant plaza to sketch each other. On another wide set of steps, they spread out to capture a building facade and play with perspective. Finally, at Rossio Square, they took a stab at drawing a giant column statue of Dom Pedro IV. Afterward, they gathered on a café terrace along the square and ordered drinks. Darla led a discussion, eager to hear about their experience.

"How was that for you?"

"It was fun," a woman named Fernanda said. "I loved seeing something appear on my page without thinking about it."

"Magic, huh?" Darla smiled.

"I noticed at first I was uptight, but after a while I relaxed," Ricardo commented.

"Did you notice a difference on your pages?"

He flipped through, paused, smiled.

"Yes, it's clear when I was able to slow down."

"Good to know," Darla said.

Others chimed in, showing specific pages and sharing what they'd learned. Darla was full, inspired, and happy to know they'd had a good time.

"Let's do this again," Keelin, a woman from Ireland requested.

Nods and murmurs from the others confirmed what Darla had felt—this was a big success.

"Sure," Darla smiled. "I'll set a date."

They hung out for a while, talking more about sketching, then moving on to discuss other things. Darla sat back in her chair, content to be surrounded by new friends on a Saturday. She really did feel like kin with these people she'd just met.

She was starting to really love Lisbon. The cobblestone streets, and the way she'd come across small potholes in the sidewalk, the small pieces of stone upturned and lying loose on the ground. The daily sun and the way the light illuminated the trees. The view from her bed of the dome of the Tivoli Theatre with the trees of the botanic gardens behind it. The view from the kitchen of the mini garden oases in people's courtyards. She appreciated how incredibly inexpensive everything was—a coffee or beer under one euro, a glass of wine under two euros. The park in Príncipe Real, with its *quiosque*, where she liked to get a drink and draw. Views of the Tejo caught when she glanced down a street like Bica. The farmer's market on Saturday mornings where she bought bunches of basil for ninety cents. The pastelerias everywhere—thousands of average Joe diner-like restaurants in Lisbon. Living in the center of the city on an incredibly beautiful street. She was able to walk anywhere in a matter of minutes.

She peeked at the pages she'd sketched. At the mirador, she had made another attempt to capture the gorgeous Lisbon skyline with the castle in it. She was surprised to feel that it looked great. She'd captured it, in her own style and palette. When she packed her art supplies, she had no idea she would come this far so quickly with her art. But here she was, in Lisbon of all places. How had Lauren known?

It was all perfect. Except. How would she be able to stay legally?

Chapter Thirty-Nine

That weekend, they went to the beach in the Alentejo for a reunion of André's friends. She wanted to be part of his whole world, not just his Lisbon life. She knew someday she would go to his hometown with him to meet his parents.

The day before they left, André informed her they would host two Globalkins from Germany. They would come to the beach with them and spend the night at their place when they got back to Lisbon. She was hurt he hadn't consulted her. What about the Love Embassy? André wasn't being a very good co-ambassador. Frankly, neither was Darla. They'd been nitpicking each other a lot. She didn't know how to bring it up, and when they were getting along, she didn't want to disturb that peace. Darla didn't want people to see them at odds with each other.

After work on Friday, André's friend João showed up with his car. Tall and handsome, he grabbed André in a close embrace. Darla hadn't seen André smile so much or seem so happy as when they hugged and greeted each other. In a flurry of Portuguese, they caught up while Darla finished packing. Before long, the Globalkins rang the buzzer. They all met downstairs, Darla and André loaded up with their camping gear and backpacks. She was excited to finally go camping.

Darla enjoyed traveling without a lot of baggage. The thrill of her first days in Portugal came back. She thought of who she was when she went to Sintra and Odeceixe with just her string bag. Darla crowded into the backseat with Astrid and Monica, the Globalkins from Germany. They were young—all Globalkins were—and friendly. Buckling up, she savored the sense that she lived in Portugal now, that she took weekend trips with her lover, and the bright day opened ahead of them. It was easier to pretend it was all working out. Darla could ignore the gritty parts on the surface of their relationship. The way they seemed to quibble a lot. She and Gregory had never argued, had carefully avoided conflict. She wondered if this is what made the relationship feel flat sometimes. A bit of disagreement was normal, wasn't it? She had little to compare it to; her single mom hadn't started dating until she was away at university.

The ride started out well enough. Leaving Lisbon, the terrain shifted—pine trees, hills, and occasional views of the sea replaced a parade of apartment buildings. A heaviness she hadn't known she carried fluttered off and out the window. She loved Lisbon, but she felt better surrounded by green.

They hooked up a phone to the car stereo. Manu Chao pushed through the speakers with his insistent exuberance. Darla knew about his band, Mano Negra, from her time studying French.

Someone suggested they speak only Portuguese for an hour. This limited conversation, but she was proud to be able to communicate. Darla had been studying Portuguese every day and practicing with André. She was making progress slowly, building her confidence. In the car, she learned a few swear words and slang, like, *"Está fiche!"*—that's cool. André and João talked between them. Despite her studies, it was impossible to understand anything. This was a handy privacy shield, to be able to talk freely in front of others without them understanding. This happened a lot at home. André would be on his personal phone, chatting, laughing, connecting with God knows who. Darla desperately wanted to know who was on the other end, but she never asked.

She gazed out the window. Mesmerized by the undulating green landscape, a wave of love for Portugal rose up in her. She was glad to get out of the city. This time in nature was what she was craving. If she left, she would miss Portugal. This thought startled her, a sneak attack on the certainty that she had finally landed and committed to a place. But now a tiny thought thread wove its way into her mind that like the other Globalkins who passed through, she might not be here for long.

The campground presented itself as a sprawling generic affair packed with people and children. Fast-food restaurants and shared bathhouses with showers. A mini village, tacky and crowded. She tried to hide her disappointment. She wished they were inaugurating their tent privately.

They'd reserved a spot in a sandy forest for their tents away from the RVs and crowds. The shelter of the branches offered a gentle respite from the sun. Darla's breath came easier after a few minutes under the canopy. They set up their tent, and before long, André's other friends arrived. They hugged and air kissed, joking and laughing together. André quickly introduced them to her. A gaggle of young handsome men, one, Tomás, a doctor in London. The friend they'd come with, João, did marketing for a wine company in the Alentejo. The women weren't as friendly as the men, barely greeting her. Darla sensed friction between one of them, Maria. She and André air kissed like the others, but Maria seemed to avoid André's eyes. She was grateful for Astrid and Monica.

Once everyone arrived, they took a short walk to the beach. They were accompanied by the endless soundtrack of waves and an urgent wind. The sight of the blue water erased all the awkwardness Darla felt around André's friends. Everyone settled in, chatting and laughing. Darla went for a swim. She surrendered to the water's ease. A moment of bliss pushed her upward. She was unbound from the earth and floating in the water between earth and sky. The waves were the right height, the water the ideal temperature, the distance between her and the others—all perfect. The sun was doing its daily fade out, dimming the day in a happy glow.

Sitting on her Turkish towel, she played in her sketchbook, drawing the bodies lying and standing on the beach. She had a growing collection of these beach sketches. Her loose drawings had given her confidence in drawing people. Depicting bodies playing, lounging, and chilling at the beach was easier than the one time she'd done live figure drawing. This was way more alive, with the water and sand and the wind constantly contributing.

She chatted with Astrid and Monica, who were in Portugal for a month. They were more approachable than André's friends. She knew it would take time to fit in to André's world. André and his mates went for a swim, then clustered near the shoreline. She wondered what they talked about. One of André's friends sat near Darla.

"They used to be together," she said. "They just broke up in the spring."

Darla looked up, following the woman's gaze. Maria was at the shore with André. The two of them stood a few feet away from the others, talking intensely. Darla swallowed. So that was it. The girlfriend he'd been with before her. She tried to read their body language. Were they getting along? Regretting they weren't together? They seemed intimate still.

That night, they hung around on blankets at the campsite. Astrid and Monica had gone to the campground canteen for dinner. Settling in, Darla moved someone's bag off the blanket to sit down. When Maria came back from the bathroom, she was incensed to find her bag touching the earth. Darla flushed hot all over, apologizing in Portuguese. But Maria ignored her.

Darla tried to shake it off, focusing on the other people. About ten of them were drinking, talking, and catching up. André and his friends removed the caps from their beer bottles and wiped the mouth of the bottle with their sleeves. Darla drank wine. They rolled spliffs and passed them around. Sitting around drinking wine and eating bread, cheese, and olives with friends should have been fun. But for Darla, it was as awkward as it had ever been that summer. It was worse because these were André's closest friends. He was ignoring her. She couldn't catch his eye. She felt like a dog he had to bring along instead of the precious lover she had once been.

The friends caught up, a river of Portuguese flowing by too fast for her to catch even a word. She bobbed in the middle of it all on a raft of complete incomprehension. Where to look? How to arrange her face? At first, she tried acting as if she were with them, nodding along, laughing a half second after everyone else. This fakery was exhausting, and it reminded her of all the time she'd spent trying to pass as "normal" in her work suits. She doubted her facade convinced anyone. She was fading.

She gazed up at the trees and the stars beyond them and tried to tether herself to her own thoughts as if she didn't mind being on an unpopulated island in a sea of happy people. She could only do that for so long. What did they think of her? Did they think she was stupid? Sometimes they'd speak English to include her, but the conversation would quickly slide back to Portuguese. André didn't bother translating. He was laughing and telling stories, absorbed in the attention his friends gave him. He had told her that learning a language requires listening more than speaking. Okay, she thought. But not speaking at all? Not truly being able to listen? Where did that put you? In and out of it all at once. Nowhere. If she wanted to listen to Portuguese, she needed to really focus. She was used to having multiple awarenesses: listening to a conversation, having her own thoughts, and taking in the surrounding environment. To really listen to Portuguese, she needed to develop a single-pointed focus.

The only thing she could say was "Obrigada" when they passed the spliff her way. A rush of lightheadedness overcame her, the hash's welcome mind breeze. She considered bringing out her Journey Blessings, but somehow now they seemed silly. She hungrily wanted to connect. She felt hollowed out inside. Only the spliff saved her; being high allowed her to crawl inside herself and find solace in her imagination. She'd done this as a child, home alone after school. Now, with her sketchbook, high, she could pretend she didn't feel what she was feeling.

Finally, well after midnight, they all went to bed. Inside their tent, the darkness swallowed everything but sound. They tucked into their sleeping bags without speaking. Finally, she spoke up.

"What's wrong?" she whispered.

He was silent.

"André?"

Nothing. Her throat clenched up. This refusal to talk pushed her further away into a solitude of confusion. Without knowing what was wrong, her mind began spinning stories. He was going through something about his friends that forced her outside of his inner circle, and he couldn't talk with her about it. Perhaps he was ashamed of her. Perhaps he was ashamed of himself. Perhaps he still loved his old girlfriend. She had to find out what was going on with him. She spoke again.

"Is it someone else?" It was hard to get the words out.

He made a derisive sound. "You're paranoid," he said. "I don't know what you're talking about."

Suddenly, the distance was Darla's fault. He wasn't responsible for it at all. She was the one with the bad ideas. She questioned herself—was she sabotaging the relationship? Was it her fault?

They went to sleep without making love, without kissing, without touching. She lay there afire, fuming, desperate to know what happened. All the wine and hash didn't help her feel any better about it. Or about anything.

Chapter Forty

She woke up with a headache. Ay, she thought. I can't be drinking and smoking like a twenty-something. She baked in the heat of the tent. André woke up and blinked several times. They made their way silently into clothes and out of the tent. Darla grabbed her bag and pushed her feet into her sandals.

The forest air was a relief from the heaviness between them. The dark mood that had filled their tent lingered around André. They walked with João and Tomás to the café for coffee and pastries. Tomás asked Darla what she did. She told him she was taking a break from work but was studying art. She showed him her sketchbook. He seemed impressed. Darla warmed, feeling a connection she'd hoped to have with André's friends. The conversation reconnected her to her art goals. Yes, she was someone doing something in the world. Even if she didn't have a job, she wasn't just on vacation. She wasn't a doll to be mistreated by André. She wanted to tell them about the commission, but the conversation shifted.

After breakfast, she couldn't bear the tension. She hated the funk that hung around them. She asked André to talk. They stepped away from the tent. Pine needles crunched under their feet. She breathed in the invigorating scent. They crouched on a log. In the distance, the sound of the waves beckoned Darla to her happy place, the beach, with its endless horizon. Another time, they would have made out in the grove, perhaps gone further, and they would have enjoyed the gentle light and breeze on their skin. Now she could only try on her own to reclaim herself.

"What's going on?" she said.

He didn't respond.

"Who do you think I am?" she said, anger rising up. "What's the problem?"

He looked her in the eye. She waited, expecting an explanation, an apology at the least. Finally, he spoke.

"Always saying thank you to my friends. You're like a peasant."

She gasped. To Darla, showing gratitude was a sign of grace and kindness. Of respect and love. But to him, it diminished her. She realized that he thought she was uncultured. That she had no class and that he was better than her. He told her to stop thanking everyone. In that moment, she realized he didn't love or perhaps even like her. Being together with his friends highlighted that she was not truly part of his life. Her stomach clenched against this awareness. She realized she'd been gripping from inside the whole weekend.

She stumbled back to the tent, numb, trying to muster a positive perspective. She was desperate to get away, but there was no way out, no way back to Lisbon without them. It was a miserable paradox—being at her happy place, the beach, while inside feeling completely disconnected. Her mind raced, trying to find an answer that would reduce the uncertainty and pain. What had happened? What had she done? Worse, what was going to happen? If it didn't work out with André, what would she do? She had no plan B—just this dream of building a home together. The thought of her mom's "I told you so" made her cringe inside. Like when New York hadn't worked out. A dump of shame overtook her, contrasting the bright and cheerful day.

The group hung out on the beach in a hazy hangover. André became more withdrawn from her and more connected to his friends. Darla smeared sunscreen on her exposed skin and tried to hide under her hat. Her body was sore from sleeping on the ground.

That evening, they loaded into cars. Tomás's grandmother lived nearby and was hosting them for dinner. Darla welcomed the change in scenery and hoped it would be better than the night before. But sitting at a long table on the enclosed patio with the beach behind them, Darla felt even more trapped than the night before. The *avo,* grandmother, brought platter after platter for them. Cod, of course. Iceberg lettuce and pink tomato salad. Some things she'd never seen before and was eager to try. The food was passed, and Tomás poured wine. Darla heaped her plate, hoping the food would soothe her. She tried to talk about the food, but André took the platter she passed and muttered, "It's not always about the food."

Darla pressed her lips together, trying not to cry. It was always about the food for them. They had shared their lust for life as it presented itself on the table or picnic blanket. But here, he had other things to talk about that didn't include her. In the clatter of silverware, conversation, and conviviality, he seemed to forget her.

The evening dragged on. She tried to drink away the pain, hoping no one would notice she kept filling her glass with the carafe of wine. At one point, a pack of dogs scampered by the patio and onto the beach. Everyone laughed as if they understood what was going on. Darla tried to smile and feel part of it all, but a lump formed in her throat and her belly tightened.

She wished to be one of those dogs, belonging, running freely together in the wild.

After dinner, they returned to the campground and headed to the beach. It was dark, the scene barely lit by a half-moon. This evening rolled a little looser than the night before, with the talking, laughing, and open beach. Darla sat at the edge of the blanket. She swayed a little and would have preferred to lie down and gaze at the stars. She'd drunk a lot of wine and smoked a spliff when it passed. The guys talked loudly, arguing over each other. Most of André's women friends had stayed back in the tents. André got out his materials to roll a spliff.

"Let me," she insisted. André resisted but then gave in. She was learning how to do it with two papers to make a giant spliff. But sitting in the dark on a blanket, the beach wind against her, she couldn't manage anything. Her fingers felt fat and wouldn't comply. She fumbled with the tobacco and the hash.

"Give it to me," André said. He crushed the wrinkled papers and pulled new ones from the pack. Tobacco threads scattered on the blanket. Darla tried to brush them to the sand. Suddenly, several men approached, beams of bright light waving from flashlights. André tucked the spliff materials under his leg. She didn't understand what was going on.

It became clear that they were police, and they wanted to search them. For what, she didn't know. André told her to hand over her ID. She swallowed. She didn't have her passport, just her American driver's license. Would they know she had been here longer than ninety days? Was this her exit from the uncomfortable weekend, escorted away by the police, brought to immigration, sent home without being able to pack her things in Lisbon? André said they wanted her to empty her purse on the blanket. She tried to hide her drunkenness and terror. Her sketchbook, wallet, and contraceptives scattered on the blanket. They stood nervously while the men searched their belongings. After a long and tense search, they told them to leave the beach. Darla didn't understand what they were looking for. But she felt more vulnerable than ever. She couldn't keep on as an illegal visitor in Portugal.

They packed everything up and headed back to their tents. Darla's hands shook. The others muttered in Portuguese. The moon lit the way from the beach up the small hill and down the road toward the campground. She pulled her hood over her head. Back at the tents, she said goodnight and tucked into her sleeping bag. She was shaken, unable to get the adrenaline to ease back. If only she could take refuge in André's touch. But he lingered outside with his friends.

After an awkward breakfast at the café, and a morning at the beach, they said their goodbyes, climbed in the car, and headed toward Lisbon. They were mostly quiet on the way home. It was like the same molecules that had gone to the beach were now arranged in a new, complex way.

At the street door to their apartment, Darla fumbled in her bag for her keys. André held their stuff, their tent, and backpacks. She could feel the weight of his impatience and hers, not finding what she sought. The keys were usually clipped inside. André set everything down to get his keys. Everyone tramped up to their apartment. André set up their friends in the mezzanine and on the couch. Darla wished he hadn't offered to host. She hated having witnesses to the dissolution of their love. After one final search for her keys, Darla had to admit she'd lost them. She thought back to the police raid at the beach. Perhaps the keys had fallen off the blanket and hidden in the sand. Someone with a metal detector would find them later, useless keys to an apartment many miles away in the capital.

In bed, she considered the lost keys a sign. She was being kicked out. She didn't belong here anymore. Had she ever belonged anywhere?

Chapter Forty-One

___

Autumn brought a moodiness that summer's brightness had fended off. It wasn't going to be easy to replace her keys, making it difficult to leave if André wasn't there. Their communication wasn't great, and she wished for their earlier connection and ease. She felt crazy with worry about what would happen to them and where she would go if it didn't work out. She felt ill much of the time, her nervous system both numb and buzzed. It was impossible to focus, and she had no appetite.

Darla found herself making erratic line drawings in her sketchbook, tangled shapes. Only color felt good. Her pages filled with splotches of her Lisbon colors: teal, royal blue, buttery yellow, and bougainvillea pink.

Darla had never felt this way before—not when she left New York nor when she broke up with Gregory. She was surprised to feel how much colors, both in Lisbon and in her sketchbook, gave her some relief from her pain.

Darla lounged around a lot in their bedroom. The breeze from the Tejo carried a new chill. She no longer kept the French doors open. She took to hanging out at the window, people watching from her tower. The ice cream cart on the corner was replaced with the chestnut vendor. Great plumes of smoke coated passersby in a cloud. These days, fewer tourist couples wandered around.

The morning sun on the Tivoli dome was weaker but no less lovely. The trees of the botanical garden glowed more yellow than green in the autumn light. One day, Darla heard a loud chainsaw from the courtyard out back. The next morning, she saw they had taken down the giant palm tree and another tree. The palm's trunk lay lifeless in the courtyard, and for days, there was a pile of giant fronds on the street waiting for the dump. Darla was already sad, and a tree coming down made her sadder.

Some days, when André left, she'd go back to bed, roll herself in the sheets, pad herself with pillows, and try to escape in sleep. Her mind refused to rest. She'd replay all the scenes where she'd gotten hangry and lost control of her emotions. If only she'd been able to have snacks on hand all the time. If only, if only.

The year had seen two breakups, but somehow, this one was worse. Everything was up for decision, but not in the fun way it had been when she'd decided to leave Boulder. Her whole trip had been built on this idea of taking an adventure, of throwing herself out there to see what happened. And she had done that, and this relationship had happened. And now that it seemed to be ending, she was back at ground zero. What the hell to do now? And where to go? She didn't feel capable of deciding from a place of abundant joy. More like restricted fear. And sadness. And disappointment. What kind of decisions are born from that swamp of emotion?

Other days, she'd wait until André left before pulling herself out of bed. Out on the balcony, she'd watch him amble down Rua São José, his gait carefree. But she knew he was waiting, as she was, for some clarity, so they could move on. Life in Lisbon kept moving. Once, she heard the flute whistle of the knife sharpener. A guy passed by on a bike, whistling out people who wanted their knives sharpened. He set up his bike/sharpener and sharpened the knives right there on the sidewalk. No need to sharpen her knives; she didn't want to cook anymore with André. She noticed more blind people passing by. People would get stuck at the dumpster or by the recycling bins, their canes leading them to a dead end. Every time, someone rushed over and gently guided the blind person back to the straight path.

André spent more time at the climbing gym. It was closing at the end of the month. He and his climbing friends had been talking about options. He wanted to try to launch a cooperative gym, a different kind of climbing gym. Things were strained between them after the Alentejo trip. Darla hoped it was just the usual stuff between couples. They were just working out how to live and travel together. They'd talked about someday leaving Lisbon, living in other countries in Europe. It sounded exciting to Darla. But now? The future was blank in a way that was not exciting at all.

One night, they were making love. It was dark, just a candle flickering in the corner. André was on top. Her hips rose up to meet him. This connection. Their hot rhythm. This was what they needed. He whispered something close to her ear. His short beard scratched against her cheek.

"What?"

He just thumped harder.

"What did you say?" She was no longer hot. But André ignored her, squeezing her tight, then releasing and rolling over. When she pressed him about what he'd said, he shook his head.

"*Nada*," he said.

"Why don't you tell me what's wrong?"

André shrugged.

"I mean, it's been weird. What's going on with you?"

"I don't know how say what I'm feeling right now. I don't have the words in English."

He pounded the pillow, shaping it to his comfort.

"Oh, now your English isn't good enough?" She scoffed.

"I need time to think."

A silence settled between them in the darkness. Darla's mind whirled, trapping her in dark thoughts. Was this the end? What was happening?

André interrupted the quiet. "I have a job offer in Switzerland."

She startled, turning toward him.

"Wow, that's great! This is what you've wanted. Congrats."

He nodded. She saw his jaw firm up. His eyes were closed. The light scattered across the ceiling.

"Where? When? Tell me everything."

"It's in Geneva. Lots of climbing nearby."

"That's perfect for you!"

"I haven't decided yet."

It dawned on Darla that he'd not referred to her. This was starting to feel like when he announced he was going to his hometown. She was not part of that picture, and her gut clenched when she realized she wasn't part of the Geneva picture either.

Friction crackled even more between Darla and André. But they hadn't said anything about ending their relationship. If he got the job in Switzerland, would she go with him? Would she stay in Europe, and how? She'd gotten used to surrendering, knowing to let André lead. And now he was leaving her behind. Now she was in the lead. What path did she want to take?

Chapter Forty-Two

Darla never wanted to be a climber. She had been fine letting climbing be André's thing. But now she wondered if becoming more part of his life would have made a difference. It was too late now. When André told Darla about a women's climbing festival in nearby Azóia, she considered it. She might be leaving Portugal and wanted to enjoy its natural beauty as much as she could. Plus, she didn't want to stay home all weekend while André went away.

They packed their tent and sleeping bags, their picnic gear, a few clothes, and her journals. She was shadowed by the melancholy of what she imagined were "last times." Last time they'd go somewhere together. First and last time she'd climb in Portugal. Last camping with André. As usual, she had no idea what to expect. After months of blindly following where André led, she knew to bring snacks and water. She thought she might have time on Sunday to relax, write, draw, and not worry about her next move. They got a ride with André's friend Pedro. They drove through coastal forests, cresting small hills and catching sight of the sea trying to outdo the sky for blue. Every time she saw the sea, Darla's heart rose. This was her landscape. This was her place. She relaxed and enjoyed being out of the city.

They arrived and parked in a giant sandy lot filled with cars. People milled about, toting climbing gear. They registered at a card table set up with badges and T-shirts. Darla got a tank top with the festival logo on it. She wasn't sure if this was something she would cherish or cringe when she saw it. They gathered their stuff and headed to the cliffs. André reminded her of the place they'd seen on their Sintra excursion. This is the most western part of the continent, he said. She followed him on the narrow, rocky path. Sintra and their boat ride in Lagos seemed so long ago. A lump in her throat formed when she thought of how connected they'd been then. And now, here they were at the true end of their world.

They approached the cliff, and the incredible view snatched away her gloomy thoughts. The sea glistened below, the sun shone, and the limestone cliff arched above her. The wind whipped at her clothes and teased her hair relentlessly. She craned to look up at the cliff. It was way, way high up there. She grimaced, hoping no one would see how scared she was. How would she get up that cliff? Everyone had set down their gear. Everyone seemed to wear the same full-faced grin.

André invited her to go first. She backed away.

"You go," she insisted. André and the others took their time gearing up. Darla sketched, observing all the steps they took to get ready. He pulled on tiny climbing shoes that seemed to bend his feet into tight curves. They set up the ropes. Pedro waited below while André climbed.

Everyone had climbed, and André turned to Darla.

"It's you now," he said. Her hair whipped in the wind, and her heart raced.

"Okay," she said, "if you think I can do it!"

"Of course you can."

His unwavering confidence boosted her. Watching women make their way up these incredible cliffs inspired her. She stepped into the harness, her legs quaking. She pulled on André's climbing shoes. She tried to listen carefully while he described what to do. But her heartbeat seemed loud in her ears, and her palms were moist when she grasped the rope. She didn't want to screw up in front of André and his friends. She chalked up, pretending she wasn't scared. She paused and sent up a prayer to the gods of the rocks. She imagined the Journey Blessing for this one: *You are rewarded for your risks.*

Reaching for the first hold, she pulled herself up. It was difficult to get started. But once she got going, a stronger her took over and pulled her along. It was happening! One move, then another, and soon she had a rhythm buoyed by the encouraging words of the others, nudging her on. Hold after hold, she made her way up the cliffside. The power of being able to do this easily caught her by surprise. Her strong feet easily gripped the rocks. She wouldn't have thought that clinging to the immutable surface of a rock would be so exhilarating. She pressed against the wall, breathing in the full-body glory of doing something so new and physical. André shouted up from below.

"Having fun?"

She glanced down. He seemed so far away. She clung to the rock, her thigh flush against the wall.

"Yes!" she shouted back.

"Enjoy the view!"

She spun on the rope away from the rock face. Dangling from the cliff, she now saw what had been at her back the whole time. The sea spread out behind her. The sun glinted on the waves, an undulating bed of dancing crystals. There was no end to it. Her heart reached out, stretching as wide and open as the sea itself. She laughed and squealed.

"Oh my god!" she shouted. She couldn't stop laughing. She was flying. She wanted to keep going. She reached up.

"No, come down," André called. "That's it!"

She took one last look around to embrace this moment in her mind and heart and cells. Here she was doing something daring, something she'd never imagined. Here, where water met rock, she'd reached beyond her limits. The armature of her life seemed to fall away. Darla imagined the structure of her past crumbling into pieces and bouncing down the rock face. She was light as the air over the sea. Joy surged through her. What else could she do? She felt limitless, light, free.

She made her way down, already wanting to climb again. On the ground, she threw her arms up in a victory salute.

"You did it," André declared. He smiled and thumped her on the back.

"Oh my god."

Her legs wobbled as she bumbled around in André's climbing shoes. Pedro helped her out of the harness and put it on for one last climb. She sat on a rock and pulled off the shoes. Her feet, sweaty and cramped, flexed at the relief of the fresh air.

They spent the whole day at the cliff. In a big, craggy cave, men climbed routes that involved hanging upside down and sideways and all kinds of crazy contortions. The women set up on the outer part of the cliffs. André left to climb with the men, a lot of buff young guys without shirts. The women all wore their long hair tied back in a ponytail. She chilled, soaking in the spectacular view. She tried to write and draw what she'd felt while climbing. She jotted Portuguese vocabulary in her notebook. She made color swatches, trying to capture the palette of the sea and the sky and how the blues differed.

People were friendly, relaxed, and focused on climbing

and encouraging others. She was wondering what to do next when a woman asked Darla who she was climbing with. She introduced herself as Alli, from Poland. She needed a partner. Alli helped Darla tie her rope and showed her how to belay. She and Alli took turns, and by the end of the day, Darla felt she could say she was a climber.

While putting the gear away, they chatted. Darla discovered Alli had lived for five years in California and a year in London. She said she didn't know why she was compelled to live in other countries, but she was. They agreed that the hardest thing was starting over again and again.

Where would Darla start again? In Switzerland with André? She didn't have any ideas on where to go next. Talking with Alli, she realized she didn't want to leave Lisbon. There was more to explore. She wanted more of the funky streetscapes, friendly people, and interesting points of view.

At dusk, the climbing community gathered in the small village. There was one bar focused on one thing: *futebol*. The club sports bar of Azóia overlooked a futebol field. Everyone drank mini Sagres beers and coffee and stood around talking and laughing. Darla deemed the mini beer one of the best inventions ever. It was just the right amount to quench a thirst, and it didn't last long enough to get warm. They snacked on fried octopus, which tasted like spicy shrimp.

Afterward, grubby and smelly, Darla and André changed clothes in the tent. When she'd agreed to come, a tiny flame of hope that it would connect them had lit in her. But now she didn't care about that. The feeling she'd had about her own freedom was bigger and better than a connection with André.

There was nowhere to wash, so they dampened a small towel and wiped clean. They trekked through a dark ravine toward the only restaurant. Tiny neon lights illuminated the path, and green sparkle lights formed a canopy in the trees. The moon was giving it her all, a glowing orange crescent dangling effortlessly over the coast of Portugal.

The restaurant was one room crowded with long tables of climbers. Some people lurked near the door, looking for a spot. The harried staff soon discovered that there was no room. They hadn't pre-registered for dinner. The group dinner was sold out.

André took this as a challenge. He somehow managed to work out a table for them in the front room. She was sad for him that he wasn't able to be with his climbing friends. He brushed it off, saying they'd have a great meal.

André always knew what to order. They got a bottle of Montes Claros white wine and *açorda de marisco* for two. After a long time and most of the bottle gone, dinner came. The waitress brought a big terra-cotta pot just for the two of them. Steam and the scent of the sea rose up when she removed the lid. She spooned some of the dish onto their plates. Darla dug into the savory bread pudding laced with cilantro and onions and mixed with shrimp, clams, and mussels. This was the ultimate comfort food, grounding after being out all day in the wind and sun and rocks. So good. So satisfying. So Portuguese.

André poured the last of the wine. Darla leaned back, content with her climbing and pleasantly surprised by the meal. It felt good to connect with André, like their early days when they'd been an adventurous team. André smiled at her and twisted the wineglass stem in his fingers.

"I have news."

She tilted her head. "Yes?"

André paused, and in the silence, Darla knew it wasn't

going to be good news. She splashed the last of her wine into her mouth, wishing for more.

"Well, it's this."

He took a deep breath and smiled again, though the smile didn't quite fit somehow.

"I accepted the job in Geneva."

Darla wondered why he'd waited all weekend to tell her. He must have known before they left Lisbon. Then it came to her, and she saw it on his face at the same moment. She spoke.

"I'm guessing since I wasn't part of this decision that I'm not going."

It was a question and a statement. But she needed him to say it.

He shook his head and reached for her hand. She pulled away, tucking it between her thighs. She wanted to slap him.

"Darla, this has been a great summer. You . . . you are truly amazing. And I think—"

"I get it. Yeah, it's been fun." Darla looked for the waitress to get the check. The once-comforting food now sat like clay in her stomach. She had to get out of there. The restaurant was hot and loud with celebrating climbers. There was no escape, just their tent.

"No, no, it's been more than fun. Our time together has been so special. It's just . . . It's time to do something else for me now."

Now all the comfy food she'd eaten wanted to reverse course and come out. The room was hot, full, loud. They sat awkwardly. Darla had never felt more trapped. Her face burned hot. The waitress passed by. Darla caught her eye and gestured for the check. She couldn't look at André.

"When are you going?"

"In a couple of weeks."

She nodded, trying to hide her panic. What the hell? Where would she go? Could she keep their apartment for herself? She was just starting to love Lisbon. She realized he'd never said he loved her. But she knew he had. It was more than just a fling. The thought that he hadn't wanted her to come to Geneva flitted through her mind and flushed her whole body with an inescapable heat. Oh my god, she thought. This is so embarrassing. I just told Mom I was in this committed relationship. And now . . . what?

They paid and left the noisy, party-like restaurant. They made their way through the night. This was Darla's favorite time. All the stars turned out to light up the sky. She always felt a reassuring sense of possibility when caught under the night sky. But now she was numb, her mind racing around what to do next. She followed André along the dark trail, their headlamps scoping out the way for them. Something rose up in her, and it wasn't the dinner. It was a hot anger. All the times she hadn't been able to speak. All the times she tried to be a polite visitor, to not be the ugly American. All of that was gone.

"Being with you," she said, "has been like visiting a beautiful country. Such good food, and wine, and beaches, and views. I love it. And then discovering it was built on a steaming toxic waste dump."

His gait shifted, slowed, and was that a stumble? She barely heard him. "Living with you has been like having a dog I am responsible for."

She resented him using dogs as a bad comparison model. They went on like this, exchanging insults and lashing out at each other in frustration. The uncertainty of where she would go unmoored her. The sea waves crashed loudly below them.

He sighed. "I thought I knew you, but we didn't have enough time for that."

"I don't know me either," she shouted. She was tired of this confusion.

"I don't think I will ever live with another woman again," he said.

She shook her head. A lovely autumn night in this beautiful place, and all she wanted was to get away from him.

Loud voices led them to an abandoned house on the clifftop. Inside, a party was getting started. A DJ had set up on the terrace overlooking the sea. The house was a madhouse, more a skeleton than a shelter. The windows were empty of glass. Rubble collected in the corners. Disturbing stencil art adorned every room. Beheaded gorillas, naked drooping women, silent cries of madness and despair. What kind of artist would come to this beautiful cliff and paint this?

She thought of Aria, her gorgeous murals and positive message. She thought of all the artists Julie worked with and how they and Julie were making a difference in the world. She wanted to be part of something like that, not this scene.

People were gathering on the terraces of the house. The sea sang in the dark below, a dark lullaby to accompany the fat moon.

"You can stay. I'm going back to the tent."

André nodded. A look flashed across his face, perhaps relief that she wasn't going to make a scene about what was essentially their breakup.

Alone in the night, she made her way to their tent, set up in the parking lot next to the bar. She could relax now, not having to pretend his news hadn't gutted her. Snaking into her sleeping bag, the tears came. Curling into a ball wrapped in the sleeping bag, she let herself cry. She had known it was not going well. Had suspected it would end. But for him to make a move like this, something they had talked about doing together . . . It broke her.

The nagging uncertainty and sadness flooded her. But underneath, something else lingered, barely noticeable. She stilled herself in the sleeping bag. There—a steady beat of relief. It was the same feeling she'd had when André left for the weekends. She hadn't noticed how much she'd been hiding herself around him. When he was gone and she could focus on her art, that's when she felt herself. That's what she wanted.

Sounds of the party penetrated the stillness around the tent, bumping music punctuated by cheers and the crowd singing along. While she had climbed alongside them and gotten along with them, these weren't her people. Who were her people? Where would she go now? Boulder was far, far away. Darla couldn't fit a picture of herself into that frame anymore. She had to admit that she didn't know who she was outside the roles she'd played for so long. But suddenly she realized she didn't need a plan. Who said she had to settle down? That was what she had wanted with Gregory, but not anymore. She didn't need a partner. The weekends without André had been some of her most creative times. She had herself, for now at least. Her mind flitted among a series of unfathomable options. Then, one idea came to land. A flare of hope ignited in her.

She sat up and checked her phone. It was late, but she sent a text.

Chapter Forty-Three

It hadn't taken much to arrange her new home. She was lucky that the cousin had gotten a job in Porto and couldn't keep his commitment to stay in Inês's place. Darla was ready to move in. She packed her stuff quickly. André stayed up late into the night packing his belongings. What would have been fun if they were moving together became a series of transactional conversations. Rui and Tiago would help her move the studio desk she had bought. It was all coming together.

She was eager to cook in Inês's lovely kitchen. She'd find new friends and hopefully a job and a life here. She hoped Lisbon wouldn't be dominated by memories of André. She arranged some roses in a vase. It made the kitchen feel like home. Lauren would approve, she thought. This was much more full ass living than anything she'd done before.

She wandered in Bairro Alto, reminiscing about her first days in Lisbon. She came upon the Queen of Hearts tattoo shop. For a moment, she considered it. Might as well go in, she thought. The shop was cool and dark inside. Pictures of tattoos lined the walls. Upbeat music pumped. The woman she'd seen when she bought *Le Cool* smiled from behind the counter.

"Welcome," she said.

"Hi there." Darla wasn't sure why she was there. "I've never been in a tattoo parlor."

"Well, this is the best one in Lisbon. I'm Maxime."

"Darla," she said, scanning the pictures pinned on the wall. Tattoos everywhere. But not the usual stuff. These tattoos were different. She couldn't find one she didn't like.

"Did you do these?" she asked.

"Some of them. This one and this one." She pointed at one that looked familiar. "Would you like a drink? Water? A Coke?"

"I'll take a water, *obrigada*." She continued to look while Maxime fetched the water.

"See anything you like?"

Darla shrugged, fiddling with opening the water bottle.

"Are you American?"

Darla nodded.

"I just broke up with a Portuguese guy. Fun while it lasted." She snorted. "This would be the worst time to commit to a tattoo."

She could barely get the words past her tightening throat. In her mind, she was reconciled with what had happened, but apparently her heart had a different experience going. She had to practice telling people this without crying. Maxime was unfazed.

"Or the best time," Maxime offered. "A breakup is the perfect time for a tattoo. To assert *you*. Your freedom."

A tiny door of possibility cracked open. Why *not* get a tattoo? What would she get, and what would it mean? Darla didn't need something so permanent to mark one of the saddest events in her life. But she was curious about the Queen of Hearts. One of the tats on the wall caught her eye. She'd seen that before. Wait. She recognized it from all her time in the salon chair. Lauren had that tattoo on her wrist. That was Lauren's tattoo.

She pointed. "What's this one about?"

Maxime smiled. "The Queen of Hearts. She represents a woman who knows her value, who has big emotions and knows how to flow with them. She's come through some tough stuff but knows who she is. She is fiercely going forward. Sounds a bit like you, no?"

Now tears were flowing for real, no hiding it. Maxime didn't seem to mind. The Queen of Hearts was Lauren. Or who Darla wanted to be. Was this why Lauren had wanted her to come to Lisbon? To claim her own Queen of Hearts? It seemed too coincidental, but here she was. Very little about her experiences in Lisbon was logical. She chuckled to herself. All the logic of her life had not led her to her true self. Only the wacky, unexpected choices had made her feel like she wanted to feel. Coming to Lisbon in the first place. Upending her life in Boulder to come back to Portugal.

Maybe she did need this Queen of Hearts tattoo. Her pulse pounded just thinking about it. She had that same zoomy feeling she'd gotten on her first date with André; when she rock climbed; and when she stood up for herself and told André how she really felt. None of the indecision about where to go and how to live was present now. Suddenly, it was a no-brainer to get a tattoo.

"Could I get a really small tattoo of the Queen of Hearts?"

"You can get anything you want, *cherie*."

Darla's heart clenched up. Maxime was so kind. Darla felt like she had a fairy godmother granting her a wish. She took a deep breath.

"Let's do it," she said, repeating what André had so often said. He'd shown her Portugal, yes. He'd also had a hand in her boldness. But she claimed this moment, deciding to be the Queen of Hearts solidly seated in her own heart.

Maxime gave her some forms to sign, and they talked about what Darla wanted. She felt supported and excited about doing something she was certain she'd never do. This whole trip had been full of new versions of her. Versions she liked and wanted to stick around. It didn't take long to get the tattoo on her left wrist. When she left the shop, she felt as new as she had when she'd left Boulder.

Chapter Forty-Four

——

Back at their apartment, Darla gathered the last of her things into her red string bag. She showed André her Queen of Hearts.

"You said you'd never get a tattoo," he commented. "Too much pain, too much permanence."

She was struck by how he'd remembered her words. How he carried all the experiences they'd shared and always would. She focused on the new mark on her skin. She turned her wrist this way and that, admiring the heart.

"It wasn't that painful. I love it."

She made one last tour of their home. André's stuff was partially packed. He was leaving in a few days. Darla could feel herself holding her breath, eager for a Lisbon without André. Upstairs, she gave one last look around the place where she'd let her artist out fully. Of all the places that had touched her in Portugal, this mezzanine, her studio, had given her the most. She didn't know where her art would lead her, but it would be different than Boulder. She suspected there would be many more home studios in her future. She didn't need this one. She didn't need André, or any man.

"Thank you, spot," she whispered.

Back downstairs, they stood in the empty kitchen. She hated goodbyes. She felt awkward with André for the first time. She hadn't realized that about him—about them— how at ease she'd felt with him so quickly. Darla had never connected with people the way she had in Lisbon. She had a lot to thank him for and a lot she still resented him for. Darla struggled for the right words. His face was so young. So many years ahead of him, so many climbs. She wouldn't be part of any of it. She recalled that feeling she'd had when they'd gotten high on their rooftop. Now she knew what she'd seen: a hint of meanness. The rigor of his teachers, the competitiveness of his work, his drive to be among the best climbers, that carved a toughness into someone. She tried to find something good to say.

"It wasn't all bad. I'd say 50 percent bad, 50 percent good."

"Not everything is a pretty picture," André said.

"Of course not," she replied.

But why not? she thought. What was wrong with wanting more beauty? She'd had such fun in Lisbon, expanding her aesthetic. Now, the funky art on the street walls was beautiful to her, the lines and colors forming a kaleidoscope of stories and people. Now, she had her own art.

"I haven't forgiven you for being such an asshole to me."

He ducked his head.

"Yet. Yet." They laughed.

"At the risk of sounding like a mom, I'll give you one piece of advice: Do better. You know better and can do better."

Behind his glasses, his eyes shone. It had been fun with André, but there was a fundamental gap they would never be able to cross. They'd never see the same perspective.

"I have to go," she said. "I'm meeting Julie."

He walked her down their winding staircase and out onto the street. They kept walking toward Julie's until they came to the São Pedro de Alcântara mirador. Darla recalled their first date and how they'd come here after dinner. The tree branches created an extra pattern, casting dancing shadows on the decorated cobblestones.

"We'll keep in touch?"

"Of course," he said.

"Let me know how it goes with the new job. I am excited for you."

He nodded, gazing at her. Oh no, she thought. It's that look. That same sexy look that had seduced her in the beginning.

"Thank you, Darla. You still are amazing."

She laughed. "Still?"

He came closer and brought her in for a hug. Darla enjoyed their bodies fitting together, but this time it was different. The tension between them—both good and bad—had drained away. She thought of that song, "Somebody That I Used to Know." Would she ever be able to think of him as just someone she knew?

She held him, trying to both hold onto and hold back all the feelings crashing through her. She loved him. She couldn't help it. But that didn't mean she had to live with him or be in touch if she didn't want. She broke away and looked over the city.

"Okay, bye."

"*Até já*," he said.

Darla met Julie at a rooftop bar. They sat on giant recliners lush with tasseled pillows. The temperature was perfect, a light breeze ushering in the evening. Their Aperol spritzes seemed to match the sun's daily painting of the blue sky orange, then pink. When they toasted, Julie caught sight of her tattoo.

"What is this! Show me!" She said it in Portuguese. "I love

it! Tell me all about it."

"I'm the Queen of Hearts now. Completely in touch with a respectful relationship to my emotions. That's one interpretation, anyway."

She shared what she'd learned from Maxime and from researching on her own. The Queen of Hearts was in favor of the emotions, in favor of feeling more, not less. Julie agreed that the tattoo was perfect. Darla caught Julie up on André.

"He's leaving on his birthday, of all days. Thank god for Inês's cousin laming out on her apartment."

"Right?! That was a crazy gift from the gods."

Darla thought about her first days in Lisbon with André. How she felt they were playthings of the gods. Was someone or something looking out for her now too?

"Are you okay?"

Darla hid behind her spritz. Was she okay? She was starting to get used to knowing what was actually going on inside her instead of stuffing it all down. But communicating what was inside was not so easy. She tried to speak, but the words clumped in her throat. Julie leaned over and rubbed her back. Tears bounced down Darla's cheeks. It took a few minutes before she could speak.

"I'm . . . I feel conflicted. I really love André, but I know it won't work. I don't know what happened . . . why things got weird."

"It's okay. You don't need to know."

"Thank god he's leaving Lisbon. I wouldn't be able to stay here with him here. I wouldn't know where to go. I kinda burned my bridges in Boulder."

"That sounds like a new age country song, 'Burned Bridges in Boulder.'"

They laughed. They talked more about André and how Darla could make her own life in Lisbon now.

"I have to get a job at some point. I can't live on Lauren's gift forever. But what kind of job can I get legally?"

Julie contemplated her Aperol.

"A lot of people teach English as a second language. Or maybe you don't have to get a job. Maybe you can make a living as an artist."

"Like Aria? She's so cool."

"Yea, she's one of my favorite visiting artists. She lives on her own terms. I love her formula—Know, Believe, Ask."

Darla nodded.

"You're doing that, Darla. Living on your own terms."

"I am?"

"Yes, of course. Look at you now compared to before you left Boulder. To think you just left for a vacation. And now you live in Lisbon."

Darla shook her head, eyes open.

"It truly is amazing. I have a hard time seeing it as permanent."

"Well, what is permanent? Nothing. Just enjoy the now." Julie waved her glass along the skyline. Most of the color had surrendered back to blue, a deep, dark water blue. Twinkly lights made the balcony glow. Music pulsed, and a few people danced. They sat in silence for a few minutes.

"Oh my god!" Darla started up from her lounge. The orange drink sloshed in her glass. "Oh my god!"

"What? What happened?"

"Maybe the craziest idea I've ever had."

She set her glass down and jumped up, waving her hands like her nails were on fire.

"Tell me!"

"Maybe I could come work at Paint the World! Aren't you looking for a grant writer? I could do that."

Julie leaned up from the cushions.

"But you write annual reports."

Darla wasn't deterred. "Yes, but there are surely skills I can use at Paint the World."

"Like . . . ?" She stood up, next to Darla, the river spread out below them. Darla had no idea what she was going to say, but words flowed out.

"Like working with different people to come together on a project. Managing projects. Taking information that may be boring and making it into a story that moves people."

Darla was picking up steam now. She'd been so locked into her job in Boulder. Of course she had transferable skills.

"I could lead things like the sketch crawl."

Julie seemed to be with her, smiling and nodding. She added to the idea.

"People would love that! I can see lots of ways you can incorporate that into collaborations with other artists and performers."

"Could you put in a good word for me? Tell me how to apply?"

Julie nodded, coming back from what Darla recognized as her thinking face.

"Of course! Of course. Let's think about the best way to do this."

It all seemed so possible to Darla. And terrifyingly good. She grabbed Julie. They laugh-hugged. Suddenly Darla was sobbing, whole body sobs that jerked her and Julie like they were doing a weird dance. Julie hung on. Darla clung to her, not knowing why she was crying. But she couldn't stop. For once, she didn't care if anyone saw her tears. They finally drew apart.

"Wow, I guess I needed that." Darla grabbed a tissue from her bag. They sat back on their recliners.

"Do you know what you just did for me?"

Julie laughed. "Offered help with a job?"

Darla laughed too. "You're such a good friend, Julie. This possible job could be so great."

"We'll see what happens."

Darla nodded.

"But it's more than a job. So much more than that. You helped me see that I can do more than just that one job in Boulder. Do you know how long I've been in that cage?"

"Too long!"

Julie waved the waiter over and ordered Prosecco for both of them.

"We're celebrating!"

Darla smiled at the waiter but inside was a bit stunned. Could it really work to have a job at Paint the World? The flutes came, and they toasted. They discussed the needs the organization had, and how Darla might fill in the gaps. Of course she'd have to apply officially, but she'd met Tiago already, so she wasn't an unknown factor.

Chapter Forty-Five

Darla queued up her playlist to unpack in Inês's apartment. A feeling of rightness settled over her, something she hadn't noticed in Boulder or Paris. Something in her had stopped searching. Her sense of wanting something else had slipped away. She'd never felt this her whole life. "To Build a Home" came on. The moody melancholy of the song was so obvious to Darla now. At first it had been so romantic and painted a picture of what she wanted with André. Now she heard the part about it being time to leave. This helped her feel like everything had its own natural cycle. She didn't control every factor. But now she knew what she wanted to do with her days.

Wandering from room to room, Darla delighted in her new home. In the living room, she imagined having friends over. Maybe Cat would come to Lisbon for a visit; she had room for guests. She pulled things from a duffel bag she'd had to buy. The Live Full Ass pillow she'd resisted bringing now brought a surge of love to her heart. She placed it in the middle of the couch, reigning over the other throw pillows. Something new coursed through her, a bright, vibrant tone. Lauren came to mind. "I'm doing it," she whispered. "Living full ass. Thank you, Lauren." The feeling pulsed in her, and she couldn't help but wonder if it was sort of a hug from Lauren.

In the third sunny bedroom, Darla set up her studio. She laid out her paints, choosing a few favorites to keep out. Her

Lisbon colors, she thought. They made her feel good just looking at them. With her studio desk and the shelving, she'd have plenty of space to work on her commissions and her own projects. She'd have to get a table of drawers for all the paper and art she would make. A printer to make photo art. She'd need a local print shop she could partner with to make her cards. She got lost taking notes about what she wanted to make and what she would need to do it. She scribbled a few ideas for another card series she could make, painting a couple of samples. She wanted to get watercolor postcard paper to make individual art pieces. After a while, she stretched and stepped away from the notebook. She photographed the pages using the light from her window. She observed that glow again, a brightness that she only experienced in Lisbon. The wooden floors creaked under her movements. It was all so exciting and energizing. And she couldn't deny that her old doubts still trickled under the surface. She wasn't sure what would happen with her art. But she knew that nothing would come of it if she didn't give it a go.

She clipped a few of her sample cards to her wall—what would become her pastiche of inspiration. She added one she had painted of her favorite coffee cup she'd bought at the arts market. At her laptop, she scanned her calendar for the next date she could host a sketch crawl. Maybe it could be a monthly thing. She thrummed with the feeling that she could make anything she wanted.

The End

Author's Note

This book is loosely inspired by my experiences when I packed up everything and left Boulder in 2008 to go to Europe. I hoped to change my life, but I did not know how that would happen. I ended up in Lisbon and fell in love with the city and one of its Lisboetas.

The manuscript began life as a memoir drafted during NaNoWriMo in 2014. I did it—65,000 words—but it was painful, and I wasn't ready. The story went into the drawer. But the idea that this was a good story, an inspiring story, wouldn't go away.

Her Lisbon Colors is fiction, and Darla is not me. Long ago, I studied with the great American short story writer Grace Paley, who taught me to "tell the truth"—the emotional truth. I sought to write the emotional truth of being a sensitive person in the world, trying to find a new way of living.

I recognize that becoming an artist and moving to another country are two of the hardest things we can embark on. Darla's experience is definitely easier than I think it would be in real life. Because this is fiction and not prescriptive nonfiction or a memoir, I took full creative license. It was fun to envision different scenarios for Darla that I did not live. It was fun giving Darla a budding career as a food illustrator.

Writing this story has been one of the most therapeutic things I have done. Taking a lived experience and turning it into a story required me to see myself as a character, step outside of my lived experiences, and accept all my human foibles.

There's a practice called narrative therapy that offers ways to view our experiences as stories, giving us new ways to frame and understand things. I loved giving Darla an ending that I did not have.

AI Usage Note

In the summer of 2023, I dipped a toe into AI to see how it could help me. I realized it did not help draft the book nor for developing characters, plot, etc. The ideas were trite, and the writing was horribly clichéd.

No part of this manuscript was generated by AI.

Acknowledgments

I was gifted with an incredible amount of support as I went through the process of learning, once again, how to write a novel people would want to read.

Kristen Tate is the best editor I could ever ask for. Her vast intelligence, generosity, and kindness are unparalleled. Thank you, Kristen, for making this novel so much better than I could have.

Beta readers Lisa Pasold and Heather Stimmler—thank you for offering and being so generous with your time and feedback. You helped enormously.

Members of my Write ON group were with me weekly as I rowed my way to the finish line. Having a writing community is invaluable, and these members are smart, kind, and make the process fun.

To the members of my Stumbling Toward Genius community, thank you! I appreciate your support as I wrote this book. Sharing progress with you each week made all the difference. Special thanks to paid members and founding member Carla Wiersema, whose enthusiasm spurs me on.

Thanks to Sara DeGonia, my copyeditor, proofreader. I love working with the talented cover and interior designers Ian and Alan. Thanks to Gigia, Koosje, Karen, and Tonja, who helped me choose the best cover design.

Early on, Susan DeFreitas read the first fifty pages and said, yeah, no, start again. This is not what anyone wants to hear, but it was so helpful and made my novel better.

Thank you to Courtney Maum for feedback during one of her workshops. I did not like your notes, but I eventually found my way to understanding and implementing them. Your weekly Substack articles made a big difference for me.

Thank you to Ashleigh Renard, who was such a big help in organizing my launch and marketing. Your enthusiasm for the book made all the difference to me. Thanks to Jane Friedman whose decades of work in the writing and publishing world has been an enormous help to me.

I found Ania Amador in a random search online for "female muralists." Her work and worldview inspired me and gave me ideas for how Darla could be inspired to go for it as a professional artist.

The people of Lisbon have been so welcoming, kind, and inspiring to me. A huge thank you to Rui and Joel of Practice Portuguese. You gave me back a love of the language and have taught me so much! Muito obrigada. Thank you to Lisbon Street Art Tours, who do such a fantastic job of advocating for art and artists.

Dear friends who have left earth too soon: Lori, Ruth, Valarie, you inspire me to live full ass. And not in an abstract way, but in a going-for-it-all-now way. This book is a tribute to you and your legacy, which lives on in me and everyone you touched. I thank my husband, Steve, who always has my back.

Questions for Discussion

What role does the inheritance with the stipulation to visit Lisbon play in Darla's transformation? Is this a device of convenience, or does it serve a deeper thematic purpose?

How might Darla's story challenge or reinforce cultural narratives about women "of a certain age" seeking renewal through travel and romance? Would her journey have been different if she were younger or older?

Darla is "a woman who has done all the right things but ended up in the wrong place." What does this suggest about societal expectations versus personal fulfillment, especially for women in midlife?

What does the age gap between Darla and André reveal about both characters? How does it contribute to both the appeal and the challenges of their relationship?

How does Darla's relationship with André change her perspective about life?

In what ways does Darla's relationship with Lisbon itself evolve separately from her relationship with André? What does this suggest about place attachment versus human attachment?

There are several mentions of Darla's experience being like a fairy tale. What elements of fairy tales are threaded through this story?

Darla is open to learning about Portuguese culture but loses a bit of herself while trying to adapt. How does a visitor to another land be respectful of the local ways and also be her authentic self?

What unspoken privileges allow Darla to make the choices she does? How might her story read differently if she faced different socioeconomic constraints?

The novel presents travel as both liberating and disruptive to Darla's sense of self. In what ways does physical displacement from familiar surroundings force her to confront aspects of her identity she might have otherwise left unexamined? Consider how the absence of her usual social context in Boulder creates both freedom and vulnerability.

Questions for Your Own Life

If you were Darla and you were given the $25,000 today, with the stipulation you had to visit Lisbon, would you put your regular life on hold to experience a new one? What if you got the offer twenty years ago? What about twenty years in the future?

Darla experiments with art even though she was told in her youth that she did not have talent. Were you given any messages around your talent or lack of talent as a child? Do any of those messages still limit you now? Have you overcome any of them? What steps could you take today to disprove a belief you were saddled with in childhood?

Darla struggles to reconcile her own unhappiness with what society thinks should make a woman happy. Has this shown up in your life? What steps have you taken to live into your own purpose when it diverges from society's expectations?

About the Author

———

Cynthia Morris is an artist, author and certified coach. She co-leads creativity workshops in Lisbon and Paris, making fine use of her French and West European Studies degrees. Cynthia is the author of ten books, including the Paris historical novel *Chasing Sylvia Beach*. Her books on creativity and writing include *The Busy Woman's Guide to Writing a World-Changing Book* and *Visit Paris Like an Artist*. She lives in Denver with her husband, Steve. Find Cynthia's other books and more about her creativity retreats and coaching at:

www.originalimpulse.com